"*The Woodkin* by Alexander James is a brutal, nightmarish trip into the heart of darkness that grabs you by the throat on page one and refuses to let go. An unrelenting, unflinching story . . ."
—**Matthew Lyons, author of *A Black and Endless Sky* and *The Night Will Find Us***

"Alexander James understands the point of horror, the point of getting beneath the surface and the skin of mundane world even if there's gore under there. *The Woodkin* is fabulously imaginative in just the right ways, a well-woven story that makes it quite clear what you'll find in the woods whether you want to or not."
—**Margaret Killjoy, author of *The Lamb Will Slaughter The Lion***

"Gruesome, exhilarating, and exceedingly lyrical, Alexander James's debut novel, *The Woodkin*, is everything horror should be. A troubled protagonist faces demons both figurative and literal, and we readers are compelled to keep flipping pages deep into the darkening night."
—**Jon Bassoff, author of *Beneath Cruel Waters***

"Pack your bags and strap on your boots and take a dark adventure through some deep woods folk horror, where the *Children of the Corn* meet *Midsommar*. This book will trap you in its cage and leave you begging for rescue—but you're on your own, kid. The only escape from the terror and pain is to travel right through. You may never be found."
—**Mark Matthews, author of *The Hobgoblin of Little Minds***

THE
WOODKIN

THE
WOODKIN

ALEXANDER JAMES

CamCat
Books

Content Warning: *This novel touches upon sensitive subject matter that may be disturbing to some readers: graphic sexuality, stillbirth and miscarriage, drug abuse, and graphic physical violence.*

CamCat Publishing, LLC
Fort Collins, Colorado 80524
camcatpublishing.com

This is a work of fiction. Names, characters, places, and incidents are either products of the author's imagination or are used fictitiously.

Hardcover ISBN 9780744302356
Paperback ISBN 9780744302417
Large-Print Paperback ISBN 9780744302424
eBook ISBN 9780744302486
Audiobook ISBN 9780744302615

Library of Congress Control Number: 2023930127

Book and cover design by Maryann Appel

5   3   2   4

To my wife,

who watched me disappear into the pages of this

novel more times than I care to count.

Heck 'em, puggerino.

GREEN-EYES

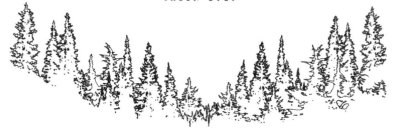

H E'D BEEN ROTTING UPWARDS OF A WEEK.

I found him by accident, buried in the depths of a hollow formed by tree roots on the riverbank. Pine sap perfumed the breeze blowing over the green-glass water, masking the sour-meat-and-maggots stench of his corpse. I almost fell over him, leaning to refill my water in the river shallows. The smell sharpened, grew sweet, the way boudin does after it's gone over.

The bank edge crumbled beneath my size twelves, sending me face-first into the shallows. When I came up for air, spitting water and profanities, I caught a glimpse of his eyes. Green as the moss covering the rocks beside him, swollen in their sockets like grapes. Most of his face had rotted away, skin curling away in tender holes where insects took little snacks.

I crab-walked backward, straight into the river in gut shock, slipping beneath the water with a sputtering scream. I forgot about what's-his-face in the struggle to catch myself from being washed downriver against the mud-slick rocks, pushing my way to the bank. I walked back to my pack, squelching water through soaked socks, approaching the nearby corpse inch by inch, covering my mouth with my bandanna.

His extremities were intact—bloated and disgusting, but whole. His midsection was a different story. I could still make out the ragged ruin of his remaining intestines hidden in the depths of his hollow. Mountain lions always go for the gooey bits, and I'm sure if I was the curious sort and pulled him out to check, his kidneys and liver would be gone.

I wasn't feeling that curious. I took deep breaths and pinched my nose to keep the bile simmering in my esophagus from coming all the way up.

His leg was bent beneath him, knee jutting a hundred and eighty degrees in the wrong direction. He must have slipped on the trail or overbalanced on his way down. Broke his leg a good two hundred feet from where anyone would have been walking, well-hidden by the pine trees, loose leaves, and scree. Probably tried to struggle back up the hill, but with that fracture he wasn't going anywhere. So he tucked himself into the hollow to overnight it, recoup a little strength for another try in the morning.

And that was where the lion must have found him—sleeping and crippled. Pretty much sliced and served on a silver platter for your average mountain lion.

I clung to the facts. Broken legs, well-hidden. It made sense, everything made sense. Because in my head, someone screamed. A hole opened in my gut, and the familiar taste of adrenaline and panic flooded through. My fingers tingled, like they were being pricked with needles.

He fell. Broke his leg. He fell. Broke his leg.

Over and over. I stood up too quickly, suddenly desperate to put distance between him and me. The horizon reeled, and for a second I thought I would overbalance and dunk myself into the stream again. I had trouble breathing, as if I had sunk beneath a black tide. The sensation dredged up memories—memories I desperately wanted to keep buried. I hadn't felt like this in over a decade.

Quick, before the tingling made its way up my arms, I looked away from the corpse. Five things I could see. The stream, green-glass water. A nearby rock, white and black like a tuxedo penguin. That pine tree, whispering to itself in the breeze. The mountains, the sun dancing on the water. Four I could touch, three I could hear. Two things I could smell.

Him. You didn't get used to the smell of the freshly dead. I muscled past it, forced myself to think. Him, yes, and the warm pine-scented air rushing through the valley. The dry dirt of the trail, rising like smoke beneath my boots. Finally, I could taste bitter adrenaline on my tongue, a result of my heart slamming a sledgehammer against my ribs. Fear, prickling my skin. Fear of the nightmares returning. Of the screaming, deep in the pits of my mind. I'd only just started sleeping through the night a few years ago.

Breathe.

I relaxed, degree by degree. The grounding lessons with Dr. K still worked. I took a deep breath, then another. I was okay. A dead body was unusual, but it wouldn't hurt me. The panic eased.

"I'm sorry." The only thing I could think to say, and it came out pitifully empty, hollow.

Could be some ID tucked into a pocket somewhere, but I sure as shit wasn't going to reach in there and roll him over for it. What skin I could see was stretched, turgid; it looked like it would burst at the slightest touch. If I'd see his skin split open and ooze whatever liquid lingered inside, I would lose my lunch.

My toes tingled; the muscles in my calves twitched with the urge to turn and run—run as fast and as far as I could. The familiar abyss

gaped open in front of me, but I stepped over it, smothered the memories before they could rise out of that darkness. Some things you left in
the past. Bodies didn't have any power over you, once they were dead.

Some lessons you only need to learn once.

I made a note of where I was so I could leave word with the next
rangers station. I was pretty sure I'd passed Image Lake a few hours
ago. I had to go off my gut and the blurry picture I'd snapped last minute of a map hanging in the rangers' station at the Locks.

I negotiated my way back up the slope toward the trail, hunched forward so my backpack didn't drag me back into the same fate as what's-
his-face. Another four hours of sweat-slicked hiking waited for me.

Now, though, the trail changed. Now the whispering pine trees
were voices, floating soft on the breeze. Faces hid in the deep-cut chan-
nels cutting into their bark, watching me. The prickling sensation
stayed, tickling the small hairs on the back of my neck. Someone was
watching me—I spun, as if I could catch them, only to see the trail.

Empty. Just me.

Every time I turned back, walked on, told myself I was being silly. I resettled my senses with the five-to-one grounding exercise Dr.
K taught me all those years ago. But the trees still whispered and the
faces still watched.

Just me. And the voices in my head.

I appreciated the shade offered by the towering trees; I was what
my dad affectionately referred to as "Irish pale," and the travel-sized
bottle of sunscreen I'd begun with ran out four days ago. Currently I
was in the "burn and blister" part of building up a natural tan. Not a
cloud in the sky for miles—great news if you were taking the boat out
on Lake Union or sipping cocktails on a Seattle rooftop; bad news if
you were Josh Mallory, trudging pink as a lobster through the spine of
the Cascades.

The Washington section of the Pacific Crest Trail was a bitch of a
thru-hike. Towering volcanoes, plunging valleys, a hundred-plus miles

of hiking glory—and I needed every second of it. When I crawled up the side of a mountain, struggling for each breath and concentrating on keeping my legs from collapsing, I couldn't picture Deb, standing in the kitchen looking like someone sucked all the wind out of her lungs. I couldn't think about the cardboard box, crumpled in the bottom of the trash can. I couldn't think about what waited for me when I'd finally emerge from the mountains.

Shit happens, right?

That's what this trip was all about.

→→⟩ ⟨←←

THE CAR RIDE was as silent as a grave for the first three hours speeding south on I-5. Deb drove, white-knuckling the battered steering wheel while I stared at the corridor of marching pine trees passing in a blur. Against the pale skin of her hand, the pink diamond in her wedding band looked red, a coal ablaze. The space between us gaped, measured in miles. It wasn't until we passed Chehalis that she tried again.

"Josh—"

"Nope."

"Josh, God damn it, listen to me. This is such a stupid plan. You can't go off into the wilderness by yourself for three weeks—"

I couldn't listen anymore. I'd listened to her all last night, alternating between shrieking and pleading, and the night before that. And the one before that.

"Life turns on a dime." I read that in King's *11/22/63*, which currently sat dog-eared and well leafed through on my nightstand. I chewed through books fast for an ex-football player and kid from Alabammy, but I always took my time with King's stuff. Read them too fast and you miss things, and the man doesn't put stuff in his books with the intention of you missing it.

No writer does, I guess.

Life turns on a dime. Which is a fancy way of saying shit goes sideways faster than you can imagine.

My life turned two nights ago because of a beer bottle.

Deb is a through-and-through believer in sustainability and recycling; she came by it honestly from a pair of patchouli-soaked hippies in Portland. We had an assortment of identical-looking bins lined up in the kitchen—plastic recycle, glass recycle, glass with paper recycle next to plain old paper recycle, compost, food compost. I put a few away (why not, thought I, it was Friday night) and it surprised no one when I tossed the bottle into the wrong bin. In my defense, in the South "recycling" meant filling your beer bottle with water so it sank to the bottom of the lake.

"Josh, that doesn't go in there," Deb said from the couch. She wasn't even looking; she just knew.

"Shoot, no one cares." I crossed to the fridge to grab a fresh one. "Want some more wine?"

"I care. Put it in the right bin. And no, I'm all right."

I rolled my eyes and affected a thick, childish lisp. "But it's all groth in there. I don't wanna."

"Tough titties, Puff Diddies," she said, no sympathy given. She set her glass of white wine down on the coffee table, pushing herself up and toward the bathroom. "Do it anyway."

"You know it's Puff Daddy, right?" I bent over and lifted the lid. Luckily for me, I'd tossed it into the paper recycling, but my bitching aside, the containers were pretty clean. "It's important to me you know it's Puff Daddy."

"You're a Puff Daddy!" Deb cackled, leaning forward from her position on the toilet. I shot her a mock glare, and she grinned.

I burrowed through the rinsed-out milk containers, empty pints of yogurt, and thousand envelopes of junk mail. I snagged the first fingerful of glass I found and pulled. The beer bottle surfaced, half exposing a brilliant purple cardboard box I didn't recognize.

"What's this?" I tossed my bottle into the right receptacle and looked at the box, frowning. The bottom two-thirds were missing, the edges jagged. A green semicircle arced over the words *Plan B One Step*.

My stomach dropped to my toes. My mouth tasted like old carpet.

I played football in high school, plus a glorious season and a half at University of Alabama (roll tide roll) as a linebacker. In a game against Georgia Tech, I swallowed a beast of a hit from a soda machine with legs. I went down hard and he came with me, burying his helmet at mach-3 against my crotch; I wore a cup, but there isn't a cup in the world capable of absorbing that much mass with no repercussions.

I earned an ambulance ride to the hospital, where a nice doctor with cold hands sliced me open and . . . saved my pocket rocket for further excursions into deep space. I forget the exact words—I'd been doped up on some heavy medication after the surgery—but the only complication arose around a bundle of ducts in my testes the doc needed to snip. He lost the battle but won the war, if you understand what I'm getting at. I'd felt so grateful I still possessed complete operation of my parts that I didn't even mind I'd never have children. For a sophomore in college, that was pretty much an ideal scenario anyway.

"Deb?" My voice shook. Cotton stuffed my head; my brain wasn't working right. "Sweetheart, what is this?"

"What's what?" she asked without looking. She tied her sweatpants, not paying attention. The television blared in the background, angry white noise. I didn't say anything; I didn't trust my voice to work at that moment. When she finally did look up, she saw my face first and concern flashed across her baby blues.

Then she saw the box.

Deb's never been a good liar. We met my first year in Seattle, both incoming first-years for the massive soul sucker Amazon. She made fun of my Southern drawl, and I made fun of the half-dead bonsai tree leaning, drunk, on her desk. Two weeks later we went out on our first date—dinner at RN74 and drinks at Canon, up on Capitol Hill. A year after that I proposed. Two weeks before I tossed my bottle in the trash, we celebrated our five-year anniversary. And in all our time together, she'd never once been able to tell a lie. It was one of the things I loved about her—she wore every emotion on her face, clean and crisp as if she wrote it on paper.

I saw utter, absolute shock, the mirror of mine, followed by a dismay scoring a dozen tiny lines in her brow. Her mouth worked, but no words came out.

Having time to reflect on it, I'm not sure what I wanted to hear.

There's a stillness that comes with certain things, big things in everyone's life. Like everything in the world is reverberating, vibrating at a bone-deep level, and when it stops . . . the silence is absolute. I felt it the night I came home from a game in high school and found my dad weeping in the living room, holding a pair of Mom's flower shears. He hadn't been sober enough to put pants on and leave the house. I felt it the night I asked Deb to marry me, hunched against the pouring rain of a summer storm in front of her apartment. On our wedding day, when she filled the silence with "I do."

I felt it that night, looking at my wife's face. Because the box I held in my hands belonged to her, and I couldn't have children.

She mouth-breathed for fifteen seconds, staring at the kitchen floor. The huge, body-racking sobs came from within, building like a hurricane dancing on a ghost of breeze.

"Are you crying because you did something you regret?" I sounded like a robot, and I couldn't do a damn thing about it. Every breath I pulled into my tight lungs was a concerted effort. The world fell still, and we huddled in silence. When she looked up, it wasn't sadness plastered across her face.

"I'm crying because my own fucking husband doesn't trust me! How dare you—"

Ding ding, round one.

I don't remember the fight that ensued. I remember it being bad, but the details stay fuzzy, as if I deliberately forgot them. That night and the two others after it blended into a misery of shouting and tears. But as it usually does with the really bad fights, it kept circling back to the same premise; a broken record, scratching at the needle. The same line Deb half shouted again in our car as we rolled down I-5 to the Cascade Locks on the Oregon border.

"You know, you have no real right to get upset at me. If anything, I should get upset at you. You don't trust me! My own husband!" Tears in her eyes, her voice cracked.

I didn't trust her, and my mistrust in her was an unbearable strain on our relationship. She found a ceaseless variety of different ways to phrase it, couched in a dozen different tones, but always with the same message. Over and over. She never once gave me a straight answer about the box and what, if anything, had made it necessary. No matter how many times I pressed. Always the lack of trust — my lack of trust.

As they say back home, "If you believe that one, I have a bridge to sell you . . ."

But at this point I'd closed in on forty-eight hours with no sleep. I lived beyond emotion. Now I was dull, blunted to her tears and hoarse indignance. I turned around and ran my hands over my pack, pretending I couldn't hear her. For my own self-preservation, if nothing else.

We sat in silence, staring at the other cars in the Locks parking lot. Listening to the tapping rain drive against the windshield, after another one-sided shouting match. After I checked my pack for the umpteenth time. After her misbegotten anger ran dry. We sat in silence.

I felt like I should say something to her, but the cotton still hadn't left my head. I had no words.

"Will — when you're done, can we . . ." Deb bit her lip, staring at her feet. Cleared her throat. "Do we have a chance, after you're done? I — I . . ."

There it was.

She'd never been able to tell a lie in all the time I knew her. I bit off the fury threatening my lips; ten o'clock already. I wanted to get twenty miles in before dusk. I opened the door, pulled out my pack, and left. The last thing I saw before the woods swallowed me was my wife, sobbing against the steering wheel.

⟫⟫⟫ ⟪⟪⟪

I WAS TWO weeks into a three-week hike, walking roughly twelve hours a day. So for twelve hours a day, I played the events with Deb on a loop. Going over and over it, shredding it and examining it from every angle. Looking at the YOUR WIFE IS CHEATING ON YOU sign hanging over my head lit up in neon.

So, yeah. It was nice to think about a dead guy for a change. As long as I played it carefully. I hunted for facts. Facts were safe ground, facts didn't change. Facts didn't disturb that long-closed box in my head.

Green-Eyes could have been a day hiker, up from Everett or Seattle, but the odds weren't in his favor. We were a day north of Stevens Pass (the last time I crossed asphalt, by the way), and the nearest jump-off point for the Cascades. There wasn't shit around for miles in the way of day hiking, unless you were coming in from Chelan, twenty miles to the east. He might have been making a bid for the summit of Glacier Peak, but if he was, he took a cockeyed approach. A thru-hiker made the most sense. Like me.

Well, sort of. True thru-hikers were the ones who did the PCT proper, starting at the Mexico border. As I was running away from my problems on short notice, I had to make do with the Washington part. Didn't quite count.

My boss had been less than pleased about my sudden and non-negotiable opt for three weeks of vacation starting immediately. The slippery fucker had probably replaced me already, but I didn't care.

My job existed in the "real world," and I wasn't in the "real world." This was the trail world, and we played by different rules here.

The valley closed in around me. The crunch of my boots on gravel suddenly seemed too loud.

"Seeing things, Josh. You're acting all jumpy." I thought speaking out loud would help, but I was all-the-way wrong. My voice floated, disembodied, like someone else's. Someone I couldn't quite see, lurking just outside of view. I stopped talking.

I wondered if Green-Eyes had a trail name. Hikers doing the "long haul" on the trail often gave themselves trail names. Ironclad, All In, Pine Tree, Rain, Lotus—it could be anything you wanted. Day hikers were a dime a dozen. Thru-hikers . . . those were a much rarer species.

I rounded a bend and froze.

He sat on a petrified tree, shedding a tattered flannel that looked like it hadn't seen the inside of a washing machine in years. As if he were plucked straight from my thoughts and placed there. A present, just for me.

It's easy to tell the difference between day hikers and thru-hikers. Day hikers were well fed and bouncy, chirping like birds about how nice the day is, or how heavy their pack felt. How excited they were to eat when they got back to town—that was a big one. Thru-hikers had an underfed look about them: too thin, eyes retreated into deep hollows, all sharp angles and dishevelment. Carved from wood. They didn't talk as much.

"Hiya." I waved, like he couldn't see me, even though we were the only ones on the trail. *Stupid.*

He nodded in reply. Stared at me. Buried so deep in his skull, his eyes glinted like shards of glass in the sunlight. Watching. "Thru-hiking?"

I couldn't tell him. That wasn't how things were done in the trail world. You didn't bring your problems to other people, you didn't make them buy into your bullshit.

Plus . . . what if he thought I did it? It wasn't that far a stretch—we weren't exactly close to a town. If someone came up to me talking wide-eyed about a corpse they found an hour behind them this far removed from civilization, the first thing I'd think was that I might be their next victim.

No thanks.

I swallowed the paranoia and fear crawling up my throat and shot for normal. How did normal people talk?

How the hell would I know?

"Yeah," I answered.

"Got a name yet?"

"Switchback," I said, feeling rather stupid. Like a kid in grade school introducing myself by the nickname I invented. His chapped lips spread mechanically, revealing a double row of shockingly white teeth. Twitching a little, like his muscles had forgotten how to move that way. He stuck out a hand.

"Boots. Good to meet you."

We shook. His grip was brittle, like I might break it if I squeezed too hard. It wrapped around mine, engulfing my knuckles in his tanned and cracked-skin ones. He looked at me as if waiting for something. Something I should say or do.

"So, you, uh . . . you been on the trail long?" I asked.

"'Bout two months," he drawled. Texas, unless my ears deceived me. Another good old boy from the South. I waited for a follow-up, something to keep the conversation going. Those Southern manners were imprinted deep in my bones; I couldn't just abandon a conversation, once it started.

Nothing. He stared at me. Something lurked in his eyes. Curiosity, like I was a novelty toy fresh out of the cereal box. And something deeper, something with edges.

"What brought you out here?" My voice cracked. I cleared my throat.

"Been wantin' to do it for a while." He shrugged. "Up and did it." A pause, growing like a thing alive.

"You?" he finally asked, a full ten seconds later. I felt like I might be going crazy. Maybe the shit with Deb was messing with my perception. Could be. Dr. K and I talked about perception at length, all those years ago. Every chance this dude acted perfectly normal, and *I* acted like the kooky one.

Breathe. Everything was fine. I was just fine.

"Oh you know." My turn to shrug, smiling wide. "Just running from my life and problems."

I meant it as a joke; something lighthearted. But my voice cracked halfway through, and the words floated between us, empty and cold. Ha-ha, my life is a trash-can fire of pain and lies, let's all laugh at it together, amigo.

"That right?" He didn't join in my pathetic laughter. He stared at me. I squirmed under that gaze. I took off my pack, sat on it and undid my shoe, pretending to hunt for another pebble just for something to do.

"Oh well, I mean . . . I was mostly joking. I'm just out here like you said. Wanted to do it forever." I said it while I scrabbled inside my shoe, looking for a rock I knew good and goddamn well wasn't in there. He stared at me, sitting on his log. I could see his arm bones in my peripheral vision, jutting through the too-thin skin.

Then, as though I imagined it, the edges in his eyes disappeared. Humanity flooded back into his face.

"Well." He slapped his knee, shooting to his feet. Another smile creased his tanned cheeks, this one smooth and warm. "Think we might pound down some miles together, what say? Weather looks like it might cooperate."

A good thing I was already sitting; the surge of relief made me weak at the knees. See? Perfectly normal. My perception skewed, that's it. Just another hiker, and a friendly one at that. *That simple, Josh.*

"Let's do it," I said.

We ambled a good five or six miles together, talking about nothing of any consequence. He didn't bring up why I came to the trail again— he probably saw the real answer on my face and learned his lesson. I swallowed any mention of Green-Eyes, kept him to myself. My own little secret. He pressed right to the top of my lips, sitting on my tongue like a foul aftertaste. A voice, whispering in my ear.

I didn't even know what I'd say. What I wanted to say. It's all a matter of perspective, that's what Dr. K said. I just had to look at it a little differently. So I didn't say anything. I talked about boot styles and brands like I didn't have a care in the world.

The hours slipped past. Around late afternoon he turned off, saying he wanted to shoot for the summit of a nearby peak.

"Okay. Guess I'll see ya." I adjusted the pack straps on my shoulders. Every now and then it slid, pinching the skin.

"Guess you will."

Too busy with my pack to notice the way he looked at me. Too busy thinking about the dead body to put the pieces together. Perception only fools you so far.

We waved good-bye. I watched him take the rougher, steeper offshoot trail, turn a corner, and disappear. I craned my neck for a flash of T-shirt between the trees but saw nothing. As if the forest swallowed him whole and left nothing behind.

"You're being silly, Mallory," I grumbled to myself. "Just downright dumb about it. So you found a dead guy. You'll tell the rangers, they'll deal with it. You got your own problems. Now come on, let's get over that saddle before sundown."

The trees dwindled two-thirds up the ridge. The trail steepened as I climbed, gaining fifty or more feet in elevation with every pivot. By the time I topped the ridge, sweat was dripping from my cheeks, and I heaved like a bellows, taking in the view.

The Glacier Peak Wilderness stretched to the horizon, forested in a carpet of pine trees. Here and there granite summits broke the green, splintering skyward. A hint of late-season snow lingered in the perpetual shadows. The sun hung three fingers above Glacier's peak; five, five and a half hours of daylight left, by my estimate. I'd also forgotten my watch.

While the ranger I registered with back at Stevens' Pass called my lack of gear "foolish to the point of suicide," I preferred to think of it as minimalist. I backpacked and hiked as a hobby, so I already owned all the basics: tent, sleeping bag, stove, pack. Nuances like watches only detracted from the experience.

Or so I lied to myself.

The trail meandered along the ridge, rising to a pass between a pair of peaks overhead. Cloudy Ridge was aptly named; an edge of bruised navy curled around the slopes, hiding the summits from sight. The trail slipped beneath the cloud layer. It dropped into the valley on the other side, if memory served, where I hoped to find a decent campsite.

Chances were good I could get far enough away from the rain clouds to find some dry wood and get a fire going. A fire made any campsite infinitely cozier, everyone knew it. My fire-making skills sucked the big one, but what I lacked in technique I made up for in exuberance. The only luxury I had time to stick in my bag was my e-reader and a solar charger. Last night I'd read the first couple chapters of Neil Gaiman's *American Gods*, and it had already hooked me hard; I looked forward to spending a few hours dusting off my elementary-school mythology while warming my socks with a toasty blaze.

I hitched my bag up higher on my shoulders and began climbing. I even started to whistle when I had the lung capacity. Why wouldn't I? The sun shone everywhere I looked, the wind soared. The corpses were behind me, one fresh and the other long-since buried. I could ignore them now.

Those were my priorities that afternoon. Remembering where the trail headed, getting to a campsite, and hoping for a fire and a peaceful evening with a book. I think back on that day and I suppress the urge to throttle the idiot who calls himself Switchback.

He missed the sign. The huge, hit-you-over-the-head-sized sign. Screaming, in big, bold letters: WATCH OUT.

2

T HE CLOUDS PRESSED AGAINST MY FACE LIKE THE TOUCH OF A GHOST.
The rain started gently, the drops ice cold against my sun-
burned skin. I stopped long enough to root around in the bottom of
my pack for my raincoat—because why would it be on top?—before
pressing on. The rain increased with every step I took toward the pass.
The wind turned sour, slinging drops against my face in a stinging
spray, like the mountain didn't want me there. A shiver little to do
with the weather slipped through my bones. The thought carried more
weight than I cared to admit.

No; it was just a mountain. Perception, that's it. Just my way of
looking at things.

I passed the last tree on my right, a scrubby and stunted pine. The
grass dwindled and fell away, turning to fine-grain silt. The Cascades

faded behind me as I pushed into the clouds, the rolling valleys and peaks disappearing. The landscape changed to a wind-blasted wasteland, cut through with a single dirt track for me to follow. I pulled my hood up and pressed on.

By the time I reached the flat saddle of the pass, rain was dripping from the rim of my hood and had soaked into my shoes. Left and right, the summits stretched into the clouds. Patchwork trails marked by stacked cairns wound cloud-ward like spiderwebs in the dirt. I contemplated wandering one of those summit-bound trails until the air flashed white with lightning, and a snarl of thunder cracked close enough to shake my bones.

Even I wasn't fool enough to tempt a thunderstorm eight feet over my head. The wind ruffled the edge of my hood, pushing it against the side of my face.

I scanned the trails, trying to guess which one led down the other side of the pass, and I saw him.

He materialized from the clouds, walking from the storm like a wraith, calm as you please. An older guy, well into his late sixties, with long white hair tucked into a loose bun and a beard to match. He wore a ragged button-up tucked into khaki shorts, knee-high tube socks and a pair of dusty Keens held together with spit and a prayer. The pack strapped to his shoulders couldn't have been more than thirty-six liters, a day bag at best. He seemed more like an apparition than a real human being.

He raised a hand, a smile cracking his leathered face.

"Great day for it, isn't it?" he shouted over the wind and rain. There wasn't the remotest hint of irony in his voice, and I liked him for it. "Watch your step, the footing is goofy up 'round here!"

"Did you just come down from the summit?" My hood struggled in my fingers, trying to pull free.

He nodded. Rain streaked his face and his shirt stuck to his knobby shoulders, but he looked unconcerned. I liked him for that too.

"Be a little nicer if it was clearer, ya dig me, but it's still a nice, tight scramble."

"How far up is it?" The thought of jumping up one of those summits still rattled around my head, weather be damned. I might have an hour or so to spare for a quick up and down.

The old man shrugged. "'bout an hour and a half, less on the down slope if you're quick about it."

Well shit, never mind. "That far?"

He nodded and grinned again. "Don't look it, right? Yeah, it's about six hunnert feet pretty much straight up, scrambling some fair-sized boulders. Unless you're dead set on it, I wouldn't recommend. Could be nasty in this weather, 'specially if you ain't got the gear."

I couldn't help a pointed glance at his busted shoes and khaki shorts.

He guffawed. "Busted for bogus, you got me. Although to be fair, I hit the trail at noon, which gave me the advantage of daylight. Which way you headed?"

"Northbound. You?"

"Same." He chinned toward a broad webbing of crisscrossed trails snaking down through the clouds. I hadn't noticed them. "Want to head down? It's getting a little less than welcoming up here."

Like magic, the air flashed, and thunder slammed all around us. By now my water-resistant shoes were pretty much soaked through, and it would take a miracle to keep the contents of my pack dry.

"Lead on," I said.

The trail dropped down the side of the mountain, steep enough to make my knees groan. The rain fell away and the wind died down. The curtain of summer fell over us once again; a valley stretched beneath us, golden sunlight slipping up the peaks around its edge. An emerald lake glimmered in the basin, nestled underneath a crown of pine trees. Cloudy Pass lay behind us, and the afternoon looked up. The older man set an easy pace, eating through the miles.

"You thru-hiking, my dude?" he asked over his shoulder.

"I am. Well, sort of."

"What do you mean 'sort of'?"

"I mean I'm thru-hiking Washington. It only sort of counts."

"It totally counts." He turned around to shoot me a smile. "Thru-hiking is thru-hiking, man. Don't sell yourself short."

I felt better equipped with this microscopic validation, even from someone I just met. "What about you? Goin' the distance?"

"Oh." He shrugged without turning around. "I suppose I am."

"Are you not sure?"

He laughed. "I started down around the northern Cali area, so I guess you could call it a thru-hike. Got bored at my desk job, so I figured why not." He looked the part of a longtime hiker; walking behind him I got a good eyeful of his legs. With every step his calves flexed, bulging, almost grotesque in their starkness. He didn't have an ounce of fat on him.

We turned a switchback, dropping down into the valley proper, which flattened around the lake. There'd be spots aplenty for campsites around those waters for sure, and from the look of the pines, dry too. A fire could be in order after all, even with my questionable skill set. I inhaled deeply, counted to five, then exhaled. Everything was fine. A good campsite and a fire, that was all I needed. Something to look forward to.

"Where you camping tonight?" I asked, peering at the sky. With the sky clearing up again I could tell time easier. Two, three hours of daylight left.

"Oh mebbe down by the lake yonder." He flapped a hand toward the basin. "I'm supposed to be further along according to my map, but my little detour this afternoon held me back. Although," he added almost as an afterthought, "that's kinda the point, I suppose."

Something about the way he spoke amused me. His vernacular carried a hint of seventies flower power, foreign to me beyond the occasional rerun of the OG *Magnum P.I.* or *Charlie's Angels*. I didn't hate it though; he was old enough to have those words bumping around his lexicon. It gave them a sort of vintage authenticity.

"Where are you planning on throwing down for the night?" he asked, giving me a glance over his shoulder. Beneath the snowy bristles of his beard, his skin was tanned to a deep mahogany, worn and weathered. His eyes beetled bright in their sockets.

"Oh, I was planning on the lake as well. Seems like a good place for it." Six or seven snowcapped peaks sawtoothed into the sky, ringing the little lake on three sides. Even from a few hundred feet away I could see the rocks at the bottom of the lake. I didn't see a single tent or hammock. Any backpacker will tell you the best campsite is one you don't have to share.

I didn't mind the thought of sharing it with my newfound colleague, though. He looked unlike any of the few thru-hikers I'd met so far. They all looked, to some extent, like they were taking a break from their lives elsewhere. Escaping into the wilderness for a few months to clean the smog out of their lungs. Running away from their problems. Looking for their soul. But this guy . . . he looked like he'd been born in the mountains. With the same pair of Keens on his feet, from the looks of them.

I didn't want to be a creeper and ask him if he wanted to throw down camp together—that strayed into serial-killer territory. After all, we only just met. Solid odds he came out here for the isolation, and didn't want to spend the night with some guy following him around—

"How's about sharing a fire tonight, friend-o?" he asked. I jolted hard enough to almost overbalance backward. Like he'd picked the thought right out of my head.

"Yeah, let's do it." I struck for casual nonchalance. I almost made it.

We were past the boulder field now. Packs of thistle and red paintbrush crept along the side of the trail, riots of red and purple. It grew warmer the closer we got to the floor of the wide valley. At the top of the pass, the occasional rumble of muffled thunder snarled in the hazy clouds. Walking and talking kept the events of earlier this afternoon at bay—Green-Eyes and Boots, the soft and gentle murmur in the back of my head that something wasn't quite right here. Walking with my new-found companion, it was easier to just . . . be. To relax. He had that kind of way about him.

By the time we reached the lake, the sunlight had faded from the peaks around us, and a distinct lavender tint of dusk tinged the horizon. We picked sites close enough to the lake for easy water-filling, but far away enough the mosquitoes around the lakeshore didn't cause issue. A fine balance to strike.

I dropped my pack against a tree, sighing with relief as I lifted the sixty pounds off my shoulders. In the morning the pack felt light as a song and breeze, but it picked up pounds with every mile. My sweat-soaked shirt clung to my back.

"Long day?" the older man asked with an easy smile, swinging his backpack to the top of a log like it weighed nothing.

I nodded, trying not to pant. "Been on it since around five, six this morning."

He whistled in appreciation, taking a drink of water from a metal flask older than I was. "That is a long day. Kudos, brother."

It took more effort than I cared to admit to hide the blush of pride at his approval.

"Oh, I'm Appletree, by the way."

"Switchback." No more first-grade embarrassment with using my trail name. I thanked Boots for it. I wondered if he'd ever made it to the top of whatever mountain he shot for. What was the name? I couldn't remember. A strange detail to forget. The electric-green of moss, growing in a dead man's eyes. It had been a strange morning, in fairness.

"Switchback, eh? I like it. Pleasure's all mine, Switchback, good to meet ya."

We each set about making camp.

My tent was a simple affair to set up; ground tarp to keep water away, tent base, two poles fixed at four corners, clip-it-vertical, done. It didn't look like rain tonight, so I left the rain fly bundled in the bag. I unfurled my sleeping pad and opened the dial to let it auto-inflate, a process I still considered almost magic.

I turned to Appletree, opening my mouth to ask what he planned on eating for dinner, but when I caught his setup I lost my entire train of thought from engine to caboose.

He stretched a plastic poncho—it looked like the eighty-eight-cent kind they used to hand out at Cub Scout summer camp—over a single hiking pole. He pulled fishing-line from one pocket, kneeling down to secure the flapping edge. His knees popped like dry air pistols as he worked his way around the base. I must have made a sound, because he looked up in time to catch me gawping.

"Like it?" He flashed me a crooked smile. "I used to do the whole tent-and-tarp biz, brother. I discovered this setup a few years back thanks to a cool cat I met in the Sierras."

"Why are you—why?" I asked, realized how rude I sounded and checked myself. "I'm sorry, I meant—what's the advantage?"

Appletree waved my apology away with a casual flip of his hand. "Weight, more than anything else. I shaved 'bout three, four pounds when I switched. And she does everything a regular tent does, keeps me dry and all."

"Does it stay warm enough?" I eyed the three-inch gaps between his "tent" and the forest floor.

"This old girl? Sheeit, no. Just keeps the rain off my hair." He laughed and patted the plastic sheet. "But I've got my bag to keep me warm."

He pulled out a salmon-scale silver sleeping bag and threw it right down onto the pine needles and dirt.

"You're not afraid of getting it dirty?"

I put a great deal of effort into keeping my gear clean, a lesson long-since ingrained from a decade in the Decatur Boy Scouts. I should match my long-haired companion's level of chill, although to be honest, I suspected it took a lifetime of effort to reach.

Much to my relief, Appletree overlooked my eighth-grade whining, shaking his head.

"Nah. I'll give it a good brush-down in the morning, but a few pine needles hitching a ride downriver don't bother me none." He sat down on a log, taking another sip of water. "Besides, that's what we're out here for, right?"

"Getting dirty?" I knelt and unfurled my sleeping bag, careful to keep my shoes outside the tent. Appletree leaned back against a tree, squinting at the gloam overtaking the sky.

"Getting in touch with *nature*, brother. That's what it's all about, right? Getting out, away from everything and back into the wilds. Where mankind belongs, dude. Not cooped up in complexes of iron and steel. I mean, yeah, everyone has their own personal reasons for being this deep in the middle of nowhere—"

My hands twitched, unzipping my sleeping bag. I said nothing.

"—but I think deep down, people like you and me all dig the outdoors for the same reason. It's back to basics—you, a few scant supplies, and the big, wide world. So what if you get a little dirt and such in your sleeping bag?"

"Kind of like paying a bunch of money to be homeless, right?" I said. Deb cracked the same joke every time I left the house for an overnighter. She laughed every time she said it. I rarely did.

"People joke about it, my dude, but some of the most content people I've ever met were homeless." Appletree folded his hands over his chest. "A lot of people see their material possessions as perks to living that nine-to-five life. It would surprise you how many people sleeping under the stars see those same things as shackles. All they need is a blanket and a doggo for company, and they're happier than a bivalve mollusk at high tide." He chortled. "Oh, and the screens! Brother, the screens these days. Cell phones, televisions, video games . . . what's it all add? What's the cumulative benefit of living a life through a little rectangle?"

"I suppose I've never thought of it that way." I slid my e-reader from my pack into the depths of my sleeping bag before he could see it.

"Ah, sorry 'bout it, brother. I ramble sometimes. Side effects of spending hours on hours on my own. Ever find yourself talking to thin air, to make sure you still can?"

"All the time," I said. "Got to make sure your voice box still works, dude." His dusted-off seventies speech turned infectious, it seemed.

"Too right, brother. Want to grab some firewood while we still have a few hours of daylight left? We're not supposed to have one this close to a lake so late in the dry season, but I won't tell the Smokeys if you don't."

"The Smokeys? Oh, the rangers, right. Yeah, sounds great."

Appletree gave the woods a cursory glance, pressing a hand against the small of his back. "You're what my pops called a whipper-snapper, so I'll be gracious and allow you to round up some big hearty stuff. I myself will focus on kindling and twigs."

"How kind of you." I gave him a sideways glance, and he dad-guffawed again. We split up; he went along the lake shore and I moved north, deeper into the pine forest where the deadfall was.

The forests in the PNW were unlike any woods from my childhood. In the outskirts of Decatur, Alabama, the woods were silent and empty, longleaf pines tangled with underbrush and sumac. Full of trash and rifle-toting rednecks pounding Bud Light, hunting whatever happened to be nearby and alive.

But in the Cascade wilds, the trees came alive. The branches whispered as the wind brushed through them, chattering beneath their breath. No choking underbrush to force through, here. Beneath the canopy each trunk stood isolated, separated by a sort of dim, filmy sunlight. A single layer of dead leaf coated the soft loam. Here were forests, not woods, and they still remember what the world looked like without people. Sometimes I wondered if they missed it that way.

Yesterday I'd found the silence and space between the trees warm, welcoming. Today twigs snapped when I turned my back, sending my heart spiking into my throat. Things lurked in the fogged-over sunbeams between the trees. Electric green eyes waited beneath every step, behind every moss-covered trunk.

Watching me.

It's all perspective. Dr. K's voice, floating across the years. Seven, specifically, since I last sat in that office just off Cleveland Ave.

I ferried two or three armloads of deadfall in varying thicknesses to our campsite. Dusk settled into our piece of the wilderness. Appletree hadn't gathered so much as a single twig yet, as he got caught up admiring the bark of a stunted oak. I grabbed a few armfuls of the delicate stuff too, trying not to huff in irritation.

"You got it?" He snapped back to reality as I brought in the last armful. Apparently, I'd earned the right to build the fire too.

"Yeah, I got it." I shouldn't get annoyed. Everyone came out here for their own reasons. Sometimes it was to commune with the trees like a flower-power hippie. Still didn't think it was super fair I had to carry all the wood and take responsibility for building a fire, but I wasn't going to jeopardize a budding kinship by saying so out loud. I scraped the edge of my pocket knife over a few sticks, producing delicate curls of kindling.

I dug around in my pocket for the little metal fire starter I'd impulse bought waiting in line at REI. I used to keep it in my pack, but it took twenty minutes of fishing around to find the damn thing. I just kept it in my pocket now. Easier.

Much to my relief and surprise, the sparks caught. Some babysitting later, the fire crackled on a stout piece of pine, and we both relaxed. I pulled out my expensive collapsible pot and filled it with a few cups of water, setting it on a rock near the blaze. It boiled faster on the pocket-rocket stove in my pack, but I wasn't in a hurry. Plus this saved my precious reserve of propane.

We sat in amiable silence for a while, watching the night come over the valley.

After a few minutes I reached for my bag, waving a pack of turkey casserole in Appletree's direction in a silent question.

"I'm all good, brother, appreciate it though." He reached into his bag and pulled out a pair of burnt-scarlet apples. He took a bite out of one and leaned back with a long sigh.

"How long you been on the trail?" I asked, eyeing the pearl-white flesh of the apple in his hand. Good God, it looked perfect. My mouth watered even looking at it.

"Oh about four months or so. I came at it kind of cockeyed—I started in the Wahsatch range, then headed north through Yellowstone. From there, bounced westward for a bit." His untraceable accent pronounced the word "Yella-stone."

"Oh really? I've never been down that way." My water finished boiling. I slit the top of the turkey casserole bag open and poured it inside. I grabbed my spoon, gave it a stir, and sealed it back up to steam.

"It's radical, man. Real trailblazer stuff, you know? I followed a settlers' trail from back in the 1750s. I felt like I walked right there with them, discovering a new America. It was wild. What about you?"

"Oh I've only been on for a few weeks. I just started down by the Locks."

"Been on this stretch of trail before?"

"Not the whole PCT. I've hit the Cascades quite a few times, but this is the first time I've stitched together the whole spine on one go."

"How are you finding it?" Appletree leaned his head back against a tree trunk, looking at the rising night. The filtered sunlight turned to navy shadow and stole through the spaces between the trees. Stole the light from the world.

I opened my mouth to talk about the beauty and majesty of the Cascades, but my subconscious had other plans.

"I found a body today." I blurted it, like the words had been lying in wait and grabbed the opportunity to escape.

The apple froze halfway to my companion's mouth. One side of his mouth quirked into a frown. Not exactly casual conversation between strangers.

"Is that right? Where?"

I nodded, staring at my shoelaces. I could still see the too-vibrant shade of green, staring at me from the loam and dirt.

"Sorry, I know it's . . . I'm trying to process. Uh, other side of the pass, few miles."

"No, it's . . ." He cleared his throat, took another bite of his apple. The shadow over his face stuck around, coloring the hard lines there. "It's fine. Process away, friend-o. Did he . . . was he, you know . . . fresh?"

"Uh-uh. Couple days, I guess? I dunno how long it takes a body to start to . . . go. Looked like he fell, busted his leg pretty bad. Went for cover to regain some strength and the mountain lions found him."

"Not an easy way to go."

"Yeah." I didn't have anything else to say. I shouldn't have brought it up in the first place.

The turkey casserole finished, I scooped out a spoonful. We ate in silence. The casserole tasted like hot dirt. I ate it because I paid for it and needed the calories.

"Hey, I'm sorry if I made things weird. I just . . . it's not every day you find a . . . you know. It's got me more rattled than I'd like to admit."

"It's all good, brother, no sweat. If I found a cold one, I'd likely need to talk about it too. Don't worry yourself." He smiled, but I didn't feel any better.

It's all perspective. The way you look at things.

Deb wasn't cheating on Switchback. Switchback didn't have problems sleeping, didn't hear someone screaming through a cloud of black smoke in his nightmares. Switchback liked hiking, liked the trail, and most important, didn't have time for Josh's crippling emotional baggage.

But Switchback found the body, and the body forced him to remember. A crack in the illusion, letting in the darkness. Because I wasn't Switchback, I was Josh. Switchback was just a different way to look at things. A way to not be hurt, for a little while. And all those walls were about to come crashing down around my ears. All those years of therapy, exercises, hard work undone. The bricks stacked one by one over that fresh grave. My heart fluttered in my chest, stuttering a skip-time rhythm.

"You good, Switch? You look like you're gonna be ill." Appletree gave me a speculative eye, rolling the other apple in one hand.

I wiped my face with the back of one hand. Cold sweat, beading on my brow, defiant in the face of the crackling fire. The grinding sound of bricks shifting overhead echoed in the silence between the trees.

Talk it out. Dr. K's voice, soft and warm in that strip-mall back office. The smell of the Dunkin' Donuts next door. *Don't hold it in.*

"Talk it out, brother. Let it all out."

I flinched, looking at him. He smiled, and for a second Dr. K's face hovered over his, an after-image. No, no that wasn't right. I was seeing things.

"Do you believe in ghosts?" The words tasted sour. I shouldn't be talking about this. Not with a stranger. I hadn't yet sorted fact from fiction. I still hadn't gained perspective.

I didn't know what I was looking at.

He hesitated. "Sure. What's not to believe?"

"I think . . ." I laughed. It sounded thin, weak. Fake. "I think I'm seeing one. Or will. Tonight. In my dreams."

The closest I could come to the truth. The closest I could come to admitting what I buried, under those bricks. Deb knew the truth. But Deb wasn't here—in almost every sense of the word. The panic attack gnawed at the edge of my brain; cold tingling started in my fingertips. It would start again, and soon. That voice, winding through the smoke. A child's panic.

The old man sat still, running a hand through the wild tangle of his beard. He stared at the fire, and I watched the flames burn in his eyes. He seemed to sink into himself, go somewhere else.

"Once upon a time, a boy lived in a small town, in the outlands of California. He was a good kid, quiet and polite, kept to himself. He liked the outdoors, choir . . . and a boy in his math class, ya dig me? So anyways, he grows up and goes to college in the big city. He meets another boy, who sings in the choir and who likes the outdoors. The two of them go hiking together, ranging all over the Sierras, Yosemite, and even the Redwoods. They like each other, like spending time with each other. They grow close, and after a spell they move in together."

I nodded. And I listened, because listening meant I wasn't thinking. The screaming muted if I listened. I was so caught up in my own thoughts, I didn't notice the subtle change in Appletree's voice. Lower now, growing husky.

"The two of them—they have a happy life. But something happens—something bad. There's a war. A war across the ocean, in a place we have no business being. People die. So many people, in fact, they start dragging regular people into the war. Snatching them out of their lives with a scrap of paper, like that." He snapped his fingers, and almost like magic the fire snarled on a piece of sap and popped loud enough to make me jump. Appletree wasn't looking at me anymore. He stared at the fire, arms wrapped around his knobby knees. I wanted to tell him to stop, wanted to tell him he didn't have to keep going, but I didn't. I stayed silent and listened. I listened to his pain, to forget mine.

"That little kid who liked choir and the mountains found himself across the world with a rifle in his hands. They gave him a choice; use the gun, or they'd bury him with it." He cleared his throat, turning to spit in the dirt beside him.

"Well by some magic, the boy survived. The war ended as it began—pointless, and stupid—and they sent that boy home. Except the boy was different now. They took something from him, in the war. A piece of his soul. Now the boy couldn't sleep at night. He had nightmares of people wrapping their hands around his neck, and he woke up screaming. Fireworks made him tremble and cry. He's scared—all the time he's scared." The fire bloomed and dropped from Appletree's eyes, spilling onto his leathered cheeks. "People nudged each other and pretended not to stare. Saying things like, 'There's the loony tune who never came back from Vietnam.' Not real loud . . . just loud enough."

"I'm so sorry, man. You—you don't have to—" I reached out, but if Appletree heard me, he didn't show it. He stared deep into the fire; I doubt he even realized I still sat across from him. I wanted it to stop. I felt like I'd stepped into a house I didn't live in, spying through a keyhole at a love beyond my understanding. Nightmares. The boy had nightmares.

That part I understood just fine.

"Things get bad. The boy has a hard time finding a job. No one wants to hire someone who can't get in an elevator without having a nervous breakdown, ya dig me? The two boys can't pay rent. They fight all the time. So, the boy comes up with a solution, you see. He waits for his partner to leave for groceries—he can't go to the store anymore, too many loud noises—and he cleans the whole apartment. He cleans the bathroom, folds the laundry. Scrubs the baseboards. Then, he hangs himself from the living room fan with a pair of suspenders."

I jumped, almost kicking my empty casserole bag into the coal bed. For the first time in what felt like a long time, Appletree looked at me. Ghosts floated in his eyes, real as the tree I leaned against. I knew the look.

"He left a note, folded on my pillow. It said, 'I'm sorry.'"

"Jesus," I croaked. I didn't have anything else to say. Appletree didn't respond. He stayed wrapped up around himself, staring past the fire now into the gloom rising around us. The last daylight fled from the sky, and the hazy dots of the first stars were barely visible through the smoke and treetops.

Talk it out. Dr. K, floating over the smoke, over the years since it happened. Since that night. The panic, building in my hands. Tingling like they were falling asleep, like I was falling asleep. I didn't want to sleep. Sleeping only made it worse.

The words bulged against my lips, stinging like acid, cold as the dirt covering that grave. Words I'd told exactly two people—Dr. K and Deb. Neither was here, neither could help. Alone.

Well, not quite.

Appletree watched me. I saw him in the corner of my eye, a pale smudge against the creeping blackness. He didn't say anything. He waited. Like he knew the words were coming.

3

A SHIFTING OF BRICKS

"I WAS TWELVE. PLAYING VIDEO GAMES ON A SATURDAY MORNING." The words floated on the still air before I realized they were coming out of my mouth.

This story. I didn't want to tell this story. Beyond the fire, the darkness fell in a black curtain, separating the outside world from our own.

"Dad said if I made the all-star regionals u-13 team, he'd buy me a PlayStation. Mom was the one who let me put it in my room; I remember them arguing about it too, in the car on the way home from K-Mart. Fencing, almost, you know how parents do when there's a kid in the car? They don't want to out-and-out fight, but they go round after round of bickering, scratching at the same thing. Dad wanted to keep the PlayStation in the living room and lock up the controller until one of them gave me permission to play. I guess he thought I'd turn anti-social and ignore them in favor of the TV. But Mom stood up for me, and when Mom put her mind to something, my Dad liked to say she was stubborn as a pit bull with a stick it doesn't want you to have." I laughed, but there wasn't an ounce of humor in it. "Crazy, isn't it? The things that set off huge events in your life? A PlayStation. It was just a PlayStation."

I shifted in my seat. There were ants in my pants, and they were crawling up my legs. I felt their tiny legs, scratching and tickling my skin.

"Anyway. I was playing video games in my room, and I heard a pop and a *whoom*—a blast, you know, like the ones you can feel in your chest? It shook the whole house. My signed Joe Montana poster fell off the wall. Then the fire alarms started going off. I wasn't scared—I was irritated, because I just wanted to play my video game. I got off my bed and went downstairs, calling for Mom. I knew something was wrong, right then. Mom kept a clean house. Like, commercial clean. The carpets were always vacuumed, the hardwood swept. Outside the kitchen window, she kept this huge gardenia bush, trimmed and neat. And I mean, huge—as tall as my dad—and when she opened the window, the kitchen smelled like flowers. Especially in the summertime. In the summertime, the entire house smelled like them."

It came back to me, every bit as strong as a hot evening in mid-August, sixteen years ago. Sweet, and full of a kind of perfume that went straight to your head.

"I didn't smell the gardenias; the smoke had grown too strong. The house was shaking, trembling."

I looked at the memory through the haze. I still remembered the details. I thought it lay abandoned; I'd boxed it and left it alone for over a decade. The broad strokes were still there, still imprinted on the bedrock of my soul, but I thought I'd left the painful details in the past.

I was wrong.

"The firefighters had to come get me from the bedroom, I think. I don't remember running out." Shards of glass coated my lips. The tingling in my fingers turned to buzzing, angry hornets trapped in my skin. Details, I'd forgotten the details. Like a dream, I couldn't remember how I got out of the house. A blank spot on the record, a skipping point. As though my brain had buried those details, trying to protect me. "The next thing I remember, I was out on the street, looking at the house. The fire was bright—so bright I needed to squint. So much smoke. Mom never made it out."

"Oh, brother." Appletree covered his mouth. I said the words out loud now, and they lived.

Something, lingering in his face. Horror, dismay . . . but no surprise. Which made sense; he had to know it was coming. The words, pressing against my lips ever since I found Green-Eyes.

I nodded, swallowing past the lump pressing against my throat. "Yeah. I tried to run in, but I didn't get ten feet down the hall before the heat became too much. Someone was in the kitchen, out of sight. I could hear them, knocking bowls and plates over. They were struggling. Struggling to get out. Buster barked like crazy."

The muscles in my neck twitched. The hungry faces pressed against the edges of the fire, eager and hungry. I scooted closer to the campfire and tried not to remember the sound of china shattering.

"The roof collapsed, toward the back. I heard one of the firefighters whisper that it was probably the kitchen. That's when I ran away. Ran down the block, to my neighbor Mr. Neery's house. I was crying, maybe. Can't remember. I remember falling into his front hallway, like I couldn't walk right. Buster was there—he followed me? No one could drive through the street, what with all the fire trucks blocking the way. Four of them, a whole fuss. Everyone came out to watch. Watch our house burn down around her."

I watched them from Mr. Neery's living room. Watched them watching. Mrs. Jones, standing in her pink and white overalls, battered

Dustbuster still in hand. Mr. and Mrs. McElroy, frozen at the entrance to their driveway. Dustin, their son, stood behind them, still wearing his baseball uniform. He and I played football in the park sometimes.

"Did you know it takes firefighters hours to stop a fire? I didn't. In movies and TV, it happens in a flash—they roll up, spray it a bit and it goes down. Unless it's a bad one. If it's a bad one it means the hero is going to show up and run inside, ignoring the firefighters telling them not to. They grab the person in danger and make it out in a dramatic crescendo. But no one went running inside my house. No dramatic crescendo. They just . . . stood next to their hoses. Watched my childhood burn to the ground."

I brought my knees up to my chest, circled them with my arms. A shiver ran up my spine, spreading goose bumps across my shoulders. The fire felt very far away.

"My dad got there about an hour later. He knocked over Mr. Neery's mailbox, he drove so fast. He jumped out of his car and just . . . stood there, staring at our house. By then the whole thing was on fire—bright enough to light up the whole block. There were news crews, policemen closing off the street. All that commotion, all that noise, and my dad stood next to his beat-up oh-three Taurus and . . . watched. After a while he came and got me. We sat together on Mr. Neery's back porch—him, me, and Buster. Sat there, watching the clouds turn orange. He told me it was Mom, in the kitchen."

Did he? I struggled to remember, to bring certain details into focus. I remember the angry orange tint to the night sky, a looming menace. I remember Buster barking like crazy beneath my arm. I remember my dad talking, muttering under his breath like he talked to himself, like I wasn't there. He stared at the grass, rocked me back and forward and whispered, "Everything is going to be okay."

But did he tell me it was Mom? Did he bring himself to say the words out loud?

"The firefighters said it was a gas leak. A pipe fitting slipped behind the oven and filled the kitchen with gas. Mom went to make herself some tea. That was . . . that was when it happened."

The spaces between the trees were pitch-black now. What horrible things loomed in the soft shadow? What things full of teeth and claws were lying in wait for one of us to get too close? To let our guard down enough for it to snatch us and rip us apart, all teeth and anger and fire, so much fire—

"Switch." The fire popped on a piece of sap and I jumped, snapping back to see Appletree leaning across the campfire, concern etched in his deep-lined crow's-feet.

"Switch, you all right?"

A memory. Just a memory. It couldn't hurt me anymore. It was in the past. I recited the mantra Dr. K and I had come up with all those years ago, and swallowed, nodding. "Yeah. Yeah, of course. I'm fine."

I held my hands out, grateful for the heat of the fire, crackling on a fresh piece of wood Appletree threw in. It seeped into my bones like a hot bath. The world warmed, and my ghosts faded back into the spaces between the trees where they belonged.

"Sorry. Sorry, I—" I shook my head. The words came of their own accord, like they did every time. In their absence, I felt bad. "I don't know why I told you that. I haven't . . . you know, I haven't told many people."

The bricks settled, back on her grave. Just like they did every time. *Just talk about it, and the pain goes away. Just remember, and you can sleep.* A price too high to pay for a kid who hears his dead mother screaming every night.

"It's all good, brother. I told you mine, right? That's awful, though. To go through so much heavy stuff at twelve . . . I can't imagine. How were you and your dad, after?"

"He, uh . . . well, you know, he kind of shut down after the fire. We went to live with my aunt for a while, and he spent a lot of time in bed. He would be asleep when I left for school and he'd still be in bed when I got back. He went back to work after a few months, which seemed to help a lot."

"Right, but how were you and he?" Appletree asked, running a hand through his bristles. "I mean to go through that much trauma together?"

Dad hid it well. He hugged me before I left for school, he drove me to football practice. Ran plays with me in Aunt Sophie's backyard. But every now and then I would catch him looking at me in the rear-view mirror as we drove. Looking at me like I did something wrong. He always looked away if I made eye contact, switched the subject to something lighter, something happier. But I still caught him looking.

"We were great. Hey, out of curiosity, how far are you going to-morrow? I've been averaging about twelve miles on a good day, but if it's hot I'll take a break in the afternoon."

"You know, it depends, man, the weather has more of a say in it than I do, but . . ." Appletree leaned back against his log and changed tack like a goddamn champion. The stars inched over our heads as we spent the next hour talking about the trail. Appletree wanted to get an early start the next morning, trying for a day trip up Glacier Peak. Around eleven I made my excuses and staggered to my sleeping bag, changing into shorts. I fell into a restless half sleep of vivid not-quite nightmares, shifting and rolling with every tiny sound outside.

After what felt like a lifetime, the blissful black door of sleep opened and I slipped inside, letting it close behind me.

→»» ««←

THE NIGHT SPRAWLED pitch-black outside my tent when I woke up again. I had to pee, but after hours of tossing and turning I'd finally gotten warm and comfortable, which is no mean feat when you're sleeping on a two-inch-thick foam pad. I abided by the tried-and-true tradition of every camper who's ever woken and faced a full bladder: I rolled over and pretended I didn't have to pee. But bladders don't like to be ignored, so it wasn't long before I woke again with an even more desperate urge. I unzipped my bag with no small amount of grumbling and staggered outside.

I knew right away something wasn't right. The forest wasn't dark—it was black. No glimmer of moonlight or stars behind the thick clouds choking the sky. It pressed close, like the shadows lurking at the edges of our campfire, but this time I didn't have a light to protect me. I had nothing to protect me.

Five days from the nearest road. I had no weapons, and apart from an old man sound asleep ten feet away, I was alone. To the average-sized predator in the mountains, I came gift-wrapped on a silver platter.

The little hairs on the back of my neck prickled.

I stumbled a few feet in a random direction and unzipped. Each way I turned my head, nothing but inked shadow and the barest suggestion of silhouettes. No birds sang, no underbrush rustled. I listened hard, but there wasn't a single sound. Like my head was muffled in a blanket. Something was off, something wasn't right, my gut whispered.

A twig snapped.

To my scraped-wire nerves, it sounded louder than a gunshot. I jumped and spun, scouring the black like I would see something. Tree trunks, silent and menacing, separated by their lengths of empty—

A silhouette, the faintest suggestion of a shape, standing between two trees. Staring at me.

A man, alone in the darkness.

"H-hello?" My whisper came out hoarse, high-pitched.

I couldn't make out where his shape ended and the curling shadow surrounding him started. Shoulders and legs.

He was small, half my height and size, almost lost to the pressing night. He held something in his hand, something long and thin.

Something was wrong, in his face. A cloud shifted and a dull, pale glow illuminated a shaft of pine boughs. His face mutated, a nightmare mask of twisted skin and malformed flesh—

I took a trembling step backward, hands buckled into white-knuckled fists at my side. Run, I needed to run; any moment now he might explode into motion and come for me, come to kill me. I took another step.

His head split into two pieces. My breath turned to ice in my throat and I almost screamed. A hole grew in his head, now; I could see through it.

I could see through it.

I waited, not daring to believe. I moved my head a fraction to the side . . . and his form deteriorated. A tree limb here, a rock sitting on a fallen trunk there. Moonlight on the indistinct lakeshore.

I'd imagined it. The sigh of relief made my knees buckle. Looking at it now, I could see the holes I'd given corporeal form, the rocks in the lake where I'd seen malformed flesh.

Not a thing out there—just me and the wilderness, and a dead-to-the-world Appletree.

I wiped the cold sweat from my cheeks. The clouds shifted again, and the scant light vanished. Shadows—empty and devoid of mutated serial killers, I now knew—crept back over the forest.

I turned and walked back to my tent, shaking my head at my own foolishness: a serial killer, out alone in the woods, staring at me?

Then, for a second, I caught the faintest reflection. Close-set, in the darkness. Almost like a pair of eyes. For a second, then they were gone. Rocks, or something else ridiculous. Just like Dr. K said: I needed to look at it the right way.

I chuckled to myself, peed against a nearby trunk, then crawled back inside, rolled back into my sleeping bag. The night turned soft again, and somewhere in the distance an owl hooted. I rolled over, and after a few minutes fell back asleep.

When I woke up for the second time, the sky through the mesh of my tent was the heavy gray of early morning. Appletree tapped against my tent.

"Whassit?" I muttered, blinking like a baby owl. I could see the outline of his face and beard through the mesh above me. The morning air was too cold against my face, and I pulled the sleeping bag up around my neck. I didn't need to go anywhere anytime soon, I could keep sleeping.

"Hey man, uh, I think maybe a 'coon got into your bag, it's kinda all over the place."

"What?" That woke me up faster than any alarm clock. I bounced to an awkward sitting position, peering outside. "Aw, shit."

My pack lay open on the ground beside my tent, the contents scattered all over the clearing. My pants were draped across a tree limb ten feet up and a pair of underwear soaked in a suspicious-looking puddle. Two of my shirts were burnt, covered in ash from the dead fire. Most conspicuous of all, though, was what remained of my food supply.

A trail of neon-colored plastic fragments waved at me from a sunken spot beneath a rock. I could see bits of dried ramen noodles and dried chili mac thrown helter-skelter. Clif bar wrappers danced in the breeze. For a brief second, I thought about the night before. Someone ransacked my bag. A chill slipped along my spine. What if . . .?

No, no, of course not. He wasn't even a he; it had been all me. My imagination and a loose collection of tree limbs didn't open my bag and throw shit everywhere. There wasn't anything out here last night. Appletree was right, must have been a raccoon or something.

"God damn it." I wriggled out of my sleeping bag, throwing my boots on. I ran to my pack first, ransacking it to see what I had left.

I came up with two granola bars and a packet of M&M's, buried way down at the bottom. Whatever critter got into my pack ate five days' worth of food. I hoped it choked on a piece of plastic and died slowly. "God damn it!"

"Sorry 'bout it, brother," Appletree said, laying a hand on my shoulder. I shrugged it off with a little more bite than was necessary. I even had a bear bag in my pack—there it was, thrown on the ground beside Appletree's tarp. All I needed to do was throw my food in it and hoist it over a tree limb. It's the most basic-bitch thing to do when you're backpacking, and I'd forgotten. Now, I had no food. I stalked around the clearing gathering my discarded clothing, swearing like a sailor.

"Hey, don't sweat it, man. You can go to Bedal." Appletree handed me my pants, and I snatched them, throwing them into my open pack.

"What?" I snapped.

"Bedal," he repeated, calm as you like. He pulled a bag out of his pocket and started chasing scraps of trash. He stepped behind a tree, still talking. "It's a one-horse place, a few miles off the trail. There's a diner and a general store. You can get back up to par today, be back on the trail by tonight. It's all gravy, man."

I took a second and ran my hand through my hair, forcing a deep breath. The air pressed cool against my cheeks and tasted of the mist curling around the edges of the lake. "Yeah?"

"Yeah, man. I read about it, and a few hikers down Oregon way recommended it as a late-trail stop. There's a dude who runs a general store, friendly to hikers on the trail."

The second deep breath came easier. "Okay. Do you know how to get there? Is there a side trail?"

Appletree shrugged. "Sorta. One of those ranger ATV access roads crosses it, down the end of the valley where it turns back north. Follow it, and it'll lead to a road. Busy one too, if the old brain box is knocking back the right info. Hiker I talked to said catching a lift north'ard to town took nothin'."

It wasn't the way I saw my day going, but life turns on a dime, right? At least I had a solution that didn't involve me scrounging for berries and edible plants, *Into the Wild* style. As I recall, it didn't work out so great for Emile Hirsch.

—»»»·«««—

I SPENT MOST of an hour pitching around in the early-morning gloom cleaning up my crap, double- and triple-checking for any trash left behind. They taught us to "leave no trace" in the Boy Scouts, and I'd be damned if I was ever the person who left garbage lying around a campsite.

Appletree had already broken down his "tent," humming tunelessly to himself. I changed into the single set of clean clothes I had left, threw the rest in my bag, and rolled up my sleeping bag.

"Hike down to the service road together?" I asked. I didn't turn around to look at him—didn't want to be making eye contact if he said no, too awkward. I needn't have worried.

"I'd consider it a pleasure, Switch," my trail mate chirped, rolling his tarp into an untidy log. His presence felt like a patch of shade on a scorching day on the trail. The thought of spending another four hours with him for company (depending on where this magical access road was, if it existed at all) was more exciting than I cared to admit.

I clipped my tent bag to the bottom of my pack. Mist and early-morning shadow still steeped the edge of the lake. Fog rolled off in lazy curls, and the leaves underfoot were wet with dew. A bird sang from a tree up on the ridge somewhere, a high, sweet sound. I inhaled; the chilled late-summer air cooled me, calmed me from the inside out.

Appletree sat on a log, pack over his knobby shoulders.

"Ready?" I asked.

He grinned wide beneath his wiry beard. "Ready."

—»»»·«««—

THE TRAIL SLIPPED down the valley floor in a series of lazy switchbacks. The forest twittered awake as the birds began to stir. The best hiking is the hour before sunrise, as the light creeps over the trail. You get to watch the forest transition from still to awake, cold to warm, dark to light. It's almost like you're walking in limbo, a world parallel to ours, just off reality. It all depends on how you look at it.

With boots on the trail again, the same unwelcome thoughts came rushing back: Deb. While not an ideal evening, it had at least been free of traitorous whispers shadowing my steps.

At least I still had the trail for another week or so, maybe ten days if I dawdled. I didn't know if Deb was still planning to wait for me at the Canadian border like she said she would. A not-so-small part of me didn't want her to. Because if she was, I would have to face the life I wanted to leave behind. I would have to admit that our marriage was over and face the music tuned up from it.

Like the story I told last night, I would have to speak my thoughts out loud, give them life.

"So what brought you out on the PCT?" I asked the back of my companion's head as we turned the dozenth switchback. "Just bored at work, or . . .?"

"I've had a sabbatical coming to me for a while." Appletree ducked under an oak tree fallen over the trail God knew how many decades ago. "I've avoided using it, but in the last year or two . . ." I heard the hesitation creep up in his voice and felt bad for asking. I didn't mean to pry. He cleared his throat and continued, "Something came up, and I figured now was as good a time as any. I packed a bag, took a bus down Mexico way, and put boots to dirt. Or I guess it's mostly sand, down there."

"I thought you said you started near Yellowstone."

He hop-stepped over a spindly tree root. "Did I? Pardon the mistake—brain ain't what it used to be."

I get that. I regularly forget important shit all the time.

"All right, Switchback, your turn. What brings you out here into the great unknown? What long-distance bug got into you?" Appletree asked.

For one cowardly and mean moment, I considered lying. Does it make me a bad person, after breaching trail etiquette and asking him about his life? Perhaps. But the thought of Appletree's tale last night made me want to tell him the truth. The way he lived his life, everything in the open, everything up for discussion. It made sharing seem less scary. It gave the ghosts from last night away, showed their ragged edges in the light of a shared fire.

"I'm out here running from my problems." No fake laughter, this time. No more half jokes like with Boots.

"Is that right?" Strange, he didn't sound surprised. Maybe he met a lot of people out here like me. Lost, confused. Maybe I wasn't the only one.

"I found a box of contraception in the trash a few weeks ago, all torn up."

A moment of silence, then a grunt of cautious understanding from ahead of me. "Mm-hmm. You and your girl trying to get pregnant?"

"Close, but no cigar. I had a vasectomy, sophomore year in college."

I waited while my companion considered this. I imagined him dancing the same dance I did, following the lines of my drama to the only logical ending point.

"Oh, so you're . . . oh."

"Yeah."

He stopped at a turnoff, turned to face me. "Ah shit, brother, I'm sorry about that. That's terrible. You talk to her about it?" He dropped his pack onto a rock, pulled his ancient metal water bottle out of a mesh pouch. I reached for my Nalgene, tucked into a side pocket of my bag.

"Tried." Talking about it right now didn't hurt as much as I feared it would. Telling it might hurt, but maybe I needed to hurt a little to heal a lot. "She flipped at me about not trusting her. Called me all sorts of interesting names. I could have handled a lot of emotion from Deb—that's my wife—in that moment. Grief, sadness—shit, even relief that the truth was out there and we could talk about it." But flipping the tables on me, making me out to be the bad guy with trust issues? Something to hide. Something she didn't want to face, so instead the fists came up. Change wasn't in the five-day forecast, back to Jim with sports.

"How do you feel about it?" Anyone else asking the question would have buried it beneath hidden questions or judgments, hinged on their own opinion. We say, "How do you feel about," but we mean "Doesn't that infuriate you?" or "Let it pass, man, kicking up a fuss will only make it worse." But my gray-haired, grizzled camp mate asked with zero pretense.

"I'm—" I stopped. It was almost funny, how a single question sometimes sums up so many things. Weeks of day-in, day-out anguish and torment. How did I feel about it? Here it was—a person standing four feet away, waiting for an answer, no time to wax poetic or couch my sentiments in context.

"I'm angry. I'm angry she lied to me, snuck around on me. She made me a fool, made our lives seem foolish. But I think . . ." I listened to the wind rush soft through the pine boughs, a bird singing. Smelled the warming sap hanging high on the breeze. I stumbled through my words and lost my train of thought.

"You think what, brother?" Appletree stepped over a lichen-eaten rock. He wasn't looking at me—why wasn't he looking at me? "Don't stop halfway. Get it all out there."

"I think that anger blinded me. Or . . . or I used it as an excuse, you know?"

"It can be so easy to hate, man. It feeds a dark and buried part in us all. Powerful but dangerous."

It would have been so easy to pull out, eject, turn the conversation to anything else—but I was in too deep. We were in this together, this voyage of pain and vulnerability. I lingered on the precipice of something.

Finish it. Say what you've been too afraid to think for three weeks. Come on, Josh. What do you have to lose?

"I used anger as a substitute. Because . . ." I forced myself to keep going, keep pushing. "Because down deep, I knew the relationship was over. At that moment, it was done, *finito*. No amount of counseling, arguing, wheedling, or crying could ever fix it. From one breath to the next, my marriage just . . . dissolved, through my fingertips."

"She never gave you a chance to fight for it, man." Appletree shook his head. "That's gotta hurt worse than anything else."

"I—" The words died on my lips. He cut straight through to the heart of it, lanced the infection with one cut. She never gave me a chance to fight for it. To fight for her. I never thought of it like that, but he nailed it. Reached right into my head, implanted a single thought.

My vision swelled and blurred, and I turned away. Being vulnerable is all well and good, but I don't cry easy, and never in front of other people. I took a second and collected myself. When I turned back, Appletree was sipping his water like it never happened.

"Sorry about . . . sorry. Do you mind if we talk about something else for a bit? It's still a bit . . ."

Appletree's smile brightened the whole valley. "Raw? One hunnert percent, man. Come on, we've got a million and one things to chat about before we hit yon access road. Top three hikes you've ever been on, hit me with 'em. And don't hit me with that 'oh I can't decide' bogus, 'cuz—"

We went back to the trail and kept our conversation there.

We found where the service road crossed over our trail a little before lunchtime. The gloomy morning broke up when the sun peeped over into the valley proper, and the chill vanished from the world. After two hours my pack was pressing against my back, soaking my shirt in sweat. The lower part of the valley was steeped in the perfume of endless acres of waving pine, sharp and sweet. That part felt similar to Alabama; I found warm pine sap uncomfortably close to hot asphalt, smell-wise. The trail bebopped over a series of streams, ducking through a boulder field.

A pair of weed-eaten gravel tracks, running five feet parallel to the trail before peeling away west, down a narrow ravine.

"Is this it?" I asked, peering down the meandering road.

"That's it."

I sighed. Fucking raccoon. I stuck a hand out. "Appletree, it was a genuine pleasure. Hope to run into you again."

The old man grasped the straps of his ancient backpack, ignoring my hand. He wasn't smiling anymore. "I'm sure it will happen. It's a funny old world that way, isn't it, Switchback?"

A cool breeze brushed through the trees, the promise of more mediocre weather on the horizon.

"Uhh . . . I guess so?"

"I'll see ya."

He gave me two thumbs up, turned, and strode down the dirt path in his easy, mile-eating amble.

That seemed like a weird ending to our time together. Which dovetailed with the bizarre circumstances in which we met, so it all washed.

I stood at the crossroads. I thought of Deb, waiting for me at the Canadian border. Waiting to pick me up so we could talk at even greater length about the torn-up box of Plan B in the garbage. I was close enough to the end I could sense them . . . the ragged edges of my life, lurking, waiting. The detour meant more time in the wilds, more time pretending I was Switchback, and not Josh Mallory.

I hefted my pack and turned off the trail.

4

THE RANGERS' ACCESS TRACK LOOKED NOTHING LIKE THE TRAIL. It cut straight west, as flat as the dwindling valley would allow; no trees, shrubs or vegetation grew in the brutal, man-made corridor. Silence reigned. Clouds didn't even float overhead. It felt like I was walking on the side of a sterile patch of road instead of the wilds. I didn't like it.

I stumbled upon the buck after an hour. From a distance I dismissed it as an odd colored hillock or a boulder buried in the dirt. As I got closer, I noticed the cohesion in shape. The too-similar proportions. What I'd mistaken for dead moss was fur, matted and clumped with dirt. I wasn't taken aback by a dead animal—good Southern boy I was, I'd done my fair share of hunting. But every part of it was still there, antlers and all. If a hunter shot it, they'd have broken the beast down and taken it home. If a pack of wolves did it, there'd be nothing left but bones and cartilage. It could have been sick. Stumbled into the corridor in a fever-daze. I rounded the huge beast's legs.

"What the . . .?"

A six-inch gash cut open the meat of its face down to the bone. A dozen more cuts ran the length of its neck, matting the thick hair with dark red. Its throat gaped; a carpet of still-slick rust matted the grass beneath. The stink of iron hung heavy in the hot summer air, stomach-turning, insistent. The huge animal's eyes bored into mine, glazed over and buzzing with flies. I popped my shirt over my nose, choosing my own stink over the still-damp blood. The lesser of two evils. For the second time in as many days I approached a corpse, inch by inch.

This wasn't an accident.

A long, thin handle protruded from the wet, crimson ruin beneath the buck's head. A hunting knife, it looked like, the ten-dollar kind you can pick up at just about any sport store from here to Seattle.

I took a step closer, reaching for the weapon almost on instinct.

A single, high-pitched laugh floated toward me from the woods.

The sweat on my back went cold. I looked up and around, but the wall of pines stood silent, still.

"Hello? Is someone there?" I called. The seconds ticked by in chilling slowness. My hand hung outward, still reaching. Like this wasn't real. Just like the man from the trees last night. Just my head, just the way I was looking at things.

Another giggle. Too high to be a man's. A child's laugh.

No way. I whipped the pocketknife from the shoulder strap of my pack. The blade was only four inches long, but its weight in the palm of my hand anchored me.

"Who's out there? Come on, this is fucked up!"

He moved out from the cover of the pines—a whisper of motion. The glint of his eyes, staring at me. A child, no older than ten. I couldn't see his face, just his eyes, creased in an unseen smile.

"Wh-what are you doing?" I asked.

The flesh around his eyes stretched tighter, his smile widening. I lowered the blade. Just a kid. I wasn't gonna hold a knife on a kid, was I?

"You come out here, right now! Hey!"

Yeah? And then what, Josh?

I'd cross that bridge when I came to it. For now, though, I wanted him out, in the open, where I could see him.

"I see you." His high-pitched singsong voice floated from the depths of the forest.

"What?" Sand packed my mouth, dried it out.

"I see you."

The knife in my hand trembled. He ducked down beneath the tree, out of sight.

I craned my neck, trying to see where he went. "Hey!"

I looked around. Too much space, too much space surrounded me, thirty feet clear of trees in every direction. Ghosts hovered in my peripheral vision, but when I spun to face them, nothing.

"Hey!"

My voice echoed in the service corridor, tremulous. A bird cawed from the shoulder of the mountain, but the pine trees were silent. I waited, adjusting my sweaty grip on the knife, heart in my throat. One minute ticked into two, then ten.

I had to get out of there. Everything about the spot felt wrong. The mutilated buck, the service road where nothing grew. The dead silence. I hitched my pack higher on my shoulders and did what I was best at; I ran.

I headed along the service road straight west, each step spiking my heart rate. My blood ran hot in my ears and every passing second I expected to hear another giggle floating from the forest . . . but none came. After a couple of empty miles I calmed down enough to put the knife back on my shoulder strap and have a rational check-the-facts.

Some kid, playing a prank. That made sense. Bedal was probably, what, twenty miles away? Odds were good it had been a bored kid camping with his family in the woods nearby, seeing how much he could scare the average hiker. He didn't attack me, didn't sprout wings or fangs. He was a kid, not a fuckin' demon. I'd done plenty of stupid shit as a kid. I inhaled a shaky breath, nodding. It checked out. The facts aligned. I had just looked at it the wrong way. I had to find the right way to look at it.

And the buck?

That, I didn't have an explanation for. That one stumped me. But the deer lay dead and behind me, and the kid was long gone, and I needed to cool my goddamn jets. I walked, breathed, and tried to calm down.

I thought of Mr. Neery's mailbox. Did my dad ever buy him another one? We moved to Atlanta with my aunt after the funeral, but we went back for a few visits over the years. I couldn't remember if Mr. Neery ever put his mailbox back up. Strange, isn't it, the things you keep with you? I could still remember my dad holding me on Mr. Neery's back porch, rocking back and forth. I remembered the look on Dustin McElroy's face, standing in his baseball uniform, watching the blaze. But not the mailbox.

The road ran five or so miles before emptying out onto the shoulder of a highway. The pavement looked fresh-laid, smooth as a new nickel, which felt unusual; if I had a dollar for every piece of shit backwoods road I've threatened my axles with, I'd be a millionaire. This one looked . . . new. Inviting. I'd never hitchhiked before, and was somewhat nervous about the prospect, but I stuck my thumb out anyway and started trudging along the shoulder. At the sound of a motor I turned and slapped on my best 'I swear I'm not a serial killer' smile, only to watch a shiny Subaru drive right past. After three-quarters of a mile another engine rose behind me. I sighed and turned to see a battered and dingy eighteen-wheeler huffing along the road.

The driver waved and rolled to a stop beside my outstretched thumb. A balding man in his late forties with a grizzled beard shot with gray and a wicked farmer's tan craned his neck to see through the passenger-side window.

"Where ya headed?"

"Uh . . . Bedal." I squinted against the sun.

A cloud passed over the driver's face. "That's where I'm headed, so it'd be kinda shitty of me to make ya walk. Hop in."

I nodded and unstrapped my bag, tucking it behind the passenger seat amid a ruin of Red Bull cans and loose CD cases. After a quick thought, I palmed the pocketknife from one strap, slipping it in a pocket. You never can be too careful. I wasn't a serial killer, but I didn't have a guarantee this guy wasn't.

"You doin' the PCT?" the driver asked as the Chevy croaked back to life. A bobbleheaded Jesus Christ stuck to the dash above the defunct-looking radio nodded in frantic greeting.

"How'd you guess?"

The driver chuckled. "You got that 'scarcely fed and walked hard' look about you. I do the local delivery route between the Canadian border and Walla Walla, so I know the vibe."

"Get a lot of us out this way?"

"Nah, not so much down here. Trail runs north, right? Up 'round Glacier. I'll see six or seven of yous around these parts, usually stopping in Bedal to pick up food or what have you before they hop back on the trail in town there."

"Oh, so there is a trail in town? Leads to the PCT?" It wasn't that I didn't trust Appletree; I just wanted to double-check.

"Yessir. I forget the name of it, but it's east of town, picks up with the Crest trail 'bout ten miles in. The owner of the general store there, Ronnie, helped fund it with the state. He said it was for th' community but between you, me, and the rattlin' Jesus here"—the driver booped the bobblehead—"I think he did it to bring in some business to his shop. He wanted to put a sign up along the main trail where it heads into town, advertisin' his general store to hikers. Imagine he weren't none too pleased when the rangers told him it's all national land up 'round them parts and he couldn't throw up a billboard."

"I imagine so." I considered asking him about the kid from the woods, but no way he'd know what I was babbling about. I'd come off as a crackpot.

It was a kid, playing a prank. The more I said it, the more I believed it. I forgot about the buck; it didn't matter, in the grand scheme of things. Things die. The buck, Green-Eyes. That's the way the world worked.

Even as I told myself this, I ignored the queasiness lurking in the pit of my stomach. I ignored the smell of sizzling wallpaper clinging to the inside of my nostrils.

Things die.

The peaks of the Cascades cracked skyward, dusted with early-season snow. I leaned back and enjoyed both the view and not being on my feet for a change. The driver ranted about something as we drove. Politics, I think. I missed the opening thread of his monologue and now just nodded my head at all the right points. He needed no conversational aid from me. The first houses began cropping up along the side of the road about three miles in. Small, tidy, and respectable, set back a way from the highway behind ivy-covered fences.

The center of Bedal was a pleasant surprise from the small-town boonies I expected. Five or so storefronts hunched around a four-way stop, watched over by a lone streetlight. A Shell station with a sign in the window advertising MONSTER ENERGY DRINKS offered gas at a reasonable $2.94 a gallon. A telephone pole sported a crow's nest crown next to a fifties-style chrome diner. CHUCKS was scrawled above the door to the diner in dead neon loops. A window box beside the door boasted a collection of thin plants straggling for sunlight. A pair of trucks occupied most of the packed-dirt parking lot.

A post office sat silent beneath the stars and stripes waving from a flagpole—in case visitors forgot what country they were in. A Ford Bronco with a too-small doughnut tire on the front right axle and a fresh coating of mud was parked out front. No police station; I guess they borrowed one from a neighboring town. Houses, set against the trees.

A two-story lodge with a sheltered patio sat across the street from the Shell. A mountain of firewood bundles filled one side behind a sign selling them for seven bucks a bunch. A little steep for tourists and car-campers, but out here you didn't have another option. The sign over the porch said GENERAL STORE.

Two roads crossed at the four-way. The highway, running north-south, and a smaller residential type. To the east, it crossed a rusty bridge over a river running low this late in the summer.

A brand-new sign stood beside the road with the PCT logo on it and an arrow pointing east, over the bridge. I didn't want to be in the real world any longer than necessary. In the real world, I had to be Josh. Josh had to deal with the shit show with Deb. Josh had to remember those nightmare-laced nights listening to his mom scream. On the trail . . . well, those things still existed, but I didn't have to deal with them. Those were Josh's problems, not Switchback's.

"This is the place." My driver-friend pulled into the hardpan of the diner parking lot. "That there," he said pointing to the general store, "is Ronnie's. He'll have whatever goods you're looking for, likely as not."

"How's the food in there?" I thumbed toward the diner. This close to the double doors I could smell rye toast and hot butter, and I had to wipe my mouth to keep from drooling. I hadn't had anything to eat since that mediocre turkey casserole the night before. My stomach rumbled.

"It's good, from what I've heard." The driver glanced at the shiny chrome diner. "Run by a lady named Sarah—try the Reuben, folks say it's the best around."

"Thanks."

"Wait—before you go."

I paused, fingers on the door handle. It looked like he was debating saying what really lingered on his mind. Real quick I hunted for a way I could politely tell him I didn't care and go, before he found the words. The Reuben danced on my mind.

"Look . . . be careful."

"Of . . .?"

"Last few months, coupla people gone missing. No one's talking 'bout it, but I seen the posters. You can keep that look you're giving me, kid, I ain't saying there's a serial killer on the loose. Just be careful. I've driven through here enough to know there's something weird about this stretch of road. Don't trust easy." He licked his lips. He had the kind of wide-eyed insistence of your average flat-earther.

All right, weirdo. "Right. Uh . . . thanks." I jumped out of the truck and grabbed my pack. The general store could wait. I'd been eating freeze-dried food in a bag for two weeks.

Papers and notices plastered the front window near the door. Pull a tab for guitar lessons. Pull a tab if you're looking for a tutor. A "looking for lodging" ad right next to an "offering lodging" ad, which I found hilarious. In the top right corner fluttered a pair of Missing Person notices, faded from rain and wind. One featured a selfie of a woman grinning from a hammock. A tattooed astronaut waved from her upper arm. The printed block letters were tough to read, faded as they were. It looked like she'd been missing from the Mt. Pugh trail since . . . holy shit, last August? The paranoid driver warned me about something that went down *last year*? I snorted and hauled open the door and stepped into a different decade.

Dead or soon-to-be politicians and actors decorated the quilted stainless-steel walls. JFK and Eisenhower, Sidney Poitier, and Jack Lemmon. The tables were spotless white linoleum dressed with napkin dispensers, ketchup, and mustard. An industrial air con spat out air cool to the point of chilly; a wave of goose bumps broke out on my arms. At the wraparound bar four patrons sat on plush bar stools, feet resting on a polished chrome rail. A bell above the door announced my arrival.

I waved, trying to stand in front of my bulky pack as much as possible. "Afternoon."

One of the patrons, an older man with wild hair and goatee to match, turned to give me the once-over. He eyed the pack I tried to shield behind my legs. "Just off the Crest Trail?"

"Yessir. Stopped in town to resupply and grab a hot meal before I get back on the trail."

"Sarah!" One of the four shouted, without turning around. "Got you another one."

The door to the kitchen swung open and a large woman wearing a blue apron bustled out, coffeepot in one hand and plate in the other. She fixed the loudmouth with a glare and scowled.

"Now what have I told you about shouting in my shop, Jeremy Ulysses Cranson? Were you raised in a barn?"

"Sorry, ma'am," Mr. Cranson muttered, dropping his gaze to his mug of what I assumed was coffee.

"Sure you are. Here's your burger, Andrew. Extra pickle, no onion." She slid the plate in front of the man with the goatee. I caught a quick glance of a toasted bun bursting with lettuce and tomato beside a mountain of fries. My stomach gurgled audibly.

"Hey there." The waitress wiped her hands on a clean white towel. "Go on and stick your bag beside that umbrella stand there, come and have a seat. Can I get you some tea?"

"Oh, uh, no tea. Coffee, if you have it, please, and thank you." I hopped up onto a stool, rubbing my hands together. Sarah slid a laminated menu across the counter as she poured a cup of coffee, which she set in front of me. It tasted amazing. Going from five cups of coffee a day in the real world to two cups of instant-in-a-bag a week had been a rough transition.

The menu was standard diner fare. Burgers and sandwiches with the occasional lackluster salad thrown in for good measure.

"You come far today?" the man who got in trouble, Cranson, asked me. I couldn't tell if he feigned his interest or offered it as penitence for his past offense. The waitress, engaged in slicing a magnificent-looking apple pie, appeared not to hear.

I shrugged. "Not too bad. Ten miles or so."

"Howf the rail 'iss time of 'ear?" the man with the goatee mumbled around a mouthful of burger.

"I'm sorry? I didn't quite—"

"You're not the one who should be sorry, sweetheart," Sarah interrupted, narrowing her eyes. "Andrew honey, swallow your food and then talk, before you choke. You know as well as I do it's Benny's day off and he's down the river fishing, so you'd prob'ly die before he got up here to give you the Heimlich. What are you thinking, dear? See anything you like?"

"I've heard good things about the Reuben."

"Yeah you have," one of the quiet patrons chimed in. He grinned over the edge of his mug. Behind his bushy black beard a silver tooth gleamed at me. "Nobody does up a Reuben like Sarah. Like heaven."

"Oh now, you stop it, Mike, you flatterer." Sarah flapped her hand, but a blind man wouldn't have missed the blush and smirk of pride. "One Reuben, coming right up. You want fries?"

"Yes please."

"Well aren't you polite." She gave me a smile, and my menu disappeared quick as it appeared. "Anybody else need anything? No? I'll be right back with your sandwich, sweetheart."

She vanished behind the swinging door into the kitchen.

"How's the trail this time of year?" Andrew repeated, after swallowing.

"Not too bad. Pretty hot, especially down around Cle Elum." I found most people asking about hiking conditions want to talk about the weather. They bore of elevation and mileage five words in, but they'll talk about your average summer storm for hours. "I was actually at a lake just below Cloudy Peak when the craziest thing happened—"

"You catch any rain up around the Pugh Lookout?"

See? The fucking weather, of all things.

I shook my head. For a brief, fluttering second I considered telling them about Green-Eyes, about the raccoon ruining my campsite, but I decided against it. They didn't care, ultimately. No one cared. It's like when someone casually asks you how you're doing. They don't want to hear *how* you're doing. They want you to say "fine" so they can tick off the little box next to your name and carry on with their lives.

"Nah, must've just missed it. What are you guys up to today? Working?"

"How'd you get into town? Didn't walk, didya?"

"Uh, no. No, I caught a ride with someone about fifteen miles down the road."

"Bad way to go 'bout it if you ask me, walkin'," Cranson murmured, sipping his coffee. "Lotta people skittish about hitchin' around these parts, but I find it to be the most effective way of getting around beyond hoofin' it."

"That's because your car is a piece of shit, Jeremy." Mike rolled his eyes. "You got no choice."

"That's not true!" Jeremy protested over the snickering from the others. "I'm waiting on that alternator to come in the mail, then the Camaro will run like a dream."

"Oh, you have a Camaro? What year?" I asked. Mr. Neery owned a Camaro, but he'd had to sell it a few years before the fire. He let me sit in the driver's seat when my parents were over visiting—I liked pretending I was a NASCAR driver.

"You've been waiting on that alternator for what, three weeks now? Where'd you order it from, space?"

"I didn't know it'd take this long when I ordered it, sheeit."

"Uh-huh," Andrew said, unconvinced. He leaned over Jeremy to me, his grin still twitching the corners of his goatee. "You gonna swing by the general store, across the way?"

"Planning on it." I took another sip of coffee. Damn, it really did taste amazing. "How's their selection over there?"

"Hey, when you do, tell Ronnie that Andy said the game's on at ten. He'll know what I mean."

"Oh there's a game on? Football or baseball?" The regular season was due to start any day now, and I had my Falcons jersey pressed and ready. Ryan's arm looked good in the preseason—I thought we had a real chance for a playoff bid. We were due for a ring any season now. Shit, if the Saints could do it, so could we. Buncha alligator-eating cousin-kissers.

"Wouldyer also tell him to quit fuckin' around and call me about that alternator?"

"Nice try, Cranson. Don't blame it on Coors, we all know you're the one that cocked it up." Mike reached for his coffee, shaking his head. When he smiled wide, the silver tooth glittered, gilded onto his grin.

"Are you—" I hesitated, not wanting to be rude. "Are you guys, like, ignoring me on purpose, or . . .? I'm not sure if I said something offensive?"

I waited for a response . . . but Andrew just blinked at me. His expression didn't change. The same smile still hovered on his lips. I leaned in, unsure if he was acting odd, or if I was the butt of a joke I didn't understand. The seconds ticked by in a silence growing uncomfortable. A gnat whined through the air.

I waited for a response . . . just like I had when I was standing in the service corridor in the woods, waiting for another giggle, my heart rate increasing, ticking like a bomb against my sternum. The air turned colder; I shivered.

The kitchen door swung open and Sarah saved us all from looming awkwardness, bustling out with a plate that she set in front of me.

"Here you are, sweetie. Eat up; you look like you need it. Mike, you want a top-off? Jeremy, ready for that burger yet?" She bustled down the bar, chatting with her customers, leaving me in blissful peace. The Reuben was delicious. Crispy, salty, and juicy. The fries were shoestring, no doubt out of an Ore-Ida bag, but I didn't care. I ate every fatty scrap, listening with half an ear to the small-town gossip from down the bar. So-and-so got caught drunk at work, so-and-so fell in the river fishing, et cetera.

"My, my, someone was hungry," Sarah said with a smile, swinging back down to my end of the bar to grab my empty plate. "How'd it taste?"

"Oh, amazing," I said, lacing my hands around the dregs of my coffee to soak up any leftover heat—still a touch cold inside. "Top three I ever had, honest."

"You're a sweetheart. Want another cup of coffee before you hit the road? Maybe some tea? I make it myself."

I did, but the morning had turned to afternoon outside and I didn't want to risk the general store closing early. Small-town shops did it all the time, especially in mountain towns. The owner has an empty shop, wants to go home and have a beer? Hey presto, closing time at three today. I paid for my meal plus a fat tip and slid off my stool.

"You guys have a good one," I said, retrieving my bag.

"Take it easy, partner," Mike said with a wave. Nobody else looked up.

The bell on the door chimed as I walked out.

5

RONNIE COORS

WAS FRESH FROM THE COLD INSIDE OF THE DINER, AND THE SUMMER day roasted, stifling hot. I crossed the street, quick-timing it to the two-story building I hoped had A/C.

Two cars were parked in front of the two-story general store. One was a Chrysler van, complete with Baby on Board stickers on the back window. The sizable cargo area was overflowing with camping equipment mixed with various family paraphernalia: strollers, toys, and a box of diapers, its ripped-open corner betraying a roadside emergency. Discarded books and toys lay scattered over the seats.

The other car was a spotless white Jeep raised on a custom suspension system over off-road tires. A black metal bar bearing a fancy lighting rig rode the top of the windshield. I loved Jeeps—I wanted to buy one way back when, but Deb talked me into the reliability of a

Subaru instead. I wandered over and glanced inside, holding my pack over one shoulder.

The inside of the car was disgusting. Cigarette butts cascaded from the ashtray. Sweat-stained undershirts, socks and pants pooled in the passenger footwell. The passenger seat acted as a repository for McDonald's bags, stiff with coagulated grease. Ladies' underwear magazines were strewn along the dash, spines well-creased, pages dog-eared. Behind the seats were two or three black duffels stacked haphazardly against each other. Industrial-strength black straps were bolted into the frame in the back—cargo holders for off-roading, at a guess. A handle of cheap whiskey glinted from a lazy hiding place in a corner, empty enough to wink sunbeams at me.

Charming. I thanked my lucky stars the window wasn't open; you could probably smell the interior five feet away.

I walked into the general store. As a person who spends a lot of time in the mountains, I'm familiar with your average mountain-town store. They're dingy, cluttered, and poorly lit, with the faint hint of racism tinging the air. A decrepit old man straight out of *Tales from the Cryptkeeper* begrudgingly rings up your total on a pre-World War I register. God help you if you asked for a bag.

The Bedal general store was . . . different. Large, clean windows lit the interior, swathing the floor in puddles of sunshine.

Shelves with hiking equipment marched along the left wall. Everything from first aid kits to bootlaces, fishing nets, and spare tarps. And not cheap generic shit, either; I spied some heavy-hitting brands. A small but tasteful section of Osprey day bags, a rack of Patagonia raincoats. The right side of the store boasted an impressive display of dried food—a whole wall close to the door dedicated to freeze-dried foods. Mountain House, Packit Gourmet, and about a dozen flavors of Clif bars for good measure. A guy my age looked up from behind a spotless white counter, holding an iPad in one hand. He tucked a strand of longish hair behind his round glasses.

"Hiya, friend!" He gave me a quick up and down. "You in from the PCT?"

Jesus, did I have a sign strapped to my neck? "I am indeed. Looking to supply up before I get back to the trail."

"Well you're in the right spot. If you want, you can put your bag down there, so you don't have to carry it around in the store with you." He nodded at a series of cubbies I hadn't noticed, lining the wall, each the perfect size for a tall backpack.

"Oh, sweet. Thanks."

Some way into the store, a woman moved what sounded like a pair of chattering kids through the aisles. I caught a glimpse of brilliant scarlet hair—either a great dye job or a genetic lottery.

"Not a problem. I'm Ronnie. Ronnie Coors. Like the beer empire, but no affiliation. Broke as a joke." He moved around the counter and stuck his hand out.

"Switchback." We shook. A port-wine stain birthmark curled around his wrist.

"Ah, trail names. Right on, man. Well, hey, I'll let you look around, holler if you need anything."

I thanked him, and he left me to my own devices while he ambled down an aisle to assist the woman.

A collection of baskets sat by the cubbies. I grabbed one and meandered to the dried-foods section. I did the basic through-hiker math, calculating how many days I had left on the trail times meals per day and snacks.

Another week left, seven days at one hot meal plus lunch and breakfast a day—

Absorbed in my musings, it took several minutes for the conversation to reach me across the store. I can't tell you why I started paying attention. Could have been Ronnie's shrill, squeaky laughter or the woman's low-toned, one-word answers.

Either way I started listening.

"—so I told them, you know, I won't stand for that kind of behavior in my store. You can't disrespect veterans or any other member of the armed services in here. And then I kicked them out. Teenagers, you know? No sense of civic pride." He paused, waiting for an appreciative murmur or a "How brave you were, you gallant man, you." He received neither. The scarlet-haired woman tightened her lips into a fake smile and steered her kids down the aisle.

"So, what brings you to Bedal? Going camping?"

She couldn't not give an answer to a direct question, and I suspect he knew it.

"Yes. I'm taking the kids to the campground down the road while my husband is away on business." She couldn't have hit the word *husband* harder if she had a bat in one hand.

"Lovely. You know, there's a stunning hike in the area, up the road. Meadow Mountain. Great views. You'd really like it."

I blinked. Wow. He plowed right past the dump truck-sized hint, oblivious. I peeked over the Mountain House bags in front of me. Ronnie had an elbow propped up against a shelf, blocking her exit. The poor woman ushered her kids along as she scoured the shelves for what she needed, hustling through the shop.

Every time she took a step, so did he.

"Thanks, I'll keep it in mind."

"It's a little steep for the kiddos, mind." Not a single glance at the kids in question. He jutted an upper lip in mock thought, then brightened. "Hey, here's a thought—just throwing it out there, seeing what sticks; I could show you the trail. Yeah, I've been a few times, so I know it really well."

Oof. The awkward moment of silence felt so palpable I physically cringed. He knew it well? It's a hiking trail, man, not the minotaur's labyrinth.

"I appreciate it, but I have the little guys here to think of."

"And a righteous mother you are because of it, m'lady."

M'lady? Oh no. He was a tipped fedora away from the single worst trope of all time.

The poor woman picked up two boxes of mac 'n' cheese and made a beeline toward the counter. I doubted she pulled into the general store for two boxes of Easy Mac, but if I were in her shoes, I'd want to get the hell out of there too. I thought about stepping in and saying something, but I hesitated. Every chance she was a strong, independent woman who could take care of herself—I didn't want to overstep. So I stared at the shelf of freeze-dried food and listened. If things devolved into violence, I'd step in; at least that's what I told myself.

Ronnie Coors didn't bother jumping behind the counter. He leaned against it, tapping away on his iPad, close enough to the woman to make her turn and fuss with a nonexistent zipper on one of the toddlers' coats.

"Two boxes of Easy Mac, two-seventy-five. Card? Not a problem." That's when he pulled out his magnum opus, his big try. Holding this poor woman's credit card so she couldn't leave. "Maybe the little guys could watch themselves? Say tomorrow afternoon? I'd have you back in four hours, easy." He flashed her the same smile he gave me: quick, charismatic. Or at least in his mind. "Unless you wanted to stay out a little longer."

I turned around, jaw dropping.

The woman straightened, the expression on her face withering.

"I'm not in the habit of leaving my children to their own devices or going for hikes with strange men." She held her hand out, flat. "Give me my card back, please. We are leaving and will not be returning."

Ronnie's face shifted in an instant. The easy smile curdled on his lips, and an ugly flush rose to his cheeks. Behind those round spectacles, his eyes turned cold.

He slapped the woman's card in her hand.

"Have a nice day, cunt. I was just trying to be nice."

"Uh-huh, I bet you were. Come on guys, let's go."

She stuffed the Easy Mac in her purse and hustled the kids out of the store without so much as a backward glance.

"Bitch!" he shouted as she pushed through the door. She turned and gave him the middle finger. I wanted to cheer.

The bell chimed, the door closed, and it was just the two of us. I turned back to perusing the shelves. Ronnie muttered something under his breath and busied himself organizing shelves. I left him alone, giving him time to compose himself. I shouldn't have been so considerate.

"Psst, you believe her?" Ronnie called across the store.

I looked around. Surely he was speaking to someone else. He couldn't expect sympathy from anyone short of a close friend in this situation, right? But no, I was the only person inside.

"I mean . . . I sort of get where she's coming from." I hate confrontation, and therefore put up a weak sort of measly defense, but I would be damned if I backed up his horrid display of arrogant . . . I couldn't even come up with a word. It went beyond sexism—like he expected her to go on a hike with him, and the asking had been a courtesy gesture. Misogyny, perhaps, might have been closer to the mark.

"I was trying to be friendly." He sidled back toward the counter. "She was the rude one—*she* was. I just asked her to go on a hike."

"Didn't she say she had, like, a husband?"

"I didn't ask her if she wanted me to stick my dick in her, man," he snapped. "Just if she wanted to go for a hike. That's it."

I wished I was back on the trail. Shit like this didn't happen on the trail. I didn't have a good way out of this conversation, so I grunted, shrugged, and fell silent. I didn't care enough to attempt to change his mind; I wanted to buy what I needed and leave.

"She'll get hers, one day," he muttered, glaring at the road in the direction the Chrysler had disappeared. "Women like her always do. Women who think they can treat men like shit, walk all over them."

If looks could kill, the window between Ronnie Coors and the parking lot would have melted into slag. Not quite the charming and organized shopkeeper he wanted to be, then. I threw eight random packages of food into my basket with two fistfuls of Clif bars. He rang me up on his iPad, swiped my card, and handed it back to me.

"Hey, can I ask you a question?" I was desperate for a change in conversation.

"Shoot."

"Is there a ranger station nearby?"

"Why?"

"I—I found a, uh, a body, out in the woods yesterday."

Ronnie didn't even bat an eye. He homed in on his iPad, tapping buttons I couldn't see. "Not here. Closest one is up the road, in Darrington."

I frowned, scratching my chin. "I guess I could hitch another ride, be back on the trail in a few hours."

"Why? Who cares?"

I half turned, thinking he was joking. He wasn't.

"Are—oh, you're . . . I mean, there's probably a family looking for him, man. It's common decency. Part of being the species, am I right?"

"I mean, it's the same as Andy McKlennon. Dude from town, went missing . . . oh, I dunno, last year sometime. His wife Beth put up a huge search party, fucking tore the woods apart west of here. Made a big hoo-ha of it all, found not a goddamn thing. I told her at the time, but she didn't listen to me. Good odds were he wasn't lying with a broken leg in the woods, he was in a Motel Six in Chehalis with a rubber band around his balls and some woman—or dude, before you give me any crap, I don't discriminate—bouncing on top of him. Tough truths, man. That's the way it be, sometimes."

"I . . . what?" I had no idea what he was babbling about. "Look, I'm just . . . I wanna tell the rangers about the dead person I came across." I emphasized the word; maybe he hadn't heard me. The dead person. As in, dead.

His face didn't change; his eyes bored into mine from behind his round glasses. He didn't say anything. He stared at me. Jesus, this dude was a real creep. Time for me to go. I was halfway through shoving the food into the top of my pack when he hit me with it.

"Hey, you seem like a chill guy—"

I braced myself; no one has ever followed that sentence with anything good.

"—wanna buy some mushrooms?"

"What?" I was determined to keep silent and not engage, but his proposal had been so batshit nuts it slipped out. "Are you serious?"

"Yeah." He adjusted his glasses, leaning back against the counter. "I grow my own strains up in the mountains. It's good shit, man, ask anyone in town. I like to brew them into tea. It's relaxing."

What the . . .? Ask anyone in town? Worst ad slogan for drugs ever, of all time.

"Uh . . . no? No thank you."

"You sure? I've got a good price—five bucks for an ounce."

My experience with recreational marijuana ended with a puff on a joint maybe twice a year. Nothing against it; it wasn't for me. But even with my inexperience, his price sounded way too low. And you know what they say: the best drugs are outrageously cheap.

"Yeah, I'm sure. Thanks, though. Have a good one." I swung my pack onto a shoulder and got the hell out of there.

"Hey, come on! I'm doing you a favor, you prick!" Ronnie's voice, high and indignant, floated over the bell chime, following me outside. "Fine, be that way!"

I made straight for the road leading back to the PCT. The hell with the real world—I counted the seconds until my boots were back on dirt.

Across from the Shell station a small group of people waited, staring at their phones, standing five, six feet apart. They didn't chat with each other, didn't talk at all—they stood like they were quarantined—

made safe by distance. Several threw glances in my direction, clocking my position even at a hundred paces away.

One stood by herself, her mousy brown hair tied in a loose bun, a thermos clutched in one hand. I put on my best "I'm not gonna murder you" smile and approached.

"Excuse me?" I waved from ten feet away, trying to catch her attention. She turned. She'd been singing to herself, or humming; a snatch of music floated away from us. She'd applied her lipstick haphazardly—it bled into the corners of her mouth like tacky blood. It made me think of the buck, and my stomach flipped. "I'm so sorry to bother you. I'm, uh . . . I need to get up to Darrington. Any idea how far it is from here?"

Her face tightened, but she couldn't ignore me. She jerked a chin to the road winding north. "About forty minutes that way."

I'd spent enough time in this town to know better than to expect a follow-up. I stared at the road, frowning. Too long—an hour and a half there and back, longer if the rangers decided to ask a bunch of prying questions. I'd lose the light, have to overnight in Bedal.

Pass.

"You a hiker?" She eyed my pack and took a sip from her thermos. A muscle flexed in her mouth. Something rattled inside the thermos, ice cubes. I got the sneaking suspicion she wasn't drinking sweet tea.

"I am."

A beat, a pause. "Good luck gettin' a ride."

I frowned. "I mean, I got one coming into town, so I don't know if it'll be that hard. I'm thru-hiking. Doin' the PCT."

I didn't think it possible, but the lines in her face deepened even further. Some of the color drained from her cheeks, and she looked at me—*really* looked at me. Like I was gonna morph into a Muppet right in front of her. "What did you say?"

"Jesus, what *is* it with people here? Some of you answer questions, some of you don't. Am I having a fucking hallucination? Do I have a giant sign taped to my back? What is your collective fascination with the Crest trail? Huh?" The wafer-thin door sealing my stress away vibrated, about to burst. She took an instinctive step back. The others were staring; I felt the weight of their eyes. Pinched, unforgiving. Suspicious.

"Sorry. Sorry, I—" I wasn't sure who I was apologizing to. Her, them, me . . . everyone. I took a breath. "I just—"

"I don't know you," she whispered, like a prayer for help. Another step back. "I don't know you. Please, just . . . leave me alone. I don't want any trouble."

"Trouble . . . lady, I just asked you a question." Ronnie's voice haunted the edges of my words, and I bit down on my tongue, struggling not to scream. I wasn't like him. Everything came back up; Green-Eyes, Boots, Appletree, my trashed campsite, swirling around me in a fog.

What the fuck was *happening* here?

A yellow school bus rolled down the road and around the corner and stopped a few feet away in a squeal of rusty brakes, unleashing a flood of kids with neon-colored backpacks. Mousy-Haired Woman took the first opportunity to flee, grabbing a sticky-fingered kid wearing a Fortnite T-shirt. The other parents snapped their kids up, ushering them into cars or up the street with sharp gestures and glances over their shoulders—at the kids, at the other parents.

At me.

Two minutes after the bus left, the citizens of Bedal were gone, safely back to their houses, far away from the main road. What did she say? She didn't know me? Of course she didn't fuckin' know me, why would she? Jesus, maybe Ronnie was the normal one, and the town was skewed way out of whack. Time for me to get the hell back to my woods. My own voice floating back to me was the only thing stopping me, following the sweet salvation of the PCT logo.

Part of being the species.

Shit. I had to tell someone about Green-Eyes, or at least make the attempt. He might have someone out there looking for him. I sure as fuck wasn't going to Darrington—too far, too much time, plus I straight-up didn't want to. But . . . I sighed and walked back down the street, shouldering through the door into the diner.

"Back again, honey?" the waitress asked. Weird; she stood in the exact same spot as when I left. I shook it off; I was jumping at shadows. One phone call, and then I could be back on the trail.

"Do you have a phone? I want to call . . ." The words stuck in my throat. I was, of course, about to talk about old boy Green-Eyes and his leftover sausage casing of a stomach. But I couldn't shake Ronnie's eyes, staring at me through his glasses, flat as the corpse lying alone in the woods. Maybe I was seeing things, or maybe something in this town stank. I hadn't been here long enough to get perspective, and I sure as fuck didn't want to be. Either way, no harm in playing my cards close to my chest.

"I have to call my wife."

Oof. The first excuse that sprang to mind, and each syllable took a slice out of my tongue.

"Well aren't you the sweetest." Sarah dimpled. "Cell service is spotty 'til about Darrington up the road a bit. We got a phone, but Jeremy here hit the telephone pole with his car two days ago. Cable company said they can't get out here 'til Monday."

The good-natured razzing from the gathered good old boys hummed, muted in my dead ears. I'd seen the telephone pole, outside— there wasn't a scratch on it.

Sarah's smile stretched her lips too far. "Can I get you anything else, honey?"

"No—*ahem*—no, I'm good. I'm just gonna . . ." I pointed to the door. I had a powerful and unyielding desire to be anywhere but there at that moment.

"You have yourself a good day now, you hear me?"

I muttered a nicety, turned on my heels, and fled.

->>> <<<-

THE TRAIL SAT less than a mile from Ronnie Coors's front porch, past a cracked-asphalt parking lot. I let out no small sigh of relief when my boots left the pavement. The woods swallowed me, just like that hiker I'd met the other day. I couldn't remember his name; I'm sure it didn't matter. He shot for an unnamed peak and left me on the trail. That's all I could remember. Like pulling leaves from the forest at midnight, scratching around in the dark.

The path wound through an east-bearing river valley, flat and wide. The water rushed past, emerald green and sparkling beyond the trees lining the banks. I passed a dozen tents on the pebbled shore and nodded in casual hello to a dozen hikers making their way back to town. The day started to wind toward late afternoon, and I was the only person headed into the mountains.

I caught glimpses of the peaks on the far side of the river, towering over the valley. I wondered which one was Meadow Mountain.

The unease of confrontation now drained from my gut, I wished I'd stood up and given that prick a piece of my mind. Asking a married woman out for a hike? What kind of man these days asks a woman he just met to go out in the woods with him, alone, for three to four hours? As my mom used to say, that's how people wind up on the news.

Only an hour from town, I could still turn around, go back to the store, and chew out the pouty Mr. Coors. But to what purpose? The woman was long gone, so no need to defend her honor—she saw to that herself anyway. Good for her. And Ronnie . . . well, something told me Ronnie had been this way for a while, and not much I said would change him one way or another.

Plus, there were only a handful of daylight hours left, and I wanted to reach the PCT sooner rather than later. Being off it was too jarring. The trail was safe, the trail was secure. You walked one direction, looked at the pretty sights, ate when you were hungry and rested when you got tired. There were no creepy shopkeepers hitting on married women or offering me drugs for bargain-bin prices. Talking shit about missing people or corpses found in the woods. No, on the trail everything was open, everything was honest. Switchback took over, and Josh could sleep.

Every few minutes I glimpsed a fluttering in the trees and jumped. I kept waiting for the wind to whisper in a singsong over the rushing river, but it never happened. And wouldn't. I don't know why I wasted so much thought on the kid from back before I hitched a ride into Bedal. He'd been fifteen miles down the road and up a ravine. No chance he'd be this far. I thought the words, but I still checked the trees.

The sun sank, the sunbeams filtered through the trees burned to a deep gold.

After about two hours of pleasant riverside trail walking, I happened upon a fork in the trail. To the right, the flat river valley meandered on to what I suspected would be a lake of some variety. On the left, the trail narrowed and straggled over rocks and roots before curving uphill. A wooden sign nailed to a tree with the official PCT trail marker on it pointed to the uphill trail. Of course it would be the difficult one.

I made it about a mile before I had to take a break, panting and sweating against a tree beside the trail. Best guess, I had about two or three hours of daylight left. I remembered the basic layout of the main Crest trail, but I wasn't *on* the Crest trail. I had no idea how many miles this tributary meandered before the two linked up. Could be over the hill, could be fifteen miles.

I had two options. I could throw down camp here, enjoy a golden afternoon with my feet in the river and *American Gods* on my e-reader. Which sounded nice, but I wanted to get back to my trail, and sacrificing three hours of daylight wasn't ideal.

The second option: I could hike the trail and see where it led me, keeping an eye out for a prime tent spot as I went. The Cascades were the most-backpacked mountains north of the Sierras. Good money said someone before me had been in my shoes and was nice enough to flatten out a section of dirt and leaves beside the trail. I could close the gap between me and the PCT, if not put boots on the main trail tonight. I decided on the second option. The more distance between me and that town, the better.

The trail turned into a gradual but constant climb, pivoting on the shoulders of one hill to climb the next. The flat river valley beneath me filled with deep, burnt sunlight as I walked. A steep streamlet chattered over rocks beside me. I was alone on this trail; the day hikers had all gone home. The sound of crunching dirt beneath my boots and the breath in my lungs were my only companions.

After three miles, I crested a ridge.

The path sloped down into a basin around a shallow lake. The basin swelled in ridges, honing to sharp, rocky faces towering hundreds of feet above me. The basin's edge (three, four miles away but seemed close enough to touch) looked sharp and distinct.

At the top, a single splintered peak rose in a spire of collapsed rock shards and crumbling cliff faces. For some reason I thought of a massive, spindly clocktower, reaching up to graze the pale lavender sky. Glacier Peak hovered over the ridge behind the basin. The PCT trundled along the base of Glacier before hooking northeast. I was close.

Behind me, the sun went down in full now, slashing the basin open with ribbons of burnt orange. It would be dark in less than an hour, which meant I would have to stop . . . until I caught a glimpse of the moon.

The rim rose behind the three-finger summit of Glacier, already bright enough to wash the mountain in the promise of a ghost glow. Not full, but close enough that it would light my way, no problem.

The trail dropped, sliding into the basin before arcing around the lake, climbing. The wind blew cool but not cold, and the stars came out as I descended. Small groups of two or three as the band of lily-blue dusk slipped from the horizon, and then dozens at a time. They glittered in patchwork spiderwebs. My neck ached from staring upward. I didn't care.

The night was young and beautiful, and it made my tired feet and legs feel new again. I hummed to myself as I walked.

The trail rose to the ridge, and I paused to catch my breath. To my right the basin fell away in a seamless, rolling bowl. To the left, Glacier dominated the skyline. A thin trail led southward down the opposite side of the basin, a stand-alone sign with the PCT logo on it. Three miles, maybe less. I'd made it.

I stood beneath the path to the stone spire, listening to the breeze. Sweat cooled on my face. The trees rustled in the valley below me. A buried river crashed unseen around the ridge. Maybe I'd take a little time and climb that tall spire. Switchback had nothing but time. Switchback wasn't in a—

A single, high-pitched bubble of laughter, floating on the wind.

I spun on my heel, whipping around, trying to see where it came from.

"Hello? Who's there?"

He moved, separated himself from the shadows of the ridge. A short man standing alone, almost camouflaged by the boulders dotting the ridge. No, not a man, I realized. A boy, no older than eleven or twelve, wearing tattered shorts and a T-shirt, staring at me.

I recognized him. The same prankster from this morning, hidden behind the pines. Except now we were far removed from any excuse of living nearby. Now we were in the wilds. No more pranks.

"What are you—what are you doing here?" I stammered.

His face was hidden in shadow, but the moonlit side—thin, too thin. His cheeks were sunken, almost skeletal. His shoulders jutted, angular, beneath his shirt. Wasn't he cold? I suppressed a shiver, and I'd just been climbing uphill.

"I see you." His lips moved, but his flat eyes never left mine for a second. I fumbled for the blade at my shoulder. The same voice from earlier today.

"Stay away from me. I'm warning you—I don't know what kind of bullshit—"

"The mountain." Now his voice croaked, dead and flat. He wasn't wearing any shoes. His feet wept carmine tracks onto the dirt.

"The mountain," he repeated, and then he smiled. Smiled so wide his lips cracked open and began to bleed. That smile sent ice water into my gut. He took a step toward me, and I took an instinctive one back.

The boy looked east, toward the three-fingered Glacier.

"What are you—oh my God, what happened to you?"

The entire left side of his emaciated face—the side that had been wreathed in shadow—was disfigured. No hair grew in a fistful of his scalp, instead showing barely-healed skin over scar tissue. The flesh of his cheek and jaw was puckered and curled in a deep cleft. One milky eye glared at me, scarred over.

My pack suddenly seemed to weigh twenty more pounds than it had fifteen minutes ago. My mouth ran dry.

He turned back to me, the smile still stretched over his cracked face. He ducked one hand behind his back . . . and pulled out the unmistakable silhouette of a hunting knife. The same knife I'd seen this morning, buried in the stag's throat, left on the trail for me to find.

He stepped toward me again, too quick. I tripped on a rock, stumbling backward, twisting to keep my feet. I turned back in time to see him lunge at me, swinging the knife at my head, his dead lips still twitching in a wide smile.

6

RUN, RABBIT

STUMBLED, LOST MY BALANCE, AND COLLAPSED, DRAGGED DOWN BY the weight of my pack. A good thing, it turned out; a silver blur passed through my vision, close enough to brush a gust of wind against my face. The boy's hunting knife, swinging for my head. It would have shattered into my temple, I would have felt the cold iron against my eyeball —

"What are you doing?" I rolled and pushed myself back onto my feet, scrambling backward, fumbling for my pocket knife. Not real, this couldn't be real, this couldn't be happening. "Hey—hey, stop it! Stay where you are!"

The boy didn't stop. He stepped toward me.

"I'm warning you, kid. One more step and I'm gonna have to get violent."

The scar cutting through his face stretched, creasing and pulling like fresh taffy. Another step, the hunting knife gleaming silver in the moonlight.

I didn't know what to do. Should I step in and get physical? Should I run? Something was wrong with him; he didn't look at me, he looked through me, like I wasn't even there. He moved again, raising the hunting knife. I panicked, made a snap decision.

I threw myself inside his reach, aiming the triangle of my shoulder at the center of his rail-thin chest. I was six-two and a buck seventy-five, even after two weeks of constant movement and not enough water. He was eleven years old and a hundred pounds including the blade he clutched in one hand. As far as the physics went, he didn't stand a chance. I dropped my own knife in the collision and stumbled to my knees, but he went sprawling ass over teakettle, knife flying out of his hands.

I shrugged off my pack and scrambled in the dirt, hoping to hit the handle of his hunting knife or my knife, I didn't care which.

"Listen, kid, I don't know what your deal is, but you need to step the *hell* back, right now."

In the corner of my peripheral vision he stretched toward the charcoal sky. His gouged cheek tightened, his mouth opened and a scream like nothing I'd ever heard before split the air. It cracked and splintered, high-pitched, angry, and challenging. So loud I abandoned my search for the hunting knife, covering my ears. It raised the hair on the back of my neck, and made my testicles shrink. That wasn't the sound a human made.

He threw himself at me, snarling. Catching fistfuls of my hair, clinging like a goddamn spider monkey.

I grabbed at his shirt, and it tore in my hand; he crawled along my back and I twisted and jerked like a rodeo bull, but he clung tight, his breath hot on my neck.

A white-hot pain lanced through my head, a flash of agony.

"God damn it!" My hands caught something solid—his throat, fingers crossed—and I hurled him off. The side of my head was on fire. My right hand came away bloody.

He scrambled to his feet, black eyes gleaming. He panted, chest heaving. His lips stretched into that horrid grin, except now they gleamed slick with red. The little bastard bit me. He spat on the rocks and wiped his mouth, smearing my blood across his face.

Warm drops splattered on my shoulder, trickling down my face. My heart hammered hard enough to send my pulse shaking through my fingertips. I started to sob in big, chest-heaving waves.

This is crazy, this is bullshit, I didn't do anything, help me—someone help me.

The boy cocked his head and screamed at me again, the muscles in his neck bulging. His chest heaved.

My stomach dropped into my toes, and my legs wobbled. I didn't think twice about it.

I turned and ran.

I FLED, HEEDLESS of trail or terrain, clutching my ear. The echo of his scream followed me, and so did he.

"Who—who are you? Why are you doing this?" He didn't answer my pathetic cry. The ridge rose and fell, writhing northward and I followed it, staggering and clutching my head.

He was fast. My blood still shone on his lips. His face was flushed with excitement. He made an odd, rasped whooping sound.

I had twenty feet on him, then eighteen, then fifteen. Every time I twisted to check the distance, he closed in on me, a shark after blood.

Ahead of me, the terrain split. To my left, the ridge rolled into a thick pine forest, dropping into a nameless ravine. To the right it dropped into the basin beneath the crumbling cliffs, an eighty-foot drop at least. I broke left, half falling, half running toward the trees promising the vestiges of safety. I'd lose him in the ravine, hide up in a tree until he got frustrated and went away.

I fell twice, my feet flying out from underneath me, scraping against the grass until I caught my balance. The little bastard screamed each time I fell, running and falling after me with gleeful abandon. I made for the forest, trying not to think about how much closer he was getting, how much he was gaining on me.

The forest swallowed me. Beneath the canopy of pitch-black pine, the pale moon was only the barest suggestion of light.

I pitched left, moving as fast as I dared, hands outstretched to ward off low-hanging branches from my face. My eyes hadn't adjusted, and I slammed into the trunk of a tree with a blinding flash of light. A dull roar filled my ears. I fell to the slope with a gasp of surprise and pain.

Run, run, you have to run.

I couldn't see shit in the darkness, but I could hear him behind me, slapping against tree trunks and ruffling the deadfall. His grunts of effort and pants of excitement followed me, hovering in my ears like gnats.

I zigzagged left and right, pitching in crazy angles across the steep ridge to lose him among the black trees. I kept moving downhill, sometimes doubling back on my own tracks. I held my hands over my mouth, trying to muffle the heaving gasps that would give me away. Tears obscured my vision, made it even harder to see. I wiped them away with clumsy, shaking fingers.

It worked; the sound of his pursuit fell back until it was a distant rustle.

A while later I slowed to a cautious shuffle, my pulse roaring in my ears. I could see now, but just. The trees were absolute black shapes, separated by inked-in shadow. My hands trembled; my breath came in rocking sobs that shook my entire frame. I swallowed them, bit them back before they could betray where I was. I clamped down on my nose and held my breath. The world spun. I lost the horizon. Ten seconds of silence, and I allowed myself to breathe again. The adrenaline on the back of my tongue tasted like shiny pennies.

At a guess, I'd made it more than halfway down the ravine. A river churned over rocks some distance below me to the right—the floor of the valley, and the fastest path out. Maybe, if I was very, very lucky, it met up with a bigger river, somewhere with campers on the banks. They could help. They could protect me.

I didn't even consider climbing back up the ridge and walking high along the shoulder of the valley. He waited for me, that way.

Trapped.

Slowly, I slunk down the slope of the ravine toward the sound of falling water. I tested each footfall before I put my weight on it, moving away dry sticks with their traitorous snaps. Rocks that would clatter and roll downhill. Ten minutes crept by, then fifteen. Still no sound of my pursuer.

You can do this. Go slow, stay calm. You've lost him, you can follow the water to get help. Stay calm.

No fresh breeze cut beneath the trees. The air sat, stifling and oppressive. Sweat trickled down my face, stinging as it met my ear.

The white-noise roar of falling water got louder.

The canopy opened about twenty feet ahead of me, allowing a measure of moonlight to light the way.

Beneath me the valley fell away into unbroken black trees and darkness. The falling water proved to be a river with a small waterfall, collected in a shallow pool fifteen feet beneath me. No chance for a trail to help me navigate that drop, choked with dead tree trunks and granite boulders. I'd have to pick my way down on my own, slipping and sliding on soggy timber waiting to betray my every footstep.

Looking at the stream made me thirsty—my tongue rasped, thick and clumsy. I fell to my knees and gulped handful after handful. I didn't even care how many thousands of microbes, bits of dirt and bugs I sucked in with every slurp, that's how thirsty I was. I'd risk the Giardia.

I splashed water on my sweaty and flushed face, blinking hard, slapping my cheeks. My heart still trip-hammered in my chest, but at least it didn't echo all the way down to my fingertips anymore.

It's all right, you've gotten past it. He's gone. I closed my eyes. My senses tripped all over the place, overworked, numb from the onslaught. Five things I could see. A tree, the river, a dark rock with a white splotch. My shoe, a dead leaf, floating lazy downstream. I wondered if I should pick my way step by step back up the ravine to where I ditched my backpack. Four things I could touch. My skin, hot, feverish. The smooth fabric of my shirt. The dirt, soft and crumbling. I came back down to myself, one step at a time.

Breathe. In the dark, in the silence, I hunted for the lessons Dr. K had taught me. I grabbed a leaf, focused on the way it crackled and crushed in my palm. I might be able to head back down the basin and be in Bedal by sunrise or sooner. Someone there would have a phone. Three things I could hear. The water, burbling. A happy sound, like a little chuckle. Laughing. If I climbed back up the basin, I would have my tent, all my supplies—

Across the three-foot streamlet, a single twig snapped.

I froze, searching the inked black shadow for a form or hint of movement.

Please God, be a squirrel. The skin in the small of my back seemed to shrink and shrivel. Nothing moved.

He exploded from the darkness like a ghost. His eyes burned with triumph, his grotesque face twisted. The knife poised over his head. I scrambled backward, screeching in incoherent panic. I crab-walked straight over the edge of the waterfall and plunged onto the rocks beneath me.

My right hand stretched out, touching the boulder that "broke" my fall. The ligaments and bones in my wrist bent the wrong way, snapping loud enough for me to hear. Glass shattered inside my wrist, and a million ants poured inside, biting.

I screamed so hard spots blinked in my vision.

I bounced from one boulder to another, then to the rocked-shallow of the waterfall pool.

The boy leaped onto a dead tree, dropping from boulder to boulder faster than my eyes could follow.

Clutching my injured wrist to my chest I flailed through the shallows, sputtering. I ran downstream, kicking up water left and right, feet plunging through water and empty air.

The boy screamed again, and this time the sound roared up the throat of the ravine, reverberating until there were three, five, ten of him. His footsteps splashed in the river behind me as he chased, panting.

"Leave me alone!" I howled. The tears were back, raw and burning as they flooded my vision. The river swam, the ravine wavered. The forest ran with the boy, chasing me, swallowing me. The ravine twisted, narrowed, widened, then narrowed again. The streambank was choked with willow reeds, slapping and tearing at my pants.

In front of me, the ravine forked. To the left it curved northwest into another nameless valley, to the right it fell to a lake. Through the gap in the mountains I could see the huge, three-finger summit of Glacier hanging over the lake, sweet salvation. The PCT lay that way, civilization—

The splashing footsteps quickened, outpacing me, racing along my right. I turned away from him, crying, thinking of nothing else but putting more distance between us. I scurried into the valley.

I ran as fast as I could, looking for an alternate path, but the landscape didn't break, didn't offer me an escape. The woods swallowed me.

The boy fell behind me, struggling against water up to his ribs. I ran until the only sound was my own heaving breath. I half sat, half fell into a hollow beneath a tree, puddled with black. I let my knees buckle and sink me beneath the dirt. It swallowed the sobs rushing to my throat. I put my face in the dirt that smelled of gentle rot and decay and cried in voiceless heaves.

Shit like this didn't happen, not in real life.

A mass of sweat-stinging blood clotted my ear, and pain bit my feet each time I put my weight down. My wrist, though . . . I probed it, biting my tongue to avoid hissing aloud. Swollen already. Even the slightest pressure from my fingertips sent pain lancing as far up as my elbow. Broken, for sure.

Tree roots cupped my shivering and shaking form in a dirt hollow, like a rabbit in a warren. Just like Green-Eyes.

The night grew ten degrees cooler. How far was I from where I found him? Fifteen, twenty miles? A day's hike, no more. Easy enough ground for a psychotic, murderous boy to cover, especially if he knew the backcountry trails.

A sudden and unyielding urge to get the fuck out of the tree hollow gripped me. I stumbled through the forest, squinting at the canopy overhead, trying to get my bearings.

I was deep in the Mt. Glacier wilderness by now—an entire mountain stood between me and any signed trail. A hiker came into the Glacier wilderness for only two reasons; to hike the PCT, or to summit Glacier. Beyond those, it turned into a dense collection of hard-to-reach valleys and peaks avoided by most.

Great.

I followed the river, limping on the banks against the current. The night breathed softly, silently except for the occasional squawk of a late-flying raven roosting in the trees.

I moved slowly. Every sound scratched at my raw nerves, every shadow a wet-wax grin on a dead face. A mouse skittered from one escape hole to another, and I swallowed a panicked *eep*. In the distance the valley pitched upward. Pale cliff faces and snow-capped summits white-washed in the fading moonlight. I'd never felt so small. Over-head, the stars burned.

He moved from behind a tree, a black-on-black silhouette.

A whine built in my throat, and I pitched into a stumbling run, the breath stilling in my hot and harried lungs.

"Go away," I whimpered, turning my head. "Please, please just go away. You don't have to do this."

No shadow broke the still mask of night, no insane grin material-ized in the stygian gloom. I shambled forward still, my child-like cry of fear still on my lips. Where did he go?

"I see you," a soft voice whispered, two feet to my left. I shrieked and jumped, twisting my head to see, but saw nothing.

He'd found me, flitting between the trees.

Something to my right moved. I jolted away from it, moving deeper into the valley, stumbling, sobbing. My ear hurt, the bones of my wrist replaced with red-hot rocks. I couldn't keep my breath; it whistled through my wasted lungs.

Something hissed behind me. Monsters in the dark with a thou-sand deformed mouths. Blood smeared on their chapped lips and hun-ger in their bellies.

A raven burst, screaming, from the black tree canopy.

I scrambled into a moonlit clearing, falling into the water of a scummed-over pond. The black faces of the cliffs and peaks glared down at me.

I couldn't. I couldn't keep running. My chest burned with effort, my legs shook. I flailed in the knee-deep shallows, turning to face him. The needling in my fingertips, the first stages of that ever-waiting panic attack.

If I'd ever found a situation that warranted it, this was it.

"Come on, then!" My strained and hoarse voice comforted me; my own echo, a hollow and threadbare shell of me. Switchback, lin-gering in the curved tree branches. "Come and get me!"

I slapped the water, trying to muster whatever courage I could. Bravado, born of desperation.

He came then, walking out of the blackness between two trees. He licked his cracked and grinning lips, and the curled cleft of his cheek gaped at me, a second smile. He didn't come for me. He stood there, smiling.

"Come on! What are you waiting for?" I'd grab one of his legs, hold it in the air. Keep his contorted face beneath the surface of the pond until he stopped thrashing. Even if he cut me, even if he took me down with him. At the end of all things, he was a boy and I was a full-grown adult. My heart pounded all the way to my toes. My pants ran warm, wet. I might have pissed myself. I didn't care.

A second shape materialized from the trees, some distance away. His mouth moved with the words that came from the other's, a corpse's harmony:

"The Woodkin feed the Feast."

Another boy. I could count the ribs sticking out of his bare chest. A black, gaping fissure gauging deep into his cheek, turning his eye into a clouded waste. He was missing half his long and lank hair, the skin puckered and scarred into a rope. He stretched his lips into the same dead-man's smile.

"What the fuck?" I spun from one boy to the other. "What are—"

"The Woodkin feed the Feast," the two boys intoned in one voice. The second one held a club in one hand, studded with what looked like nails.

They didn't move toward me. They stood still.

Another emerged from the forest, this one a full-grown man. His teeth chattered clear through the same cleft in his cheek, and his milk-eye glared at me.

"What are—hey! You!" An adult—I could reason with an adult. The last vestiges of reason left in my screaming mind. "Help me— please, I'll give you anything you want!"

He moved with the rest of them, staring through me. They said it over and over, in one voice:

"The mountain. The mountain."

They appeared one after another, shadows come to life, men and boys. Each carried the ruination of scarring, each spoke the words. Some carried clubs, others knives. They surrounded the pond and me. With each repetition, the words got more and more heated, angrier. The words became a chant, and the chant became a howl, rising to surround us. They beat their chests, they slapped themselves, leaving raised red welts on their skin.

The first boy, the one who'd attacked me on the mountain, stepped out of the crowd. His words came alive:

"The Woodkin will feast in His glory."

His lips moved with the others'. Nothing in his eyes but me.

They fell on me at once, closing the trap. I ducked under one of the fists, but the second one caught me dead in the jaw, sending a blinding flash through my eyes. I threw myself into the water, trying to swim, but they caught me, clutched me. One of them rabbit-punched me in the kidney. My turn to scream. They dragged me out of the water, dumped me on the bank and beat me, a flood of fists and feet. Someone slammed my head against the ground. Blood burst into my mouth, bright salted copper. A foot connected with my balls, and I writhed into the fetal position, crying.

This is how I died. In the dark, in the shadows.

Something blunt and heavy crushed my temple and the darkness swallowed me.

I'm sorry, Deb.

7

HIS FEAR IS SHARP

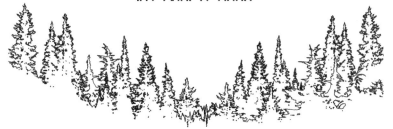

SOMEWHERE IN THAT BLACK SLEEP, I BEGAN TO DREAM.

I dreamed Deb and I were going to the movies for date night. I can't remember what we were seeing, but Deb was all smiles. I felt happy; I remember that with painful clarity. Whatever divided us had vanished, and we were whole once more. We joked, we laughed. I threw popcorn at her, and it got stuck in her hair. She broke down in giggles. She raised her hand and we high-fived—but it hurt. A rush of pain shot through my wrist and hand, just for a moment, enough to make the cinema lobby bolt and shudder. Deb asked me if I was all right, I said I was. She kissed me on the cheek and whispered, "I love you, Puggs."

But her cheek against mine felt odd, felt different. It shifted in strange patterns, like cold and sticky fingers. When she pulled away, her face was a ruin of scarred flesh, slashed, the raw muscle of her face exposed. One of her baby blues stared at nothing, milky white. She grinned, and I could see her teeth through the hole in her cheek. Filed to splintered and fragmented points.

"Do we have a chance, after you're done?" Her ruined mouth moved, but it wasn't her voice anymore.

I shook my head, confused. "Deb? Babe, are you all right?"

She looked at me and smiled. The skin around her eyes bulged and warped, sloughing like a spider's husk.

"The Woodkin feed the Feast." She lunged at me, biting my hand, and the splintered ends of her teeth drew blood. I screamed. The dream collapsed around me.

Her words still echoed in my ears when I woke up.

Oak limbs outlined against the patchwork stars in many-fingered silhouettes. My head sagged and bounced. I couldn't orient myself; the horizon dipped and wavered. I wanted the dream back—it hovered in the darkness beyond my reach, fading into the trees.

They clutched me by my limbs, grunting in unintelligible words, moving me over dead trees and across streams. A thousand splinters of glass twisted in my injured wrist. Something grasped it, holding it too tight. I groaned and pulled, trying to free it, but whatever held it tightened even more.

Their scarred, tight faces floated above me, spots of blurred white in the black shadow. Some as young as the boy who had chased me— young, why were they so young? Why me? Where were we going? I couldn't focus on any one detail, couldn't hold the strand of a single thought.

We stopped, and they dropped me like a sack of flour. I put my hands out to catch myself on instinct. Something hard beneath my palms, before the bolt of lightning shot through my wrist again. No scream, but a whimper. My throat burned from screaming. One of the men pulled something open beside me, and the squeal of rusty metal grated against my ears. Metal—a cage? The moon finally dipped below the mountains, stealing the last silver half-light. Silhouettes surrounded me, I smelled blood—mine—and the sweet rot of molding leaves. Something else lurked beneath the sweet rot, as well. It was distant, difficult to make out. Sweet at first, but bitter, far too bitter. I couldn't say what it was, but it made my stomach churn. My pulse pounded in my ears.

They hauled me by my armpits, dragged me inside a room. I tried to fight and kick, but my limbs moved slowly, sluggishly. My legs slid over wood boards, and what little light I could see shrank to a rectangle. One of them gave me a kick in the gut for good measure, and I crumpled like an empty beer can. He spat, and something wet splattered against my cheek—I didn't move to wipe it off, didn't make a sound. Metal on metal screamed again. Footfalls moving away, then silence. No rustle of tree limbs, or chirp of crickets, or scurry of squirrels through the leaves.

I didn't move for some time. I stayed curled in the fetal position, wet spittle cooling on my cheek. They would come for me again. This was a trick, had to be. One of them waited in the shadows, waited for me to relax. They would come for me, beat me, materializing out of the shadows like ghosts again. I stayed in the fetal position and twitched at my own imagination.

When no attack came, I cracked an eye. I clenched my gut, sure the boy would erupt from my peripherals, snarling and biting.

Nothing.

My eyes adjusted to the filmy black shadow, putting fuzzy and incoherent details in place. Distant starlight filtered through a grid-marked rectangle. An iron door. I was in a cell, a prison cell of some kind. The air tasted sour with the reek of strong mold, unwashed sweat, and iron, either from the still-wet pool of blood soaking down the front of my chest or the metal of the barred door. The line where the floor met the wall blurred. Dead leaves.

I grasped at these things, these pieces of logic and cold fact, clung to them. A gibbering, slack-jawed panic fomented at the edges of my thoughts. This wasn't real, couldn't be real. And yet, my wrist burned. My ear stank of hot blood.

I could smell and taste and hear and touch.

More time passed, and nothing burst from the shadows or fell from the rafters. My pulse slowed, and I inched onto my back, moving to wipe the sticky spit from my cheek.

In the far corner of the room, in the darkness of pooled shadow, something stirred.

"Who's there?" My voice cracked even at a whisper. I scooted backward until my back touched a wall. "Please leave me alone, please, I don't want any more trouble, I'm sorry—"

A pale face appeared. Long, too long, and for a fraction of a second I thought it was inhuman until my brain clicked the shapes into place. It wasn't long, it was framed by a beard, a white beard—and I'd seen the face before.

"Appletree?"

The face disappeared, shrunk back into shadow without an answer. I licked my lips, chapped and swollen.

"Appletree, is that—is that you?"

Still no answer. My eyes almost adjusted to the darkness of the room, but the corner he remained in stayed out of focus. A warped square of silver light spilled onto the wall above him. Unwilling to part with the security coming from having something solid against my back, I scooted along the wall. After about two feet, my hand scraped against a bundle of sticks, buried beneath the wet leaves.

God, if only I had my . . . the thought stopped me in my tracks. I fumbled with my good hand at a pocket, hoping against hope, clumsy with excitement. I pulled out my keys, dropped them carelessly, kept digging. It was still there. My little impulse-buy fire starter, still in my pocket.

"Thank you, God," I whispered, kissing it. I could have a fire. Fire meant warmth, and light. Fire was safe. For the moment I forgot about Appletree.

It took longer than I'm proud of—even in a decent mental state, my fire-making skills sucked the big one. The sticks were thin, the thickest as big around as my thumb, and pretty wet. I spent five minutes shuffling through the deadfall, trembling with cold and pain. I scraped the fire starter three or four times, then leaned in and blew. I got a lot of wet, miserable smoke smelling of dead rot and no flames, but I kept at it. On what felt like my five-hundredth try, a tiny finger of flame curled upward. More smoke than fire, but it did the job. I fed it leaves one at a time with trembling fingers.

After a few minutes, a guttering orange glow lit the inside of the room, threatening to go out at any minute. I turned back to the corner.

It was Appletree. A tattered and stained blanket pulled up to his chin, blending his torso into the sagging wall behind him. His face turned away, staring at the waterlogged timbers. At first I thought the lighting changed his face. The eerie half-light from the fire cast dancing shadows across his cheekbones. He looked harsh, gaunt.

"Appletree? Bud?" I worked my way across the floor. "Are you all right? Can you hear me?"

It wasn't the fire. His skin, tanned and leathered from hours of exposure on the trail, now looked pale, slack. It pulled away from the sharp lines of his sunken cheekbones like overboiled pasta. The flesh of his forehead sagged over his brow in heavy folds. Livid bags seared beneath his eyes, and a fine tremor shook the fingers clutching the edge of the blanket. Those, too, were thin, with the skin falling in folds over knobby knuckles. Like he was rotting away, right in front of me—like his body had died and decayed with him still trapped inside it. He looked . . . ill. But I'd seen him this morning. Just twelve hours ago.

"Appletree. What happened?" We were a dozen miles away from the PCT, at least. "Did they attack you?"

His mouth moved, small utterances too far below his breath for me to understand. I scooted closer, trying to make them out. I made sure to keep my hands out where he could see them.

The words spilling from his lips were breathy, incoherent. He babbled. In the slew, I made out two, strung together in the middle of a sentence.

". . . the Woodkin—"

"Yes! That's what the boy who attacked me kept saying!" I whispered. "Something about the Woodkin, and the mountain, and a . . . a feast, I think! Do you know what it means?"

"The Woodkin—"

I leaned in to hear but got nothing but mumbled gibberish. "I can't understand you. Hey."

I waved my hand in front of his face, trying to snap him out of it. His gaze ricocheted against the wall, darting here and there. I moved closer, clutched the blanket. We could work out an escape or figure out a way to get a signal to the outside world. If he knew their comings and goings, if he watched them, it was possible. "Appletree—"

He recoiled from my touch, crying out like I'd branded him. His bare feet scraped against the floor as he pushed himself farther into his corner, away from me, leaving slick rust-red trails. I glanced down.

Cuts, shallow and scrawling, covered his bare feet where they peeked out from beneath the blanket. A dozen, two dozen, along the toes and heels, ankles, all weeping thick strings of blood.

"Jesus," I croaked. He looked at me, and with a single glance I understood. Saw it in his red-rimmed eyes, gleaming with tears of confusion.

Fear. Not the fear of a man, but the fear of a child. A child who sees but doesn't understand. I knew the look, because I saw it once, a long time ago. In the mirror above the sink, in Mr. Neery's bathroom, the day my mother was burned alive. Fear, because he knew something. Something he would never whisper to another soul, because there were no words. In the shadow beyond the fire, a truth long buried came back to the boy, staring at himself in the bathroom mirror. A secret that should have stayed in the dark.

"What happened to you?" I whispered. Neither the boy nor Appletree responded. He whispered still, and this close I could hear it. I knew what he was going to say before he said it. The blanket writhed in a burst of motion and his hand gripped my wrist, white-knuckled.

"The Woodkin"—quiet, barely breathing the words—"feasts."

Tears stole the rest of his words from him. His eyes locked on mine, pleading.

"I'm sorry." All I could say, the only words. He whimpered and flung the blanket over his head.

—————

I TRIED SEVERAL more times but got nothing else out of him. I cajoled time and time again, assuring him I wasn't going to hurt him, there was no one else but me. After a while his sobs quieted, and he lapsed into silence.

I didn't disturb the blanket; I doubt it would have helped.

My pathetic fire lasted another ten minutes or so before devolving into a pile of clumped ash. Autumn came early this high in the mountains. I wrapped my good arm around my knees, pressed them tight against my chest and shivered.

My body ached and my eyelids dragged, but sleep lay entirely out of the equation. Tired, but couldn't sleep. Thirsty and hungry, but no food or water. Wrist pounding, heavier with every heartbeat, but I couldn't bring myself to look at it.

"What the hell are we going to do, Appletree, old buddy?" I whispered. I didn't expect a response. I leaned my head back; the wall behind me, slick with mold and fungus, gave a little. Outside, in an unseen tree, a pair of birds twittered to each other. If I closed my eyes, it sounded like every cool morning in the reaches of the cascades. If I closed my eyes, I could lie to myself, pretend I wasn't here. *Perspective*, Dr. K whispered, across the years.

After a minute, another sound rose, barely audible beneath the chirping. Guttural, droning—like a river, or a waterfall, but sharper. I blinked, sat up. I knew that sound. It grew, rising in pitch until it drowned out the birds, sent them cawing and fluttering away. A car engine. I shot to my feet, staggered to the door, and stuck my good arm out, waving like a madman.

"Hey! Hey, over here! Appletree, get up! There's someone here!" I shouted at the top of my lungs. I didn't care if the whatever-they-were heard me. An engine meant the real world. Appletree, or the trembling half person he'd become, cowered beneath the blanket across from me and didn't budge. An off-roader, out late? A hunter? I didn't know, didn't care.

The sound cut out thirty or forty feet away, and a door opened and closed.

"Over here! Please! Please help me!" Feet crunching over sticks and twigs, running. Tears of relief stung my eyes. The footsteps echoed over the wood boards, approaching the door. A silhouette rushed into view, breathless.

"Is someone there?"

I squinted, trying to pull the details of the face I knew would have round glasses and longish hair. "Ronnie?"

Ronnie Coors gaped at me, his expression almost a mirror of the one I'm sure was plastered across my face. "You? Oh my God, what are you doing out here? What the—" He shook his head, blinking like I'd disappear. He gaped like a fish out of water.

"I'll explain later. Can you open this door?"

"Can I—yeah, of course, there's a latch right here—" A familiar squeak of metal, and the door swung open. He stuck his head in. "What the hell is going on?"

I ran to the corner. "Appletree! Hey! There's someone here, some-one who can help us. We have to go, right now. Come on."

No response.

"Appletree!"

"Who are you talking to?"

"He's there, in the shadow by the corner, you can't see him. Ap-pletree!"

Still nothing. I ground my teeth, struggling not to panic. Ronnie showing up was a literal miracle, but we didn't have much time; the Woodkin must have heard the engine, just like me. I grabbed the edge of the blanket, hauled it off my cellmate, hissing. "Appletree, come on—"

He shouted in fear, too loud, grabbed at the blanket in my hand. He whined, a deep-throat sound of misery, intent on nothing else but staying hidden from the world. Like he wasn't even a person anymore. Like the last vestiges of the man I knew were gone, snuffed out.

"Appletree, please—"

"What are you doing? Let's go!" Ronnie whispered. He peered out of the door, adjusted his glasses. Behind him the cloud layer grew a shade brighter, lighting the world in cold shadow. "We should get out of here, while the getting's good."

"I can't leave him—" But the words sounded puerile, even to me. What did I owe Appletree that weighed more than my own life?

"We don't have time for this!" Ronnie hissed. "Come on, let's go."

He jumped from the cell, broke right out the door. I threw one last look at Appletree. I owed him nothing—I repeated the words to myself like they could seal the breach of betrayal. Just a guy I met yesterday, nothing more. I was leaving him to die, and I knew it. But if I stayed with him, I'd die as well. Kill, or be killed, that's how I needed to look at it. Josh would never leave a man to die. Switchback, on the other hand . . .

"I'm sorry."

I left. The dawn chill surrounded us. Ice-cold drops of rain pattered against the dead leaves in a thousand tiny taps.

"Fuckin' thing—I got no signal, I keep calling AT&T but they
keep telling me there's no way they can make it stronger. Oh my *God*
I can't believe it's you, you're *here*." Ronnie clutched an old-school
flip phone over his head, whirling it like service started six feet in the
air. The white Jeep was parked at the end of an oblong clearing, and I
made for it. Ronnie followed, raking a hand through his hair, talking
at a breakneck clip. "I wanted to get out for a morning drive, before
the shop opened. I saw a game trail through the woods I hadn't seen
before so I thought fuck it, why not, and then—"

"Can you call anyone? Do you have service?"

"I'm tryin', I'm tryin'." He had something in his hand, raising it
over his head.

I spun in place, gaping. Cold dawn lit the clearing in shades of
shadow and navy, and I saw my surroundings for the first time.

Mold-eaten houses, sagging to one side, roofs collapsing, dotted
the clearing. A dozen or more, some so decrepit they had collapsed
back into the forest and were covered in ivy and crawling weeds. Old,
held up by sun-bleached and warped timber. Pale patches of rock-
dotted clay or foraged sticks covered with dirt dotted the roofs. Trees
grew close, punching holes in rotten timber walls. Hiding the town
beneath the thick canopy. In the center of the clearing a single pine
tree loomed, twice or three times the size of any other. A rope hung
from one of the limbs. An old mining town, had to be. Couple hundred
years old, if not more.

"Ronnie, look at this. Where are we? This is—this is unbeliev-
able." I panted. We'd almost made it to the Jeep. We could turn around,
drive out of here. Salvation, at hand.

"Believe it, dipshit."

I didn't see his outstretched foot until too late. It hooked under my
ankle and sent me sprawling face-first with a shriek of surprise and

pain. This time I didn't stretch my hands out to break my fall—fool me once. Pine needles prickled and stabbed my face, and I spat out the bitter taste of dirt. I rolled over and he towered over me, an all-too familiar smirk on his face.

"You utter moron," he snorted in his shrill, girlish laughter and adjusted his glasses. "Oh my God, you fell for it. Why do you fuckin' people always fall for it? Dumbass. 'Oh, my savior! Please won't you let me out of this cage?' Pathetic. This isn't even a real phone! It's a fuckin' toy some kid dropped in my store!" He wiggled the cell phone-shaped piece of plastic in front of my face.

"What are you doing?" I didn't understand. I rolled, still spitting dirt and pine needles. A boot pressed against my shoulder, put me back on the ground.

"Man you are a stupid hick, ain't ya boy? Surprise!" Ronnie's upper lip curled back against his teeth. He leaned in, the toe of his boot digging into the soft spot below my shoulder. I moaned and ground my teeth, but I didn't cry out. Behind the round glasses his eyes shone with glee. He reached down and tried to haul me up by my shirt front.

"Get off of me!" I hammered a fist against his wrist, and he dropped me with a curse. I slithered backward in the dirt, trying to get away. I spun over, scrabbled for my balance, got to my feet.

I made a beeline for the trees at the end of the clearing, hooking around the Jeep. I'd make for the river, follow it downstream. A solid chance the river flower back to Bedal, I could get help—

A figure slid from behind a pine trunk twenty feet in front of me, silent as a shadow, his scarred face malevolent and still. In his hand he clutched a rusty piece of iron, jagged and lethal at the end.

I cried out and altered my course. I could still make it, I could outrun one of them, now that I knew what the alternatives were. I'd have to. A boy manifested from the dark haze, stepping out of the forest, dead in front of me. He looked like the boy from last night, but he carried a rock lashed to the end of a stick.

"God damn it, leave me alone!" A bird squawked at my scream, but the forest swallowed my words.

Three more stood in front of me, shoulder to shoulder. I turned, and another shifted from the darkness of the woods.

I spun in place, panting, trying to find a way out. The bruised clouds pressed the sky low, stifled the air and made it heavy. I couldn't breathe. Everywhere I looked, scarred and ruined faces glared at me. Filmy and sagging eyes full of raw anger. None of them wore shirts, only tattered shorts or pants. They were all thin as walking corpses. Each chest breathing with harsh angles of ribs pressed tight against sallow-looking skin. Within the shared disfigurement of their faces, cheekbones jutted outward.

They closed in from the clearing on all sides, weapons clutched close. They didn't speak. Nowhere for me to run. They stalked me in almost-unison, closing the trap.

"Switchback, meet the Woodkin," Ronnie called, spreading his arms wide.

"What—why are you doing this?" I pawed dirt from my face, shrank back from those terrible cold faces, those milky eyes. "What did I do to you?"

Behind me Ronnie snorted. "There you go, champ, start firing off questions, I'm sure that's the recipe to success."

A man stepped out from the ring of bodies. He held no weapon. His scar cracked his face, a livid red channel, showing white flecks of bone and threads of unhealed muscle gone to atrophy. On the left side of his face, his lips turned down in a perpetual frown.

"There you are." All traces of mockery slid from Ronnie's face. "Finally. I've been entertaining myself with this fool. I'm back—I need more stuff."

The man said nothing. Ronnie waited, tapping a hand against his thigh. No one else spoke—only the birds tweeted, and the moan of a cold day's wind blowing through the clearing. After a minute the corner of Ronnie's mouth curled in, betraying his irritation. He spoke again.

"I, uh, see you've got yourself another one. Full house, so to speak."

"We're blessed by the Feast." The man's hoarse voice creaked like ancient floorboards. White stubble clung to his cheeks. His skin was so pale it looked like he'd never seen the sun. Like he manifested from the shadow beneath the trees.

"I know this one." Ronnie jutted his chin toward me. "He stopped in my shop yesterday. Ain't that a bitch? I mean, what are the odds? How'd you snag him? Trapped? Hunted? Come on, man, gimme some juicy details!" He clapped his hands, rubbed them together.

The man stood still, silent.

"He was on his way back to the trail, last I heard." Ronnie held himself ramrod straight, mirroring the other's stiff posture. "I know how much you guys like thru-hikers—ain't nobody gonna miss him, right? Those people, out on the trail . . . nothing waiting for them."

That wasn't true. Deb would miss me, wouldn't she? Maybe she would. Or she'd hear her husband went missing in the spine of the Cascades and she'd be relieved. Because then she could stop lying, stop sneaking around. She'd be free to fuck whomever she pleased.

The older man said nothing. A breath of air moved through the valley, and I shivered. Ronnie pulled his long-sleeved flannel a little tighter. None of the scarred men moved at all. Like the cold didn't touch them. Like they were already dead.

The seconds ticked by, and the sick excitement in Ronnie's eyes curdled to annoyance. He threw his hands in the air. "Fine, whatever. I need more stuff. I'm out."

"You're early." No inflection in his words; not even the slightest hint of emotion or intonation. Flat, dull.

"I don't care," Ronnie snapped, pushing a strand of hair behind one ear. "I'm out, and I need more."

"You took too much, last time. We haven't had time to harvest—"

"No—no! Don't say it like that, as if I stole it from you. You gave it to me, remember? I asked, and you gave it to me." A hint of petulance now.

"We offered what we could spare, and you took more."

"That's because I needed it! We've talked about this! I'm—" Ronnie's eyes darted to me. "The boys need more, you hear me? We're out. Otherwise, you know what's going to happen."

"You're early."

"I don't give a rat's ass!" His shrill voice cracked and echoed through the clearing. A red flush built in his face, along his neck. He glanced at me again, and the flush grew. "You know what? You aren't showing me the suitable respect. Not working with me to further our plans, not addressing me by my proper title. I have always been a friend to the Woodkin, but it doesn't seem like my friendship is being valued at all. Maybe I'll take my support"—he lingered on the word, his tongue darting out to moisten his lips—"and go back to where it's valued."

He crossed his arms. The old man stayed silent for a heartbeat. I watched his face but got nothing. No flicker of irritation in his one working eye or clenching of his jaw. None of the microexpressions giving each of us away as living, breathing humans.

He nodded once. Incremental, like gravity forced the gesture. "As you say. We'll collect it by this evening. It will be ready before the ceremony."

I didn't like the choice of words at all. I especially didn't like the way Ronnie's eyes lit up like a kid on Christmas eve.

"It's tonight? No kidding. What timing I have, eh? Good thing I came out, I thought about skipping today, coming up later in the week." He craned his head, looking around at the silent wall of broken faces around us. "Where are they? I want to pick a few out for later."

"They have duties to attend to before—"

Ronnie shook his head, interrupting. "No, no. I want to see them now. I waited last time. Not today."

Another pause. They stared at each other. Ronnie ran hot; excitement burned in his eyes and stretched a smirk across his slack lips. The old man was the antithesis of the emotions scrolling through Ronnie's face. Even the wind seemed hesitant to ruffle the few strings of lank gray hair hanging by his temple.

The old man broke first. He turned his head to the side and muttered something the wind stole before I could make it out. One of the boys stepped out of the circle, ran toward the trees. The smirk on Ronnie's lips widened. He turned to me.

"You see, Switchback—"

My fist cut off the rest of his words in a whoosh as the air rushed from his gut. He folded like a lawn chair, and I went down with him, punching and kicking with my good hand and foot.

"You son of a bitch! You knew? You fucking—"

My vengeance was short-lived. A dozen hands closed around my arms and mouth, muffling my indignance, throwing me to the ground. A foot connected with my ribs, and I cried out, writhing. Another kicked me in the neck, and my head snapped forward hard enough for my teeth to clack. A foot connected with my face and my nose crunched in a way it wasn't supposed to. A warm spray burst onto my face, running down my mouth and chin.

"All right, all right that's enough. Hey! I said enough!" Ronnie shouted, elbowing his way into the circle. "He's no good to you dead. Back away. Back up, God damn it."

His left cheek was swollen and puffy. *Yeah*, I thought as I spat blood and what I hoped was dirt and not teeth fragments, *that'll show you.* A throbbing pain radiated from my left kidney up to my shoulder. Ronnie looked down at me, pressed a tentative finger to the swelling around his eye.

His smile stretched, cold as ice.

"Good for you, Switchback. Keep that anger—you'll last longer. Get him up. Hold on to him this time, for fuck's sake."

Three of the scarred men hauled me to my feet. I spat out more blood and breathed through my mouth.

Newcomers arrived at the other end of the circle. A group of women. I blinked, trying to focus on their features. Seven or ten of them, ranging in age from gray-haired to younger, my age. They didn't share the same starved look the rest of their companions did. No bone-thin upper arms over swollen elbows. They wore normal clothes—none of the tattered rags the men and boys wore. Unscarred, each of them. If I squinted, they looked like regular people.

Except the harsh cheekbones casting shadows on their faces. Except for the way their eyes watched me, like I was a maggot wriggling in the dirt.

"There they are!" Ronnie spread his arms. "Ladies. So good of you to join us. Sorry you had to witness that. A little lesson in humility, for the boy. Father tells me the ceremony is going to be tonight. Imagine, imagine. Very exciting stuff, very exciting." He turned toward each, weighing, analyzing. "Of course we all know what ceremony night means. I'm still sore from the last go-round. That was a good time, as we all know." His high-pitched giggle made the hair on the back of my neck stand at end.

I could only see the back of his head, but it didn't take much effort to imagine the way his piggish eyes leered, stripping the women's clothes off one layer at a time. One—no, two—of the ladies were pregnant, their swollen bellies pushing against their clothes. The shape didn't match their faces; it was like they'd stolen the muscle and fat right off the others' bodies. Sliced it with knives, slapped it on themselves. A build-it-yourself nightmare.

"I want the stuff in my Jeep before we get going tonight. Double what I needed last time. They're proving . . . difficult to keep under wraps."

The silence was palpable. It moved through the clearing like a thing alive. I hunted the older man's face for an emotion—any emotion, any betrayal of actual humanity. Nothing. Still as a silent lake. Not so much as a ripple.

The man Ronnie had referred to as Father bowed his head. "As you wish, Reaper."

My skin chilled at the nickname. It didn't match the ever-widening grin on Ronnie's face, or his overall air of almost childish exuberance. If anything, I would have guessed that the old man was the Reaper. And Ronnie was just . . . Ronnie.

"That's what I'm talking about!" Ronnie clapped and whooped loud enough to make me flinch. "Hot damn! And you called me by my title. Look at you, finally learning the new order of things. Better late than never, right? Is everything ready for tonight? Need any help from the old boss man?" He cackled.

For the first time, Father's face moved. His thin lips spread into a smile colder than the touch of frostbite. Pushing high up his face, cutting into his pale skin like a pair of razors. A wave of goose bumps spread across my belly.

"His fear is sharp. He is ready."

Ronnie's answering grin attempted to match the casual maliciousness of the old man's. It failed in spectacular fashion; he looked like a buffoon. "Excellent. You three! Take him back to the cell. You have yourself a good time there, Switchback. While you still can."

They did as they were told, ignoring my injured thrashing. The door squealed shut, and the sound of the pin falling into place echoed in my ears.

"Hey! Hey! Let me out of here! This is bullshit!" I hammered on the rusted iron door and screamed until my voice grew hoarse and scratched my throat like nails. "Ronnie! God damn you!"

My words turned into raw screams, which turned into shaking sobs. The darkness came for me, rising within. I fell to the floor, curled into myself.

This was it. This was how it would end.

His fear is sharp.

They were going to kill me. I stuffed myself into the corner, listened to Appletree's whimpering, and tried not to imagine the creative ways my death would find me. A razor blade, whispering along the veins in my feet. My skull shattered with a rock. Hanging from a tree struggling for the evaporating breath in my lungs.

His fear is sharp.

FACES IN THE TREES

T HEY LEFT US IN THE CELL TO ROT.

Midmorning it began to rain, drowning the forest in white noise, cutting us off from the rest of the world. Rainwater dripped from holes in the roof above us, tapping on the floorboards. Outside the cell door, hazy forms stalked through the downpour. They seemed like ghosts. Wraiths from the spaces between the trees.

Fingers of rainwater streamed through the pine needles, moving south. South, toward the river. Toward Bedal.

At first I paced, too jittery to sit. I stuck my face between the bars. Shouts ripped at my raw, dry throat. No one even threw me a glance. They shuttled through the fog.

Maybe they weren't ghosts at all. Maybe I was the ghost. Panic tightened in my chest, squeezing my voice to nothing. Maybe I'd be the one to just . . . fade away. An in-between, haunting the forests for-ever, locked behind bars. Rust ringing my fingernails, ripping grooves into wood.

I gave up. Something sharp stabbed my mouth every time I swal-lowed. When was the last time I drank water? I couldn't remember. I couldn't remember a lot of things. I hunched in a corner, tried to sleep. Nightmares of split-faced men cracking my skull open with a rock came in waves. My skin crawled and I slapped at writhing cen-tipedes that seemed there one second, gone the next. Reality dipped inside-out, and for a moment I stared at the world through my dream-eyes, trapped in the wrong side. Fingers clawed at my feet through the dark, here. Whispers that smelled like smoke and ash screamed from a great distance.

"Think we're going to die here, bud?" I spoke so I'd hear some-thing, pretend I wasn't alone. Appletree hunched in the corner, an empty shirt. He couldn't help me. No one could help me.

"We're already dead."

Did I say that? Did he? A hoarse whisper, a shadow of its former self. I scrambled to my hands and knees.

My voice started and died in my throat, spasming, twitching like an animal in death throes. "Holy shit, you're awake. I thought you were . . . I don't know, catatonic or something. Sweet Jesus, man, what happened to you?"

"A kid." He stared through the wall, a thousand yards into nothing. He groaned, a high-pitched whining, pulled the filthy blanket tighter around himself. "A kid, I thought . . . I thought he'd gotten lost, needed help. I reached out to hold his hand." He looked at me, the loose skin of his face dead white, eyes shimmering. "I wanted to help, man. He attacked me—I screamed and ran, but he caught up, so fast, I—" What little coherence he'd possessed devolved into whining sobs.

"It's okay man, it's okay. Stop crying. You gotta stop crying." The razor-thin margin of sanity I'd managed to scrape together narrowed.

We needed to come up with something, come up with a plan. And here he was, crying like a little kid.

"God damn it, dude, shut the fuck up!" He recoiled like I slapped him, pressing his head into the corner, trying to retreat. "That's not helping. Now that we're both here, we can think of a way out."

"No. No." Appletree sniffed, shaking his head. "They'll come for us, they'll chase us, bite us and eat us."

"Eat—what are you talking about? Come on, they're not going to eat us. I didn't mean to yell, I—"

He turned to me. His wet eyes drilled holes into my soul.

"We're already dead, you and I. Ghosts."

The filthy and stained blanket shifted, moved, fell away.

His hand was gone. In its place where the hand met the wrist gaped a mess of ragged yellow tendons, weeping blood onto red and swollen skin. There, a dozen tiny, semicircular puncture marks, buried deep. Teeth marks, but too small to be an adult's.

Baby teeth.

"Oh my—" The paltry contents of my stomach emptied, climbing the torn ladder of my throat. His bloody wrist seared into the back of my eyelids, haunting me with every blink. I shook, my arms weak.

The air reeked of iron, now that he'd taken the blanket off. Like the clearing with the buck. Tortured. Left to die a slow, wheezing death. Were they going to stick a hunting knife in my throat, or cut my hand off?

Another wave of watery vomit forced its way up my throat.

Ronnie said it himself, elbowing through the Woodkin members that were kicking me into submission.

He's no good to you dead.

A cold pit that had nothing to do with hunger grew in my gut.

Behind a thick layer of clouds, the sun set. Shadows pooled at the bases of the trees, growing thick and deep. The smell hit me first. The same one I smelled when they dropped me in front of the cell door.

Spun sugar, flowers. Cloying, like my mother's perfume . . . and beneath that, a bitterness. Like getting a faceful of smoke at a campfire. It smells sweet from a distance, but when it blows into your face, you realize it's not sweet at all. The sweetness is a lie, a cover. It's the bitterness that's real.

"Appletree, you smell that?" I stood with a groan. A blue-black bruise had spread over my ribs, and a dozen other places creaked with every movement. I walked over to the iron door, looking out at the deserted clearing, sniffing. Stronger now. "It smells like . . ."

Through the navy-blue shadow, through the spitting rain, torches winked. In, out, in, out—through the trees they wound closer, coming for me. Like predators' eyes, exposed by a flashlight beam. The cold in the pit of my stomach grew colder—the touch of what lay in wait.

"Appletree, get up. Get up. Something's happening." I pressed my face against the bars. They wound through the forest, nearing.

A group of hunters entered the clearing. Beneath the smoking, guttering light, their faces were swathed in hard shadows. They approached the cell, drew the bolt back with a heavy clunk. Surrounded the door, silent and still.

"It is time," one of them said.

"You will come with us." Their voices were the same timbre of apathy—flat, uncaring. As though they were taking me to the bank. Beneath the uncertain torchlight they looked the same. Set apart by the differences in the scars that traced the left side of their faces. Based on the twin reflections of fire, one of the men had the use of both eyes,

"Me?" I swallowed sharp bile and panic. My hands shook, even balled into tight fists. "Or both of us?"

"Both."

"I don't . . . I don't think he—" I stuttered. Words failed me. I looked back at the blanket. It shook like a leaf; no way he didn't hear us, didn't know what was happening. "He's—hey, hey! Be careful!"

One of them, a boy no older than sixteen, slipped past me, crossing over to Appletree's corner in two huge strides. He ripped the blanket away. The old man cried out in rusty terror, covering his face, curling into a ball of whimpering cries. The kid said something angry and short, a command too quick for me to catch. Appletree didn't respond. He stared into the floorboards. I wondered if the fat droplets tapping around me were rain or blood.

The kid struck so quickly I almost missed it. I caught the impression of blurred limbs, heard Appletree's cry of pain and surprise. The old man sprawled on the floor. The left half of his face gleamed scarlet.

"You didn't need to do that!" I flung toward Appletree, but a pair of hands clamped down on my upper arms. The other Woodkin dragged me out the door, inexorable as a machine. I kicked and struggled, but with the use of one wrist it wasn't exactly a fair match. "Hey! Come on, leave him alone, he's an old man!"

The kid knelt over Appletree. It looked like he was whispering. I craned my neck, trying to see, but the hunter pulled me out the door. I caught my foot against a rogue root, twisting it in the wrong direction. I hissed a sharp inhale of pain.

"God damn it, getoffme!" I grunted, punching behind my head. My knuckles brushed something hard, and I got a knee in the hamstring for my trouble, sending me sprawling for the third time that day.

I rolled over, red-faced, angry. "He wasn't hurting anyone! You could have just picked him up. That kid didn't have to hit him!" I couldn't hear the old man, but that didn't mean they weren't doing something awful to him, muffling his muted struggles and choking the scream from his lips. "He probably would have come along just—"

The rest of my sentence stuttered to a wheezing stop.

A group of scarred men stood, shadow-eaten in the darkness. Five of them, twisted features distorted in the shifting blackness. My words turned to ash on my chapped lips. I stopped thinking about Appletree and started thinking about myself.

"What do you want?"

"Get up," one of them said. His one working eye glared at me, but didn't flicker, didn't track my movements. As if he stared through me. Like I wasn't even there.

Already a ghost.

Another jutted his chin toward the edge of the clearing, the direction they'd come from.

"Walk."

I got to my feet slowly, bones snapping into place, muscles screaming for water. In the unsteady light a rough path wove between two crumbling houses, leading into the forest. At the edge of their firelight, the world vanished into rain-soaked darkness. A dim hum began building in the back of my brain, like a swarm of far-off hornets rising. I bit down until I tasted copper, a whine of low panic in my throat.

"Walk." Someone shoved me and I stumbled forward, off balance. We walked together, following the path between the shells of abandoned mining huts. A window, or rotted-out slab of wall, had collapsed under the weight of decades of rain. Dead leaves covered the floor, rustling as if a specter paced inside.

The shadows traced our footsteps, running in front and behind us. Slipping into nothingness behind rock, moss, and the corpses of dead trees.

The rain came back, drizzling in a thousand bursts of applause against the canopy overhead. My shirt clung to my shoulders, rain soaking through my skin to chill my bones. I clenched my teeth to keep them from chattering. The path undulated across the uneven valley floor, meandering. I found and lost the trail half a dozen times—it blended with the ferns and shrubs underneath, impossible to find if you didn't know where to look. We climbed one side of a hollow before dropping to cross a dry creek bed.

I thought about making a run for it. There were only a handful of them, right? I could outrun them if I had to . . . but even in my head, the thoughts rang hollow. No, I fucking could not, that little voice whispered. I couldn't even outrun a single one of them last night.

North, following the walls of the valley as they surrounded us, closing into a narrow gully. The air pitched cooler, the smell of shale rising from wet earth. I kept my head down, careful of where I put my feet—the footing shifted, nebulous, ensnaring. I stumbled a handful of times, catching myself on the gully walls. Why bother, I thought, after stumbling yet again. They only needed me for another few hours? Fine. Maybe I'd break my ankle on purpose, force them to carry me. I had a vision of two of them grunting with effort, sweating as they picked over the rocks. Fuck 'em. The fantasy gave me a hateful joy, bitter as smoke.

Time wound away from me. My shirt clung to me from shoulders to hem, and my hair was plastered to my forehead, dripping onto my face. I shivered. We turned a corner.

A box canyon half a mile long at its widest sprawled in front of us like hands cupping a ravine. The walls rose tall enough to rub shoulders with the sheared-off slopes of the pitch-black mountains. Somewhere, a waterfall roared in blank static, close enough to drown out any speech. The rain clouds rolled close overhead, sealing the sky in roiling charcoal gray.

Trapped.

A path split the darkness, lit in pinpricks of flickering orange. Torches. At its end, a bonfire rose ten, fifteen feet into the air, winking at me from between the trees. A clearing, at the high end of the canyon. Lit like the pits of Tartarus.

A slab of granite so large it almost appeared to be a mountain hunched over the clearing. The edges gave it away—too sharp, too thin, like knife blades. A sullen orange glow from the bonfire spat fluttering light along its black depths, sending pockets of shadow dancing along the imperfections in the rock face. The smell I'd caught back in the cell grew stronger here, cloying and sweet.

My feet slipped and skidded, the muscles in my legs locking up. An animal led to slaughter, unwilling to move another inch.

"Move," one of them growled.

The path twisted down, steep and dangerous, cascading over boulders, sliding down tree trunks. A split-log tree bridge spanned a frothing white rapid, slick from spray. Patches of electric-blue mold grew where the spray lightened, offering decent footing. I tried not to look at the water fifteen feet beneath us, carving its way underground. Tried not to let my balance shift. I could see my fate if I fell, shattered against the rocks. Perhaps it would be a mercy, drowning in slow-motion, clutched in the black water.

Perhaps it would be better that way.

I don't know what kept my feet on the bridge, as I slipped from one patch of mold to the next. Cowardice, or the cold and perpetual bubble of hope that something or someone would save me. Some miracle. My shoes touched dirt on the other side, and I exhaled the breath burning my lungs.

But there was no rescue party. No helicopter blades spearing the air. Crude torches made of bundled sticks lit the path on either side. Moving past one, I caught a glimpse of a torn and burnt collar. The gleam of an ivory button winked at me.

Clothes. They'd topped the torches with clothes.

"Oh my God," I whispered. I shot a look over my shoulder. The Woodkin accompanying me wore some combination of shorts or long-legged capris, cut ragged. I remembered Green-Eyes from just a few days ago; rotting bare-chested in the river.

I heard the music first, long before I saw the first signs of the clearing. Wordless, hammering in harsh bass and quick, irregular rhythm, joined now and then by ear-piercing vocals that made the skin on the back of my neck shrivel. I couldn't quite place the music; something about it had an eighties vibe, but in a series of cascading minor keys. An indistinct voice growled, blown out and grainy. The speakers hung from trees, wound with nooses of black wire. Looking at them—the joining of two things that should have stayed separated—caused a schism in my brain. This lurking, scarred cult didn't deserve technology. It felt . . . asynchronous, looking at it. Like it didn't belong there.

Or I didn't.

Black silhouettes danced in front of a huge bonfire to the music, heedless of the pounding rain. Round and round they whirled, shuffling like lost souls on their way to hell, limbs akimbo.

More members of the Woodkin gathered around the edges of the flame, watching. Above us all, the towering piece of granite stood sentinel. I didn't like looking at the huge piece of rock; something about it made me uncomfortable.

"Switchback! You made it!" A familiar voice split the music. At the opposite end of the clearing, a bench of sorts was dug into the joined roots of three trees. Here sat the familiar scowl-faced patriarch, cracked face silent and angry. And . . .

Ronnie's pale face flushed tomato red beneath his glasses. He staggered off the bench, sending the woman on his lap to the ground in a heap. Judging by the way she shot up and scampered back to sit on the opposite side of the clearing, she didn't mind too much. He clutched a flask in his other hand.

The men who escorted me drifted off. Their eyes kept flickering to me, tracking my position. No doubt if I took off into the forest, I'd make it about eight feet before they'd catch me. Good odds they'd break something to keep me in line.

"I was just saying how long you were taking to get here." He stank of trapped sweat, his breath ripe enough to trip my gag reflex. The bottle I'd seen in the backseat of the Jeep, if I had to guess. Even looking at me, he swayed in place. He adjusted his glasses with a clumsy hand. "Any later and you'd miss all the festivities!"

He gestured, staggering off balance. I didn't reach out to catch him; if he fell, maybe I could kick him where it counted before anyone grabbed me. My satisfaction would be short-lived, no doubt, but hurting Ronnie would be worth every split second.

Ronnie threw a companionable arm around my shoulders, treating me to a close-up of his pit stains. The flask in his other hand sloshed, spilling all over his fingers. God, he smelled terrible. He leaned in close, whispering.

"I have personally fucked three women tonight. Took them right into the woods and bam! They can't say no—they love it. A chance— just a chance to have a son of Ronnie the Reaper. That's me—you like it? Ronnie the Reaper." He beamed, his grin slippery and loose. "I gave it to myself. Being with the Reaper is like, their whole dream, these women. Isn't that awesome?" He leered at a woman standing across the fire about twenty feet away. Her black hair fell across her shoulders in thick ripples. Dark shadows flickered along her arms as she stood near the fire. She was one of only a few not dancing. She watched everyone else. I narrowed my eyes—yes, she actually watched them. Her eyes traced their movements, their furious pace as they writhed around the bonfire. Unlike the hunters who'd grabbed me, whose eyes drilled into the soil and trees behind me, unseeing. Ronnie leaned on my shoulder, whispering too loud in my ear: "See her? I'm gonna—"

"Get the hell off me." I smacked his arm from my shoulders. The heads of a dozen men whipped in my direction, eyes narrowed. *Careful, be careful.*

"Don't be such a sourpuss, Switch. It's a party! Lighten up, man, you look like you're at a funeral or something."

"What is all this? What am—what am I doing here?" I stumbled on the question, like it glued my tongue in place. My mouth still tasted like carpet. But I had to know.

"This"—Ronnie gestured to the clearing again—"is the night. *The* night, you hear me? The Woodkin call it the Feast." He looked over at me, grinning. "Like that one, dontcha? My suggestion. Or, well . . . yeah, sure, let's say it was mine. 'The Feast.' Sounds like a movie title or some shit." A rogue belch rocked his whole frame. "They think they're all big and bad, but really they're just a bunch of podunk pretenders," he whispered, "but don't tell 'em I told you that. The women are fine enough if you close one eye."

I tried to hide my recoil, a gag searing hot in my burned-out throat. I muscled through it. More important things to worry about. "What is the Feast?"

"What is the Feast?" The mocking, high-pitched voice made me want to punch him in the throat. "God, what are you, a parrot? Asking all these questions. Calm down man, get a drink. Enjoy yourself! This is a hedonist wonderland. Take a lady for a stroll around the trees, if you know what I mean."

People left together, dipping into the velvet darkness of the forest hand in hand. Sometimes two, three, or more, faces tight with anticipation. Some came back, loose-slinking, relaxed. Everyone partied, everyone cut loose . . . but the only drink in the clearing was in Ronnie's white-knuckled grasp.

A scar-faced man pitched too close to the bonfire and staggered backward with a surprised shriek. He collapsed, trying to slap away the fingers of fire eating the ragged hem of his trousers. Ronnie burst into squeals of laughter, slapping his thigh and pointing.

"Oh my God, look at that fuckin' guy. What a moron!" He laughed alone, snorting in drunken hilarity, too loud; he drowned out the music. They turned to him, too quick; a second or less before they turned away, back to their dancing. *How can he not feel it?* I wondered. Feel the weight of two dozen eyes on his skin, the combined condescension.

I stepped away. Sidled a few inches to the side as if to say, *It's him, not me*. Ronnie raised the flask to his lips, taking a deep swig.

"Want some, Switch? Old boy Switchie? Suh-weetchback?" He tried out my name on his tongue, thick and clumsy with the cheap whiskey rising from the open mouth of the flask like a redneck genie. He giggled and swayed where he stood.

I shook my head, tuning him out. The music slamming from the speakers thrummed their menacing beat faster. Two circles of revelers whirled dizzily around the bonfire at a fever pitch, their eyes glassy, pupils blown wide and dark.

A second party entered the clearing. A shuffling figure, hunched, still wrapped in the filthy towel I'd left him with. Appletree's one working hand wrapped around himself, tucked deep in his armpit. He didn't even look up at the cavorting black shapes spinning around the flames.

His gaze dug into the dirt at his feet, and he shook.

Ronnie's hand on my arm stopped me before I realized I'd moved.

"Don't do that, Suh-weetchie. Uh-uh. Not smart."

"But look at him, he needs—"

"What he needs, you can't give him. Leave him, Switchie."

"No, I can't, he's all alone over there. Get off me, I have to—"

"Look!" Ronnie snapped. He shook me hard enough to rattle my teeth. The smile slipped off his lips. "You look. Not at what's-his-face, forget him. Look around you. Look at the trees. Use your eyeballs and not your mouth. Concentrate."

I looked at the trees.

At first, I didn't know what the fuck he was talking about; they were trees. Pine, some scattered oak, I don't know. I wasn't a fucking tree scientist—

I squinted. Now that I looked at them, really looked at them, something seemed off. *A trick of the light, that's it, or my perspective fucking with me again.*

Something shifting. The shadows pulling away from the bonfire tangled in patterns, tap-dancing across the patches of bark. Like a sculpture of darkness and light. Except the shadows didn't look quite right; they weren't forming in the right tree-like shapes.

But no. No, the longer I looked, the more I saw. It wasn't the shadows that were off.

It was what they were forming against. The shadows were merely the negative space. I blinked. My perspective shifted, the world adjusted just a degree to the left. I blinked and peered closer, trying to see. The twining rivulets, curved into ovals about two inches wide: faces.

They were faces.

Hundreds, thousands of them, covering each tree as far as I could see. Spreading beyond the torchlight, surrounding us. Carved with mouths open in silent screams, black eyes full of suffering. They shrieked at me, eyes boring into my soul. Michelangelo couldn't have put more emotion into those twisted and agonized features. They wore earrings, piercings, scratched tattoos.

The detail packed into their tiny, tormented features raised the hair on the back of my neck. A man with pinched jowls and deep eyes howled for his life between two branches of an oak tree. Beneath him, a woman's face twisted in guttural, bone-deep surprise. I could see her shock in the scratched corneas of her eyes. I'd blink, and those mouths would start moving. I'd start to hear those silent screams, echoing in a crushing wave. Rivers of agony, flowing from the trees.

"What the fuck?"

Thousands of eyes, glaring at us from the darkness. These faces, frozen in their torment. These faces, watching me. My breath caught in my throat, keen as shattered glass.

"You see 'em?" Ronnie clutched at my arm, using me to balance his drunken swaying. He glared at me—or at least, in my general direction. "See? Each of them, each of those faces—they've been right where Appletree was. They stood right where you stand. There's nothing you can do. Nothing any of us can do. If you get in the way—"

"What?" My turn to snap, spinning on him. "They'll kill me? Is that it, Ronnie Coors? I'm sitting in the batter's box for the spot, aren't I? I'm next in line. They go through him, then it's my turn. It's true, isn't it—don't you fucking lie to me. I see you about to try. What'd you say earlier? *He's no good to you dead?* You son of a bitch!"

The wafer-thin tether to my self-control slipped beyond my reach. I shoved Ronnie in the chest, hard enough to send him stumbling, arms flailing. "Don't help him, because no one's going to be around to help you."

No one paid attention to us, this time. They turned to Appletree, who stared at the ground and shook.

"Feast. Feast. Feast." Their mouths moved as one, in whispers of horror.

I didn't hear the chanting over the roar of blood in my ears. I didn't notice the music stop, or the dancers freeze in place, dead eyes staring unblinking at Appletree. Only their mouths moved, forming shapeless words in my peripheral hearing.

"Feast."

Appletree shrunk away from them, pulling the blanket tighter around his shoulders. Trying to disappear beneath it. Trying to hide.

I surged toward him. If nothing else, I could stand beside him. I could walk with him all the way down. He wouldn't be scared alone, not if I was there.

"Hang—hang on there, big fella." Ronnie lurched to his feet, hands held out. He swayed, dangerously close to falling on his ass without any help from me. The flask in his hand gleamed silver in the firelight. He took a big mouthful, gulped, wiped the amber liquid from his chin with the back of a wrist. "Look—listen. It's already started. Here comes Priest."

"Feast."

Then I noticed the lack of music blaring from the speakers. Too late to run in and protect Appletree, standing there shaking, all by himself.

Writhing behind the kitchen door, all aflame.

He came from the darkness beyond the bonfire, walking as silent as the dead. Greasy hair hung from his head in twisted ringlets, colored amber from the fire. The priest's torso looked distorted, full of sharp edges and curves. His ribs looked like the sharp lines of a xylophone, his collarbones pushed up from the skin, creating twin bowls at the top of his chest. He wore black pants that fit snug to his legs and a creased jacket of oiled leather, open over his scrawny body. His chest was bleached white like he'd never seen daylight. Like an upside-down version of the priests from my childhood—the pace, the costume, the gospel just behind their teeth. The Good News, but this time, *all wrong*.

The priest's scar engulfed his face, deeper and crueler than any of the others. White bone glinted in the firelight. Twisted, atrophied muscle, wide pores cratering its surface. Then he entered the circle of light and I saw the skull in his hands. A stag head, bleached white, complete with an enormous set of antlers, stretching a full two feet on either side of him.

As soon as he set foot in the clearing, the chanting rose, quickened. The world shrank to the snarling of the bonfire, the combined voices of the Woodkin, and the blood roaring in my ears.

The buck, bled to death and left to die in the woods. Left for me to find. Now it came back, back to haunt me a second time. Death, coming back for me, as a bleached skull stretched in a perpetual grin. The buck's teeth gleamed in the firelight. I'd been running from that skull my whole life.

The priest stopped at the edge of the clearing. Waiting. One of the Woodkin approached, holding a leather bag like it contained a pit viper. He reached in—maybe the bonfire played tricks with the air, but it looked like his hand trembled. He pulled out a finger-full of something I couldn't make out and held it up to the priest's lips. The priest opened his mouth, and the man dropped his offering on his tongue, communion-style.

Whatever it was, it didn't go down easy. The priest chewed, staring at the ground with twin lines of effort scratched into his narrow face. It took more than one swallow to choke it down.

"I love this part." Ronnie turned to me, heedless of the icy stares he drew. He didn't bother to whisper. The woman from the other side of the fire had moved closer to us, only a few paces away. Ronnie motioned at her, trying to get her attention. When she didn't respond, he hissed. "Psst! Hey, you. Girl."

The skull-bearing priest wound partway around the other side of the clearing. Marching toward the center of attention: Appletree.

"Hey. Psst!"

She stood resolute as a statue, letting Ronnie's words rush past her. Her eyes stared at Appletree like the rest of them, her mouth moved with the rest of theirs, following the same words. Except . . .

Her shoulders stiffened. Such a minute gesture, so small it shouldn't have mattered. But it was the first sign of normal behavior from one of them. It almost looked . . . human.

Ronnie noticed. The corners of his lips curled up, digging divots into his cheeks. "I know you can hear me. I know you know who I am. You can—hey."

Her head turned, ever so slightly. This close, the fire turned the edges of her raven hair auburn tongues of red-orange. This close, she didn't look like one of them.

She almost looked normal.

"You know the weight of your refusal. You know what it could cost you if I decide to make it so." He dug an elbow into my ribs, a snicker clutched tight in his face. "Come here. I've got . . . I've got an itch I need you to scratch."

She parted with the circle with reluctant steps. I craned my neck over the whiskey-soaked shopkeeper, trying to keep Appletree in view. If only he would look up, look over here, we could make eye contact and he'd know at least I was here. He wasn't alone.

The priest continued his march, closing the distance to Appletree. His cracked and warped lips moved, and it almost looked like he was caressing the skull in his hands—

"Oh yeah," Ronnie sighed. "That's right. Just . . . there."

I heard a pause the length of a single heartbeat, and then a sudden hissed intake of air, stretched around a hoarse scream. When I spun around, Ronnie's face was red as a tomato, with lines of agony etched into the flesh.

"What's the matter, Reaper?" the woman whispered. Her hand closed around something in the vicinity of his groin, the muscles of her forearm stark with effort. "Isn't this what you wanted?"

Heads turning, eyes catching glimpses of our little drama. I wanted to sidestep, wanted to back away, but I also wanted to make sure Ronnie got everything that was coming to him and more. Ronnie whispered something, but it disappeared in a fizzing gasp as she squeezed harder.

He dropped the flask, dancing on his tiptoes with pain.

"I'm sorry, I didn't quite catch that," she whispered.

"Please." His words were smoke. He looked like he was about to vomit. Personally I hoped he would.

Another second, and she released him. He sagged backward, falling to his knees. Something pale and shriveled flapped through the open zipper of his jeans. She turned back to her fellows.

"Traitor!" Ronnie screamed. A vacuum sucked the air out of the clearing. The priest froze in his steps. The old man shot to his feet.

Ronnie pointed a finger at the woman, staggering back to his feet. "She's not one of you, Woodkin. She's faking it. She's a liar!"

The woman's face went as white as a sheet. She turned, protests falling from her lips.

"I'm—I don't—don't listen to him, kin, he doesn't know—" She turned her gaze to the old man. "William—I mean, Father, I swear to you, I'm not . . ."

The Woodkin closed in around us. Around the woman.

"Ooh, girl you done fucked up," Ronnie whispered, radiating sharp-cornered glee. "You know what your refusal cost you. Beg me to save you. Go on. Offer me anything I want. You know I can do it—quick, girl, quick, he's coming, and I'm the only chance you've got. Offer me whatever I want, and I'll think about saving your life."

She looked at him like he was a cockroach, tears in her eyes. Back to the old man, closing in on her.

With a cry of shock and pain, the priest recoiled. He clutched the buck skull to his chest, bent over it, muttering nonstop. Slammed both hands over the empty eyes, like he needed to keep something inside.

He chose the perfect moment. Confusion, chaos. All eyes on the woman and Ronnie. No one was watching Appletree. No one but me.

I looked over—and Appletree's eyes were on mine. Wide, pleading, desperate. And then a swift motion, like he was miming cutting off his own head. There was a loud crash, and the clearing exploded. Appletree disappeared. I thought he fell, then I thought someone attacked him. The three men surrounding him collapsed to their knees, crying out. One of them tugged at the old man's fist, pulled something out of it.

My keys, covered in blood. The keys I'd dropped in the cabin, fumbling for my fire starter. They hauled him up, trying to stem the red river flowing down his shirt, with little success. I could see the punched red weals spreading across the white cartilage of his windpipe. He did it himself—he'd waited until the last minute. The bonfire danced in his blank eyes.

He was dead.

Appletree. My heart broke for my campfire companion. He didn't deserve this. No one deserved this.

I spun away from the grisly sight and collapsed to my knees, holding the contents of my stomach back with gritted teeth. A hive of bees buzzed inside my head, threatening to take me apart at the seams. People screamed, the priest shouted. The old man watched, his face as still as the corpse lying in the dirt. No surprise, no anger, no emotion reflected in his split and deformed face. And above it all, Ronnie.

Laughing.

"Ho—holy shit, Switch, did you—did you see it?" he wheezed, bent almost double. The drunken flush turned his cheeks scarlet, and there were tears in his eyes, he was laughing so hard. "Just—whoop! One and done! Bravo, sir, Bra-fucking-vo! Way to stick it to the man!" He applauded, still chortling.

His applause floated over a silent clearing. The men and women, the old man—they all stared at Ronnie, held in a moment of icy stillness. The drunk man swallowed his laughter with much effort, raising his head to return their glare.

"Can I fucking help you? What are you all staring at? Come on, it's funny. Switch, don't you think it's funny?" He turned to me. The expression on my face must have finally keyed him in to the vibe. I watched the drunk hilarity drain from his eyes. He spun back to the Woodkin, hands up, empty apologies scrawled on his slack features.

"Take him." The old man's flat, dead voice rang around the clearing.

They sprang like jackals. He fought, or at least tried to, but there was only one of him and a lot of them. They dragged him to the ground, seized his thrashing limbs.

"Switchback! Help me!" He writhed, looking up at me. "Stop! You can't do this! I'm the Reaper! Hey! God damn it!"

I didn't say anything. A sick squirm of vindication swirled in my gut. He deserved the worst, but a quiet voice in the back of my head whispered that he might not deserve this.

They carried him kicking and screaming to the priest, whose gaunt face was shiny with sweat. He hadn't opened his eyes once or moved his hands from the eye sockets of the deer skull. They shook with effort, pressing hard against the white bone.

"Get off! Get off! I—you—I'll kill—!"

The Woodkin began to chant again, pressing close around Ronnie's thrashing form.

"Feast—Feast—"

"Please!" Ronnie squealed, the righteousness and rage churning into panic. "Don't do this to me! Please—!"

The priest leaned his head back and sighed, utter relief lowering his shoulders. He took his hands from the eyes of the skull.

9

BEAST OF BLACK SHADOW

DON'T BELIEVE IN GOD.

I should; I grew up in a Christian home. Church every Sunday morning, et cetera, et cetera, but the honoration never clicked for me. The crux of my disbelief came from putting my faith in something incorporeal. Something I couldn't see or touch. Existing because my pastor or my parents told me it did. I was a stubborn child; if I couldn't touch it, see it, taste it, or hear it, it didn't exist. The Sunday mornings I woke up early to spend an hour and a half in a sweltering brick building were an exercise in keeping my parents happy, not faith. I never understood what the people were singing and dancing about.

Praying for health, good fortune, protection—it never happened. They stayed in their miserable circumstances. God never helped anyone.

"No, no no—I—you—please—"

Ronnie's squeals grew in fervor and pitch, losing what little coherence he had left. He stared past the priest, his eyes stretched so wide I thought they might burst. The splotchy, beet-red flush returned, blooming across his cheeks. A long vein pulsed in his forehead, below his hairline. He was looking at something at the farthest end of the clearing, where the mass of sheared rock swallowed the horizon behind the trees. I followed his gaze.

It poured into the light, pooling, spilling over the tree roots and pine needles. It poured from the eyes scratched into the trees, a thousand pinpoints of agony frozen in time. It poured from their lips, thick as blood.

It didn't billow out or flatten; it moved with purpose. I couldn't see where it started. Beyond the firelight somewhere. Almost like it came from the base of the enormous granite slab.

Smoke, black as the shadow lurking between the trees. Black enough I couldn't see beneath it, see inside it. It moved toward the man in the leather jacket, pooled beneath his crouched form. It rose, sliding up his legs and torso.

"No—" Fat tears burned bright on Ronnie's cheeks. Snot gleamed on his upper lip. "No, I don't—I can't—"

The smoke touched the skull in the priest's hands, caressing the bleached bone. It slipped inside the deer's gaping mouth, moving in thick strands, bulging like muscle. Gathering inside the hollow space behind the skull's eyes.

"The Woodkin feast," Father whispered. The dozen hands on Ronnie picked him up, held him in front of the skull. His eyes locked onto the dead leaves and dirt at his feet. He shook, head to toe.

"Please." A sniveling, low and pathetic.

It took someone's hand grasping Ronnie beneath the jaw to tear his vision up.

"Look." The priest hissed a whisper, held in a moment of rapture.

The darkness oozed from the deer skull toward Ronnie's snot-and-tear-covered face, slow—too slow. It poured into him inexorably, streaming into his open mouth, his nose, the corners of his eyes. He fought against it, thrashed, choked, spat, to no effect. It forced his mouth wider, silenced the already-muffled protests in his throat.

The hunters clutching his limbs dropped him like a bad habit, backing away in a rush.

Ronnie fell to the ground, jittering and twitching like he'd touched a live wire. His mouth appeared to scream around the choking black vine pushing into his lungs, but no sound came out. His eyes stared at the sky behind his glasses, blank. I watched, as they clouded over, turning dull, gray. Lifeless.

Moving like a puppet, he rose to his knees. His movements were faltering, jerky. Smoke fell from his eyes and nostrils like thick liquid. His head swayed, bent between his shoulders. Like something filled him, weighed him down.

The night stilled. The bonfire grew silent, burning down to a dull red glow.

It started in his fingers. The first boils, red and angry, pushing against the sallow skin of his hands, little pinpricks. Then on his palms and wrists: the size of marbles, stretching beneath his skin. They moved up his arms like plague pustules, red at first, turning black. He opened his mouth in a silent scream. As if someone had pressed the mute button.

Not even a hoarse whisper of breath.

The boils opened, and delicate wisps of black plumed out, hanging heavy on his limbs. The transformation wasn't the bang-and-flash of movie visual effects; it was incremental, torturous. Ronnie's muscles clenched and spasmed, struggling in uncoordinated agony. The shadow consumed him, grew from him, swallowed him. It covered his neck, his jawbone—it slipped into his mouth, choked him. It slid over his eyes. The man disappeared, and only the smoke remained.

Is this why people prayed for protection in church? What they prayed against?

The shadow stretched into heavy limbs, crushing the pine needles, digging deep furrows into the ground. One leg, two, three. There were also arms. Huge and only getting bigger, crowned with ingrown claws, stabbing into its own flesh. There the inked shadow congealed and grew thick, shiny. No blood fell from these self-inflicted wounds — just a scattering of dark flakes, like rust, evaporating as soon as they touched the wet earth. Already as tall as me, getting bigger, drawing strength. Its torso stretched three feet across, a mass of dark shadow around slick patches of shiny hide.

I backed away, stumbling.

A head formed, pulled out of the torso like taffy, snapping into place as the shadow cracked like bone. It didn't solidify; it stayed indistinct, a thick, boiling mass of coiled black, like snakes writhing on top of one another.

"Feast." Father's voice floated from a great distance. The Woodkin fell to their knees, faces pushed into the dirt and dead leaves, groveling. In the corner of my vision I saw the woman—the one who'd turned Ronnie into a squealing pig—clutched between two hunters. Her face was every bit as white as mine felt. Her eyes were filled with terror too.

They might have been chanting, but beneath the furious beat of my own pulse in my ears, I couldn't hear a thing. My heart sledged against my rib cage; sweat dripped down my face. I wanted to scream, wanted to run, wanted to do something . . . but I froze in place. This had nothing to do with perspective. I wasn't dreaming or high. I couldn't rationalize the monster that bloomed in front of my eyes.

It turned. With each movement of its nightmarish limbs, the bent-backed Woodkin surrounding it scuttled out of its way. The ball of wriggling snakes swiveled, tasting the sour air of the clearing. Its body went taut, convulsing, snapping excitedly—a malevolently abstract Picasso. I stared at the beast's head, watching it change again. It stilled and shifted, churning into a face. A face with longish hair and round spectacles. A mockery of Ronnie Coors's face, screaming. It pulled his face into sharp lines too clear to be anything other than utter, endless agony.

"Jesus wept," I whispered.

It swiveled, finding me in the crowd. The dark, splintered pupils behind those glasses found mine. My bladder loosened, and everything went warm. Teeth—there were too many teeth. Long and thin, like needles, rows on rows of them packed into that dark mouth, stretching open. I heard that howl again, a high, sharp sound. It came from all around me, echoed in my head, in my very thoughts. It sounded like my mom, screaming through the fire that burned her alive.

Did I hear her? I clenched my teeth, blinking the sudden tears away. No. I was not in the house. The firefighters had taken me out of the house.

Right?

The face changed again, shedding Ronnie like a dead husk. Slim brow, pronounced cheekbones. Sharp eyes. The same face I'd taken to a first date at RN74. The same one I'd stood in front of and said *I do*.

I'd never seen Deb's eyes full of so much loathing, so much disdain.

The beast exploded with a roar, crushing my eardrums and ringing me like a bell. I collapsed, clutching at my ears. I think I was screaming, but I couldn't really tell. The world spun on its axis, a confusion of movement, light, and darkness. The shadow moved like a gale carried it, growing thin in places, evaporating.

A glimpse of Ronnie, hidden deep in the depths.

At first, I caught nothing but a pale form, hunched over, arms wrapped around his knees. He'd lost his glasses, and his dead eyes stared holes in the dirt beneath the tips of his shoes. A stream of muttered words fell from his lips. He looked small, lost. The smoke broke for a fraction of a heartbeat, and he looked up.

Straight at me.

His eyes widened. In a burst of confused motion he sprang to his feet, leaping toward me, hands outstretched. His face, cut deep with hard lines that hadn't been there five minutes ago. Like the faces in the trees.

Help me.

I read the words on his lips but couldn't hear him. Red marks covered his palms and fingers, angry and livid streaks like burns. The beast swelled around him and grew, tall now as the bonfire, snapping into grotesque limbs, shouldering into the charcoal sky. Ronnie disappeared, consumed by shadow again. The beast stretched toward the clouds, rising ten, fifteen feet into the air. It roared.

A pause, a hesitation. A moment, where its growth shuddered.

The snarling black hooks jutting from its hide dipped for a second. The look of enraptured zeal on Father's face slipped. He and the priest exchanged a worried glance.

The scream clawing its way through my ears changed in pitch, became lower, more desperate. The twisting mass of black tendrils bucked, pitching to one side and then the other, thrashing. The tendrils grew smaller, shrinking, like a candle suffocating.

The shadow twisted into sharp angles, crawling into itself like burrowing maggots, shrinking. The scream built into a crescendo, so loud I was sure it would split my skull. I clapped my hands over my ears and writhed in the dirt.

It stopped.

I sagged into the pine needles. My shirt was stuck to my chest, either from rainwater or sweat, I couldn't tell. I'd completely forgotten about the rain. I dug a finger into my ear. I could still hear a high-pitched ringing, an echo of the scream lingering far longer than was welcome. I rolled onto my side. The shadows disappeared. I squinted against the sudden glare from the bonfire, burning brighter than before.

Where the darkness failed lay a familiar body, facedown in the dirt. Blue chambray shirt, open and fluttering in the cold wind. His eyes frozen wide, his lips tight, stretched over his teeth in one last scream. Angry red weals crisscrossed the skin of his face and neck. His hands stretched outward, taut and white-knuckled around fistfuls of dirt and rock.

The smell in the air again, stronger than before. A bitter tang, like gardenias, like the aftertaste of ash. The wind rose and the scent danced past me, filling my nose and throat. I flipped over, inhaling through the pine needles. A flash of white and scarlet, lying on the ground. A pair of blank eyes, digging into mine. Two corpses for the price of one.

Appletree. I'd forgotten about him. The images came rushing back to me, picture fragments that didn't line up. The gleam of fire on my keys, dripping blood. The commotion, yelling and screaming, and wave of panic. The wave of red liquid gushing over Appletree's neck and chest—

Father approached the corpse of Ronnie Coors, a scowl clutched deep in his disfigured face. I backed away.

You could make a run for it. The thought came sly, cautious. *No one is paying any attention to you.*

That much was true. The collection of twisted faces looked around, vacillating between bewilderment and disappointment. They gathered in small groups, all tight faces and whispers. Pointing to Ronnie or Appletree. A few of them actually wept, wiping tears from their cracked cheeks.

Father stood over Ronnie's body, hands balled into fists at his side, looking down at the dead man. The priest walked up, sidling to one side, fingers drumming an anxious pattern on one leg. He looked like he'd finished a long sprint with a sudden stop. Dirt and ash marred his cheeks, which were outlined with sweat streaks. His chest, flushed beneath the leather jacket, gleamed in the firelight.

"A thousand apologies. I thought He would—" The priest shot a surreptitious look over his shoulder at the remains of the shopkeeper.

"It's not up to us to guess His intentions," Father said. His voice wavered like an untuned instrument. "He has a plan. Trust Him. All of us!" He raised his arms, spinning to face his audience. His cry echoed against the low-hanging sky, pressing down, closing us in. "We must trust in the Feast, for He is our one and true savior! It is He, who will ferry our souls across the river of bones and blood yet to come! Another Feast shall arrive. Another chance, to spread His gospel."

They hung on his every word, breathless. Nodding, mouths moving in silent agreement.

"Only He knows the truth; this world will drown in its sins and misdeeds. We, the Woodkin, the faithful, will receive the gift of eternal life for our suffering. Our hardship. Do not let your faith falter, beloved. For we are closer than we have ever been to our greatest triumph." He looked down on them, benevolent, confident. The split-faced men and women clutched one another, some mouthing a raucous cry. Like a pack of gibbering animals, hunched around their leader.

All except one, held fast in the fists of two hunters at the edge of the firelight. Her face was pulled into a mask. She was a fraction of who she was before Ronnie broke her. But it was different, now. Now I saw what that mask covered.

"I see your struggles. I see the sacrifices you make, for the Feast. Never doubt, children; He will rise. He has a plan, and we are all . . . His glorious machinations."

The priest jutted his head forward, lowering his voice to a conspiratorial whisper. He looked nervous, or ill; a sheen of sweat beaded on his upper lip. "The guards who were watching him failed you. They're the ones you should punish, not I. They were the ones—"

"I'll punish who I see fit. Quit your sniveling." The old man cut him off, and the priest fell into immediate silence, drawing back as though Father had slapped him. The two of them stood in silence, staring at the fallen Ronnie, boring holes into the dead man's back. They'd forgotten about me for the moment, allowing me to fade into the background. Fine with me.

The Woodkin gathered behind me, gliding silent as sharks through water, coming to stare at the fresh corpse. Still and silent masks slipped over their features as they took in the man who'd called himself Reaper.

"What went wrong, this time?" The priest leered at the body. Poor Appletree lay where he had dropped, forgotten. It could have been a trick of the light, but his body seemed much smaller, lying in the dirt by itself.

Father nudged Ronnie's corpse with his foot, a frown pulling twin lines deep into his brow. He shook his head.

"He was too arrogant to know true fear. His fear was the fear of a small man who thought himself big. He had his uses at the beginning, but his time had long since passed. Use one of the others to take his place."

A twitch of movement caught my eye; a member of the Woodkin, wiping his mouth with the back of a dirt- and sweat-slicked hand. He left a smudge of black loam on his chin. Beside him a woman with a swollen belly stared at the fresh corpse, unblinking. A palpable shift of the energy in the clearing, now.

They gathered around Ronnie. Pressed around their Father in a semicircle inching smaller and smaller.

At first I thought it might have been a shadow, uncertain light thrown by the dimming bonfire, or my own eyes, playing tricks. On the upper arm of one of the women, standing nearer the firelight.

A tattoo. An astronaut, waving at me.

My heart stopped. I remembered that tattoo. Fluttering in the corner of a corkboard in front of the diner in Bedal. Missing Person.

Found 'em.

"What now? The time is past. We can't try again for—" The priest squinted skyward, hunting the pale clouds for answers.

A man with teeth visible through the raw gash in his face shifted, catching a moment of light. He wore shoes. Not scavenged, torn-up tatters, but laced-up hiking boots, old but 100 percent purchased in a store. A piercing glittered from his ear.

My vision wavered and spots danced in front of my eyes. I saw one, three, half a dozen. More tattoos, more piercings.

"One more day," Father answered. "The time will ripen again, quickly. He is close; His strength only quickens, and He has tasted blood." For the first time in several minutes, he turned his gaze away from the corpse and looked at me.

His mutilated face split open in a huge smile—a smile too big for his face, too big for anyone's. A double image wavered over it, a blurring distortion of reality. His mouth warped, bleeding at the corners. Bending around an impossible number of suddenly razor-sharp teeth.

"Good thing we have a spare."

The priest uttered a single syllable and they fell on Ronnie's body in a crazed rush, snarling and growling like animals. The sounds of skin rending and bones popping out of sockets filled my ears and made me gag. They tore at him, clawing open his skin with their bare hands, slathering his blood over split faces. His flesh tore like wet cloth, ripping to expose the bones.

10

THE PRIEST

I N MY DREAMS I STUMBLED THROUGH KNEE-DEEP SNOW AS MY LIMBS turned black. Every breath hurt.

I woke back in my cell, the gently rotting room stinking of blood and fear. The world passed me by just on the other side of the door. The day dawned, raining again. Water dripped through soft spots in the roof, pattered against my already chilled skin. I didn't care.

They ate him. They fucking ate him. I couldn't credit the few and far-between pictures floating to my muddled consciousness. A dozen or more bloodstained faces, strings of muscle bulging in the spaces between their teeth. Human muscle, muscle that used to be a walking, talking person. A garbage person, but a person, nonetheless.

This was no issue of perspective. No other way to look at it. I couldn't pretend it had happened to Switchback, and not Josh. Two lives I desperately wanted to stay separated drifted toward each other. Collision course.

In the corner across from me a pile of leaves shuffled in a frigid breeze. Appletree had hunched there yesterday, hiding from this place behind a tattered shred of cotton.

A glimpse of baby blue among the rust red of the dead leaves. Appletree. Ronnie Coors. I'd crossed paths with both, and both were now dead. For all I knew, they'd devoured Appletree's remains when they were finished with Ronnie.

My stomach lurched hard enough to send me into the corner with the dry heaves.

Another cool morning, the freezing damp clinging to every surface. Fifty degrees, tops, and raining to boot. I clung on to the little bit of acidic bile left in my stomach and shivered, gooseflesh rising over my upper arms.

Something iron slammed against the door to my cell, loud enough to make me flinch and cry out. I stuffed my spine into the corner—they couldn't sneak up behind me then; at least I'd see them reach for my throat with their bloodstained fingers, reaching to tear me apart like they'd torn apart Ronnie.

Two men stood on the other side of the door, wearing identical expressions of casual disdain.

They didn't speak. One gestured with curt motions, a "come here." The other spat over his shoulder, bored.

They were people. They might have been an insurance adjuster, or a chef—fuck, they still might be. But their faces . . . their scarred and twisted faces couldn't be fake. Anywhere they went, people would point and stare, whispering about them. They were monsters now. Swallowed by the woods, by the outstretched arms of the old man. By the distorted column of smoke and malice.

"You can get fucked. I'm not going anywhere with you." I thought of the small and lonely form of Appletree, surrounded by a red corona of dirt. I hunched deeper into my corner, and concocted a wild plan of darting between them, out into the trees—

The rusty squeal of hinges told me they didn't give a good goddamn if I wanted to go with them or not. After my clumsy dive through the legs of one, they had me by an arm apiece.

A familiar woman crouched beneath the sprawling limbs of the enormous pine tree, shivering in the cold. The one who'd refused Ronnie, who slipped up and revealed something she wasn't meant to show. The rawhide rope hanging from the tree closed around her throat. She stared at me, eyes flat and disinterested.

"Hey—hey!" A hand that tasted like sweat clapped over my mouth, sealing my surprise. She turned, watching us pass with flat eyes. Like a dead body sitting upright.

They dragged me through the same path in the woods. Between the two leaning houses, through the woods with their many-fingered oak trees. Into the narrow ravine. The box canyon loomed, every bit as threatening in the daytime. The massive slab of granite filled the horizon, heavy and glaring. Everywhere you looked it lurked in the corner of your vision, waiting. It pulled at your gaze.

We took the same path down the rocks.

The first face stared at me from the bark of a pine tree, watching the river roar beneath us. I frowned. It lacked real proportions or any grace in form or texture—almost like a crude child's drawing. I spied another, scratched into a tree some feet away from the rough game trail we followed. This one, too, was a poor-quality imitation of a real person's face. The eyes were black holes, punched so deep into the bark they wept cracked amber tears of sap. The mouth was a thin slash of curled bark, not even arched into a frown—just a straight line.

They spread by the thousands as we climbed the hill, growing over the trees like boils of a plague, sharpening in distinction as we neared the clearing. Mouths formed from straight lines, growing lips and teeth, stretching in wide screams. Punched boreholes turned into eyelids, brows, wide-eyed, terrified. With every step toward the slab of granite, they grew closer together, sharper. The agony and fear captured in so many strikes of a knife. The eyes watched us. Closer to the clearing, the real faces emerged.

Murder begets skill. They had plenty of practice.

We finally made it to the clearing, all of us breathing hard and slicked in a faint sheen of sweat. I looked around. Some part of me expected to see the bleached white bones of a human skull grinning at me. A hunk of leg-sized meat hanging from a tree, where the bears couldn't get at it. But the clearing was empty. A ring of soot-covered black rocks from the bonfire sat in the center, but there were no bones, no moldering corpses. As if they'd scrubbed last night away, footprint by footprint. As if it had never happened. As if I'd imagined the whole thing. The slab of granite towered over us and stretched to either side, vanishing into the trees. I craned my neck, trying to gauge how tall it was. Hundred feet, easy. Two dozen holes, some as big as fifteen feet across, some smaller than tennis balls—gaped at me in the weak sunlight. Perfectly round, gouged into the rock.

He sat cross-legged on a boulder at the base of the slab of granite. The priest, wearing the same leather jacket. I rubbed my arms and tried not to be jealous of the extra layer. It grew colder. A gust of wind touched my sweat-soaked shirt to my back and I flinched.

The man on my right pushed me toward him. "Go on."

"And do what?" I snapped but received no reply. I approached at a snail's pace. A stack of pale logs sat beside him, partially obscured, sending plumes of blue smoke into the cool air. He watched us enter the clearing, watched me come closer. He still wore the smudged ash and dirt from last night. Smeared and faded in large streaks, it revealed pale skin beneath. The scar on his face engulfed his left eye. A curled mass of filmy scar tissue, like cauliflower, gaped from the depths of his socket. The sight of it made my stomach clench.

"Come closer. Sit," he said. He gestured to a nearby boulder.

I thought of Ronnie's corpse and the way the priest eyed it last night.

I stayed where I was. "I'll stand, thanks."

A muscle clenched in his dirt-covered cheek. He gestured to the boulder again in a curt snapping motion. "Sit. I'm not the one you should be afraid of."

I laughed. Nothing to fear. Right.

"Sit or I'll have one of them come over and break your ankles and you won't have a choice," he snapped. He sounded like a normal person in the cold light of day. The charade was thinnest here.

I cradled my wrist and sat, shuffling on the hard rock. He stared at me, weighing. Analyzing. Was he a lawyer, in his not-far-enough-behind-him previous life? A banker?

"I know who you are. I saw the secret." I went with a straggling kind of bravado. Why not? I figured. Go for broke.

"We are the Woodkin."

"No, I—not that. I mean, I've seen the tattoos, the piercings. The way you all act like you don't speak the lingo. You fucking speak the lingo, don't you? Like you, specifically. Not everyone, but you—" I thought of the Father's terrible double-face from last night. "You do. I know you do."

"We are the Woodkin," he repeated, but he didn't try to hide the smirk tickling at the corner of his mouth.

"What do you want from me?" I asked the question but didn't want the answer. "I didn't do anything; I was hiking—"

A fist-sized chunk of rock skittered down the massive boulder face, echoing from the trees. I flinched, put my arms up to ward off any stray shards, which fell hard enough to leave divots in the dirt a foot away. The mountain, answering my pathetic whining. When I looked back at the man in the leather jacket, a smile stretched across his face. It wasn't a nice smile.

"To make you see the truth."

"What the fuck does that mean?"

He snapped his fingers.

One of the men approached, head bowed and eyes cast downward. He bent to the pile of logs on the ground and fumbled with something out of sight. In less than a minute the smoke turned white and curled upward, heavy, perfumed. The man straightened, handed something to the priest. A palmful—brown, black.

Mushrooms.

Ronnie's voice floated a dozen yards behind me, whispering behind the tree trunks. *I grow my own strains, up in the mountains.*

He wasn't the one doing the growing.

"The truth," the priest repeated, looking back at me. His expression didn't change. His mouth still stretched wide, but his one working eye was cool, humorless. In a single motion he slammed the ruffled fungi back, chewing with effort. His shoulder shook, and for a moment I thought the mushrooms were coming back up. He gritted his teeth and inhaled through his nose. His hands clutched his knees with pale knuckles, and he shook, like a kid trying not to upchuck in the car on the way home from school. The moment passed, and he relaxed.

"Look, man, I don't know what your deal is, but I just want to get the hell out of here. Can you—" I licked my lips. The smoke grew thick, now a dirty gray color, and drifted into my face. "Is there anything we can, like, work out?"

"You can't leave," the priest said. "You are . . . necessary."

"Fuck—necessary for what?" I cleared my throat; a sour taste coated my tongue. The smoke didn't seem to be obeying the breeze moving through the leaves. It gathered around us in thick clouds. I realized the two men who took me up here were gone, I couldn't see the way back. My body grew heavy. Movement—even wiping my eyes from the stinging smoke—seemed to take much more effort.

"The Feast," the priest said. He took thin, shallow breaths. His cheeks were paler than five minutes ago—sweat gleamed in the hollows.

"Feast?" I felt dumb, thick. The trees grayed out, thinning, lost in the smoke. *Shadow, Josh. Concentrate.* "I don't understand."

No, not Josh. Switchback. Switchback, now. Perspective.

Shadow, wearing the face of Ronnie Coors. That I remembered. The buck skull, the smoke. Ceremony. Death.

Sacrifice.

"The truth. You'll see," the priest answered around a suppressed cough. A red tinge spread around his working eye, and a trickle of sweat dripped down the hollow at the base of his throat.

A tingling spread in my fingertips, like they were falling asleep. My legs and hips stopped complaining about the rock shards jabbing at them. My balance faltered—or at least I thought it did; thoughts came slow and heavy.

The opening notes of a panic attack, familiar. *Not here.*

"What—" I swallowed, struggling. "What is the thing?" Not what I wanted to say. I tried again, but my mouth wouldn't cooperate. I searched for the panic, the adrenaline, but it wasn't there. "I—"

"Can you feel it?" The priest's voice hissed, sharp. He sounded close, right next to me. I flinched, but my body stayed still. I tried to cry out but made no sound. His eye stayed open, blood red, glaring at me. I swear his lips didn't move when he spoke. No—that didn't make any sense, did it?

"He's here. Close." That time, his lips definitely didn't move. My heartbeat spiked, distant and removed, like it pounded in someone else's chest. How did he speak without moving his lips? I didn't understand. I struggled for every breath. I coughed, and my vision shook.

The face of the granite slab glared down at me, somehow more massive than before. I couldn't see the sky around it, the trees, the mountains. Only the pockmarked granite, staring me down. Like the black holes punched into the tree, weeping sap. Just another face, hiding in plain sight. I was spinning now. Reeling like I'd been drinking, but with my body frozen in place. I sank into my own head. I felt like my brain had turned to liquid and drained down my spinal cord. I tried to open my mouth and scream, but none of my muscles worked. Was I breathing? I didn't know. What if this was how I would die—locked in my own body, unable to draw breath?

Spots danced in my vision as it blurred and dimmed at the edges. Would my lungs burn for air?

Did hers burn when she went rushing into the kitchen?

Something lingered there, some deep truth I didn't want to remember, attached to the thought. I didn't see her rush into the kitchen. I didn't see her do anything.

I was not in the house.

"There we are. Much more comfortable now, aren't we?" The voice inside my ear sounded like glass splinters scraping along a blackboard. I wanted to recoil, wanted to run away from it. It stabbed deep into my head.

"Come, come now, it's not all so bad. Just . . . relax. I need you to relax." The warm scent of honey and gardenias slipped into my nostrils, and my heart slowed a fraction. The second time around, the voice wasn't so bad—it was familiar. It had an accent that tickled the back of my memory. The priest spoke too. His lips moved with the voice in my ear, framing the words. Curious. I think I should have been upset or scared to notice that, but there wasn't any fear. I reached for it, but it slipped beyond my grasp.

"Welcome. I've been expecting you." His lips moved, but I wasn't talking to the man across from me. I was talking to . . . Jesus, it sounded like I was talking to Dwayne Phillips, the varsity football coach at Austin High. The same purling, south-Savannah laziness dripped from the words. I couldn't be afraid of Coach Phillips, right? He brought home-baked snacks to practice. He taught me what a back-sweep position was on the football field.

"I'm—I feel strange." My tongue rasped like sandpaper, rough against my lips, scratching.

"No, that can't be right. You're fine. Isn't that right?" Coach Phillips whispered. His bushy white mustache dominated his face.

I took a breath, prepared to protest . . . but the air stayed in my lungs. No more coughing. I inhaled again—testing, shallow—but again, no coughing. I still felt like I was floating, attached to my corporeal form by a few dozen threads, but at least I could breathe. There, there. Things were going to be all right. Switchback felt great. He had perspective. Josh . . . well, Josh could handle being in the backseat for a while.

"I brought you here for a little chat," Coach Phillips murmured, settling onto his boulder. He wore his varsity coach jacket, orange and black, pushed up around his beefy forearms. The bear was missing. He'd had a custom, snarling bear head on his jacket, a more ferocious take on the high-school mascot. Rumor around the locker room was that his wife had made it for him.

For a fraction of a heartbeat, I thought I felt something slink in, way in the back of my brain, above my spine. A cold, curious finger, like a breath of winter air slipping through a door left ajar—

"Whoops. Gotcha right here, son. Almost missed it." Coach tapped a fat finger against the jacket, where the embroidered bear snarled. I relaxed.

"Coach, what are you doing here?" I remembered a clearing, trees and mountains and a village, set deep in the trees. It didn't seem important now. I couldn't focus on the details. Like a water slick around a tub, the only evidence of a bath.

"I went for a walk, found you. I wanted to sit down so we can get to know each other for a bit. Doesn't that sound nice?"

I laughed, a stupid and slow *huck-huck* sound. "Coach, come on, we already know each other. I've been to your house, remember, with the boys 'bout six months back. Doris made us tea, you remember . . .?"

Coach Phillips smiled, letting me ramble on. It wasn't until I paused to draw breath that he reinserted himself, neat as a pin.

"So, I understand some things happened yesterday. Some things that . . . might not make all kinds of sense to you."

Black smoke, streaming from the buck skull. Ronnie, screaming and thrashing as it consumed him. Seeing him, hunched over in the black mass of shadow.

"I thought we could sit down, the two of us, and discuss it. You know, hash it out." He looked at me, his eyes full of sympathy. "Do you want to talk about it?"

"I just—I don't get it." My breath caught in my throat. I did want to talk about it. He knew me so well. "Why is this happening to me? What is all this, what was that thing, last night?"

"Oh, that?" He laughed, his tidy little beer gut pushing against the yellow polo tucked into his khakis. "Just a little fun, that's all."

An image of deformed monsters floated to mind, melted skin around a scar dug in each of their faces. "Fun?"

Coach Phillips twisted the ends of his mustache with one hand. He did that when he got excited. His eyes gleamed. "Aren't you having fun, Josh?"

The beast of black shadow, writhing and growing. The touch of it as it brushed past me, dragged back into the unwilling form of Ronnie. I wanted to tell him I wasn't Josh anymore, my name was Switchback now, but I didn't have the words. I shook my head, trying to clear the packed cotton slowing down my thoughts. I wanted to cry.

Coach tutted in sympathy, shaking his head. "Ah, Josh. Always the last one to figure it out, am I right? This must all seem so confusing to you. See—" he leaned forward, gesturing for me to do the same. My body moved mechanically, ratcheting forward, mirroring his—"you're a smart guy. Smart guy, who thinks he knows what's going on here. Parts of it, at least, right?"

I wanted to be wrong, wanted to think of something else. But every thought led back to Ronnie, reaching out to me from the cloud of black smoke. Fear etched in every line of his face.

What did he know? What did he see?

"Look at me," Coach Phillips said, but for a second it didn't sound like Coach—his voice grew deeper, hungrier. He didn't sound that way in real life. He sounded friendly, nice. "Josh. Look at me."

I squinted at him, trying to focus—my eyes didn't seem to want to work right. Smoke filled them.

I looked at Coach Phillips, all right. Same balding hair, watery eyes, and bushy walrus mustache. The varsity jacket pushed up to his elbows . . . wait. No, but it wasn't a varsity jacket at all, was it? A shadow, beneath the cream-colored fake leather.

"There I am. You see it, don't you? What's hiding beneath." Coach grinned wide, a silver molar winking at me. "I need your help with something, son. A special . . . errand, let's call it. A special task. And in order for you to help me with my special task, I need you to see."

Parts of him grew see-through, the longer I looked. Beneath his fake jacket, behind the wide-stretched grin. I could see through the boulder he sat on, beneath the rocks and dirt below. My vision stretched as something unlocked it. Veins of water running quick and silent a dozen feet below the ground. Tree roots, bent and knotted as they plunged deep, shifting tons of dirt and loam.

Look at me.

The massive slab of granite. It went deep into the soil, deeper than I ever imagined. Riddled with holes, each perfectly round and large enough to swallow me whole. It looked like a tooth, suffering from an infection below the gum, rotten all the way through.

Look.

There, buried deep beneath the rock, hundreds of feet below the surface, I caught a glimpse of something black, split into dozens of wriggling, writhing limbs. Blood and slime slicked its hundred tendrils, riddled with holes like the rock above it.

I shut my eyes and screamed, and Coach laughed. Except it wasn't Coach, and the laughter stabbed like needles in my brain.

"Are you scared, Josh?" Coach whispered, leaning close. He stared at me with stolen eyes. I wanted to look away, but it wouldn't let me. "What are you scared of?"

What was I scared of?

Tears burned my smoke-stricken eyes, and the smile on Coach's face widened, cracking at the edges. Blood beaded and trickled down his chin, seeped into the edges of that fat white mustache, but he didn't wipe it off.

A boy, twelve years old with soot stains on his *NSYNC T-shirt, standing in front of a mirror in his neighbor's house. His face streaked with tearstains and coated with black, greasy ash. He's crying, his entire frame shaking with racking sobs. Not from grief—that comes later—but something else. He looks in the mirror, and swears he'll never tell. From the living room he hears his father cry for the first time in his young life, and he knows he'll never utter a single word.

But the boy knew. He was crying out of fear—fear that he'd be found out, that someone would tell. Tell his secret. The firefighters pulled him out of the house. Dragged him, kicking and screaming. If he says the words over and over again, he could change them. He could make them real. He could lie.

"Oh, dear," Coach Phillips whispered, the bloodstained grin still stretching over his fat jowls. "Now, we have a few things to work with. See you soon, Switchback."

He leaned back and disappeared. One second he was there, and the next he vanished, replaced by the priest, bent over, panting like he'd just finished running sprints. The fire beside him struggled. The edges of the clearing blurred, suddenly white and thin.

Beneath the smeared dirt, the priest's already pale face was gaunt and gray. He bent double, caught his breath. When he turned back to the land of the living, his one working eye locked on mine. It glittered with fever, bright as a beetle's shell. A bead of cloudy liquid bloomed at the corner and fell down his cheek, thick as blood.

"Take him. We have everything we need. His fear will be sharp."

They dragged me out of the clearing, limp and listless as I stared at ghosts. My heart hammered in my chest, clawing its way up my throat. The truth, long buried, back again.

No one pulled that little boy out of the house. No firefighters came and snatched him. He smelled the smoke and came downstairs. He saw the kitchen door, slipped from where it was usually hooked to the wall.

And he did nothing.

Nothing.

I did nothing.

She burned, and I stood there.

I could hear the sound of china shattering in the kitchen. They sounded like bricks—the same bricks I'd stacked on that grave, one by painstaking one.

11

A TOUCH OF DEATH

LMOST FULL NIGHT HAD FALLEN BY THE TIME THE TWO WOODKIN members got me back to my cell. My heels dragged against the dirt in twin streaks, leading into the shadow looming behind us. When we reached the decrepit shack, they dropped me in a heap.

I didn't sleep. Each time I closed my eyes, the fire crawled toward me, splitting the wallpaper of my childhood home into fingers of ash. The dull, scraping sound of someone kicking against wooden floorboards reached my ears. Once, when I closed my eyes, I heard a scream, and I started to cry.

I heard her over the sounds of the PlayStation. Faint confusion at first, like she was calling for my dad with questions. Except Dad wasn't home.

And her questions turned to shouts in a split second.

I remember walking out of my room, heart in my throat. Tingling in my fingertips, hornets under my skin. A small child who didn't understand. I walked down the steps, stood in the front hallway. Looked at the kitchen door, slipped from the hook on the wall. I knew it was heavy, knew it had to be tied to the wall or it would lock.

And I knew Mom was trapped on the other side.

Her screams still echoed in my ears. Just like that day, standing in my front hall.

An echo shivered through the chilled air, and I blinked. That one wasn't in my head. That one was real. I held my breath, unsure if I was about to slip back into my nightmares. Was I Josh or Switchback?

Which one was I?

The scream came again a few minutes later, this time blasting into my ears loud enough to raise the hair on the back of my neck. I snapped back to full consciousness. This was no dream.

Outside the eighteen squares of my cell door, a commotion was taking place in the clearing. I swallowed with no small amount of pain. Too long since water had passed my lips, my starved and dehydrated system answered. A full day, or two. A dull pounding beat in the back of my head that didn't bode well. Dying of thirst didn't seem like a great way to go.

Another scream. I looked at the first thing I could to distract myself—my injured wrist. Swollen, bright purple, and straining against the cuff of my filthy flannel shirt. It didn't look good.

The next scream was longer, drawn out, and ended with a faint huffing. Like someone preparing to run a sprint was lifting four hundred pounds. A scream of effort, more than suffering. I dragged myself to the door of the cell, looking through.

A woman was kneeling, naked, her body lit by two torches jutting crookedly from the dirt. Her shirt lay discarded in the dead leaves. She hunched over her swollen belly, clutching it, teeth bared in a grimace. The muscles in her neck stood out in harsh relief, thick cords from the effort. Her eyes held a static place in the distance, narrowed in concentration. The firelight gleamed off the rivulets of sweat trickling down her arms. A sun with an eerily realistic face stared from her shoulder, inked in dark purple and reds.

A dozen other women surrounded her in a ring, kneeling, hands outstretched. In supplication. In worship. Not one of them lifted so much as a finger to wipe the sweat clinging to the woman's brow or reach out and hold one of her twitching hands. They supported her in presence only.

Her, or her baby. At this moment, they were one rolled in the other, hand in hand. Like Josh and Switchback, except they weren't fighting for control. The woman braced herself through another wave of contractions, breathing intentionally, carefully.

With each wave she half fell to the ground, panting in effort, only to pull herself back up to her knees afterward.

The wracking waves came closer together now, ceaseless, insistent. She flipped over onto her back, heels kicking the dirt. I felt like an outsider, witnessing a private moment. A moment between a mother and her child, a moment of toil and labor and love.

And the ring of supplicants with hands outstretched.

I took a shuffling step away from the door and her belly moved.

A knot of flesh rose from her stomach, bulging outward, surrounded by a corona of livid veins. Even after it disappeared, a red eye of broken blood vessels remained. She screamed, arching her back and hammering a fist against the ground. The tight concentration on her face shivered, wilting. This was different. Something changed. Just like that moment in the clearing, with the beast of black shadow. One split second, and everything was different.

Still, the other women did nothing.

I sagged against the weak walls. I thought I might be sick. It wasn't human, couldn't be human. The air reeked of low-tide rot, dying sea creatures buried in the sand. Of the layers of dirt and sweat coating my skin. The chanting grew louder. Every eye watched the thrashing woman, but no one broke ranks to help. She lay exposed, alone. The message was clear; she has to do it herself or die trying.

I put my back against the door. I couldn't watch—my stomach already churned in cartwheels. Images of the beast from last night floated in front of my squeezed-shut eyes. Writhing and bulging with limbs stretched like pulled taffy.

The chanting and screams surrounded me, painting their own garish pictures. I wrapped my good arm around my knees and bent forward, trying desperately to think of something, anything else.

Cotton candy. The taste of a cheeseburger, where I was in the book American Gods. *I think Shadow Moon just got to that town—*

A scream from the woman shot up in pitch, and the chanting stopped as if cut with shears. For the third time in a day I lurched into a corner, stomach heaving. I ran beyond empty, so nothing came out but a weak string of sharp-tasting bile. That didn't stop my gut from trying to squeeze out every last drop.

Don't look, it's not going to help, it'll only make things worse, don't do it—

I wiped my hand and turned, resting my head against the bars of the cell door. They were mercifully cold against my hot and flushed skin.

It lay on the pine needles. Surrounded by the afterbirth, blood-slick and covered with dirt and leaves. It wasn't moving. The woman lay a few feet away, trembling from head to toe, and looked anywhere but at the mess between her legs. Her stomach was a riot of bruises already turning a dark wine red.

Father stepped forward, manifesting from the darkness. His face was as still as a grave. The women in the circle pressed their faces in the dirt, arms outstretched.

"Give it to me." Father addressed the new mother, who was still panting from effort and dripping with sweat. He stopped at the edge of the ring, folded his arms across his bare chest.

"Give it to me," he repeated. Other men detached themselves from the pooled shadows behind him.

She pulled herself onto all fours, heaving for breath, and crawled to the red mass lying in the dirt. The muscles in her arms spasmed, twitching like they were attached to strings. Even from here I couldn't miss the livid-colored flesh, the twisted limbs of the not-human form, still slicked with blood.

Not a child—something else.

She lifted it with a locked elbow behind its neck and got to her legs, shaking like a newborn calf. Father watched and said nothing, made no movement to help. A smattering of familiar-looking longish-brown hair coated the creature's head, the only sign of faint humanity. I wondered how many of the swollen bellies of the Woodkin were a direct result of Ronnie's drunken lechery, versus . . . the other thing. That creature of pockmarked shadow, buried beneath the granite slab in the clearing.

Stillborn—clear as daylight, even from my cell. No screams of indignation or rage escaped its lungs. It didn't writhe or kick in protest against the cruel, cold air.

Father turned his head and spat into the dirt. "He was weak in life. Why should his seed be any different? Another failure. Another."

His hands tightened as the lines in his face scratched deeper. For a second I thought he might do something unspeakable to the creature in his frustration. His bleak facade cracked, and the anger seeped through. Then, as soon as it appeared, it vanished, and he fell still once more.

The sky spat thunder, heralding a late-summer storm. Father lifted his face skyward, spoke too low. They took the child from his arms, whisked it away into a group of hard-faced men. The scene broke up; the child went in one direction, the men in another. The group of women carried the one who'd just given birth away despite her snuffled protestations.

The woman tied to the tree had looked on. I caught a glimpse of her, peeking around the massive pine trunk. Wide-eyed. She was just like me: a prisoner by any other name. We locked eyes . . . and she faded back behind the tree.

"You." His voice was inches away and I jumped, jarring my wrist against the iron door.

"Motherfucker," I hissed, clutching at the rod of molten iron twisting inside my wrist.

Father crouched in front of the door to my cell. His arms were slick with blood from the child—or the mother, I'm not sure which. His eye glared at me, unblinking.

"You're coming with us tomorrow."

"Come with you where?" I hissed through clenched teeth. Sweat beaded on my forehead.

He threw something between the bars of the cell. It thumped heavy against the rotten wooden floorboards. Rolled with a distinct sloshing sound. My heart leaped into my chest.

"Up. Into the mountains. Drink. You've got a long hike ahead of you." And with that, he left. The torches were gone, the clearing dark and empty.

I fumbled for the object. A bag, made out of some kind of leather or hide. I pulled the stopper open.

Despite the frantic screaming in my head I took a small, cautious sip, prepared to spit it out. I needn't have worried—it was just water. It tasted of faint river silt with a hint of algae, but I didn't care. I drained a good chunk of the skin in one go, until my lungs burned for air and white spots danced in my vision.

I made a pile of leaves in one corner and fished around for Appletree's blanket, spreading it over my legs and hips. It was surprisingly warm, and only stank of unwashed bodies if I brought it close to my face. He'd had it wrapped around himself by the fire, and for a second—just a second—I wondered who had brought it back to my cell and why. I seized the precious skin of water and clutched it to my chest. With a belly full of water and a night free of screams or murder, I collapsed into a black and dreamless sleep.

I woke to the sound of tiny thumbnails being dragged in the soil.

I sat up in a rush, fast enough to smack the back of my head against the wall of my cell. A vise tightened around my skull. Through the eighteen rectangles holding my freedom from me, the night grew cold. The thumbnails I'd heard against the ground were only leaves, skittering in the face of an early-autumn wind. They swept the clearing, dancing through the spaces between the decrepit and leaning shacks. A thousand shadows forming jagged silhouettes. Like tiny many-faced shards of glass.

Dead, and free to fly on the breeze as they wanted.

I pulled Appletree's blanket tighter around my shoulders and pressed my head against the iron door. It felt good against my hot and fevered skin. Like the touch of an alpine lake on a brutal summer's day, after hiking all afternoon. So cold your skin ripples in goose bumps, your breath catches in your lungs and threatens to drag you all the way to the bottom.

I breathed now like I did then: controlled, slow. Trying not to sink below the surface. Switchback was doing just fine. Switchback was surviving. A couple of scrapes and bumps—or a broken wrist—but he was still alive. He was still here.

A few breaths later, and the skin of my forehead started prickling. I looked up.

A pair of eyes stared at me from the shadow of the pine tree. Floating, disembodied for the moment. I blinked, rubbed my eyes. I stood up, and crept toward the door. A sense of déjà vu—the night I'd rolled out of my sleeping bag to pee and saw a silhouette watching me. Except this time, it didn't break apart when I took a step to the left. No moonlight split its growing shadow, no rocks and distant lake speared the pieces my imagination gave corporeal form.

She was watching me. Sitting, like she couldn't feel the chill of the night air, the early teeth of autumn. She didn't say anything. Didn't so much as twitch. Like a statue, or a shade conjured by my fevered brain. The only thing that tied her to reality was the noose, strung up to a bough.

We stayed like that for a time. Staring at each other. Two animals, ensnared.

"Can you hear me?"

I don't know why I spoke. I didn't mean to—the words slipping out from between my lips surprised me as much as they did her.

She didn't blink. Didn't budge. Gave no indication that my words reached her. And then . . .

"Yes."

She might have nodded. There was no way for me to know; shadow shrouded her face, her dark hair blending into the dark trunk of the tree behind her. A pale face, floating in black. Staring at me.

"Are you okay?"

She looked at me squarely. "Great. You?"

Despite everything, the still-snarling pain in my wrist, the low ache-turning-into-pain in the back of my head, despite the cold and certain knowledge that I was cattle waiting its turn at the slaughtering pen, I laughed. *What a stupid fucking thing to ask, Josh.*

Or Switchback.

I stared at the ground. At the charred remnants of my sad attempts at a fire. At the dead leaves curling into static mildew in the corners.

"How did you get here?" I asked. It was the first question that popped into my head, the only voice in the growing darkness. I rushed to fill the gaps, to seal the places in my question where the water would drain out. She had answers. She could teach me things. "Not, like, here, here. I mean . . . like . . ."

"How did I get with them?" Her voice detached from her, floating between us. Just another leaf on the wind. Just another piece of us, dead and free. One of her hands reached up, testing the rope. Delicate fingers, pulling at the coarse fibers. I imagined them pricking at her skin like tiny wires. How many necks had that rope held fast? How many lives swayed at the base of that pine tree?

Another batch of faces, carved into the bark.

The skin on the small of my back twisted in a shiver that had nothing to do with the cold. She stayed silent. I slumped to a crouch, pulling the ragged edges of my—Appletree's—blanket over my shoulder. Another stupid thing to ask, I suppose.

"I was doing a midnight hike. Heard about it from some guy in a town when I stopped in for gas. He was pretty insistent. Best views for miles, he said. I'd been having a tough time at work lately, and that day I got written up for making a simple mistake. I just . . . needed to get out for a bit, so I figured why not. I was planning on doing Mount David, south of Glacier. The moon was full, and I wandered off trail to get a better view of it rising over the valley. I made it about fifty paces when I heard the voice. It sounded . . ." She paused. Considered her words. She stared at her hands in her lap. "It sounded like my boss. Begging me for forgiveness for something, I can't remember what. I followed it. Off the trail, down a hill. I felt . . . I don't know. Different. Looser. Like I was dreaming, I think. I walked off the trail, followed the voice. The woods felt better than they had at the top. Warmer, closer. Like a hug. I know it sounds stupid."

"I don't think it sounds stupid," I said, quickly. I did, a little bit, but I didn't want her to stop talking. As long as she was talking, I wasn't alone. At least she wasn't hounded through the woods like a petrified rabbit, running for its life. Although, given our current circumstances, it was tough to suss out if that was a net positive or a negative.

"I walked for a long time. The voice kept pulling me, talking to me. It changed. From her to my old man, to my grandma. People I cared about, people . . . people I hadn't heard in a long, long time. It promised me things. Things I knew should have been impossible, that

I shouldn't—shouldn't—have wanted, but I wanted anyway. By the time I got to the valley, I was sunk."

"Sunk?" She was like a reclusive animal just stepping out of its pen. I didn't want to scare her. Didn't want to scare her back into silence. The noose was already doing a fair job of that, I imagined.

"That's how I think of it. It's hard to explain. Like . . . like your brain sinks backward into your spine. Draining, all the way down. Something else took the front seat for a while. Something . . . not great. I think that's how it got a lot of us."

"Who?"

"Feast."

The word slipping from her lips sent a chill through the air. We sat there in silence for a little longer. Separated by the night, by the chilled air. By the leaves tap-dancing between us.

"How did you get out?" I stared at my own hands. The fingers of my right hand were swollen, tinged red. My wrist bulged in spots I was fairly sure it wasn't supposed to.

This time, she was silent for so long I thought she wasn't going to answer me. I thought the moment between us had passed, and we were alone with ourselves again. The woman with a noose around her neck and the man with the broken wrist. Animals both, trapped. Waiting for the final touch of the knife. Cold steel, cutting flesh.

"My old man wasn't great. He had a thing for . . . he was . . . he liked pain. For himself and . . . others."

"Fuck." I didn't mean to say anything; the expletive fell from me, hollow and already bruised.

"My mom, mostly. My brother and I slept in the basement, Mom and Dad's room was on the top floor. Some nights, you could hear him through the vents. What that dickless wonder said—'I've got an itch I need you to scratch'—that's what Dad used to say too, before going a few rounds with my mom. The same words. Like it was Dad, standing in the clearing with me, and not that douchebag."

Once more and likely not for the last time, a wave of nausea at the thought of Ronnie Coors rose through my chest like a trash-filled tide.

"I hadn't heard those words in . . . God, decades. But I still remembered them. I still remember how they made me feel, lying in that shitty twin bed in that stifling basement. Telling myself that everything was okay, that they were just talking. That it was the TV in the background, and not him. But when I heard Ronnie say those words . . ." The icy breeze plucked at her words, sending them fluttering around us like deadfall. "It all just hit me. That my dad was a bastard. That I'd been lying to myself this whole time. I finally got it. I guess."

"Lying to yourself." I whispered so only I could hear it. Like Josh Mallory, holding the box of Plan B over the trash can. Telling himself that he could fix this, that he and Deb could find a way out.

The silence returned, steeping the night. The wind moved through the trees, rushing almost water-like, and tiny creatures ruffled the grass beyond my cell door, but the two of us were silent.

Lied to. Trapped. Like a pair of stars caught in the gravity of a dying sun, we'd both run into the valley. She had been promised something she desperately craved. Me, running from the smoking ruin that was my life outside the trail. Briefly I wondered why I didn't hear the same voice she did. Why I wasn't called from the trail, to 'sink.' Maybe it was just as simple as I was food, not fodder. I lacked something, anything concrete to my life. I wasn't even an entire person; Josh, Switchback, Josh, Switchback. Round and round we go, where we stop, no one knows.

It had to be the lie. The reason we were different, the reason we weren't . . . like the rest of them. It was the only place our stories synched, the only common ground. That moment where you whispered to yourself that you weren't what you were, that things could be different. That you could change your life just by looking at it differently. That you could make the pain go away simply by wishing it wasn't so. But look at it differently, pretend it was something else, run from it—the truth always waits for us. Waits to sink its antlers sharpened like knives into your spine. The truth will set you free, or death will. Everything in between is simply the hunt.

One more question pushed against the inside of my lips, chitinous and bulging like a cockroach shell. It tasted sour. It tasted like death.

I had to ask it, or I was sure it would end me.

"What's going to happen to us?"

"They're going to kill us," she said simply. She was leaning her head against the tree, staring up into the boughs. "I'm not sure how they'll do me. But I've got a pretty good idea of what they'll do to you."

I swallowed. "Yeah. Me too."

The image of Ronnie's face, frozen in terror and agony. His hand outstretched, begging for help.

We didn't talk after that. The wind died down, and the exhaustion welling up inside my chest finally dragged me to the floor of the cell. This time, the nightmares waited for me.

This time, my mother was already screaming before my eyes closed.

THE CAVE

T HERE ARE SEVERAL UNPLEASANT WAYS TO WAKE UP. THE SOUND OF
a hunting knife slamming against iron bars has to be in the top five.

A voice somewhere in the floating ether of the world above
me snarled in inarticulate anger. I blinked, trying to sort reality from
distorted sleep-vision.

A face swam into focus; twisted and malformed, scarlet in flushed
anger. Someone standing outside the door. He hammered the butt of
the hunting knife against the door again, a sharp, ear-splitting noise. I
sat up, wincing.

The hinges of my cell screamed as the door opened. His iron grip
on my arm encouraged me out of the cell and into the cold day. It was
raining. Again. Fat raindrops plopped in random spurts from the dirty
gray sky, touches of ice against my bare skin.

Father and his entourage waited for us in the clearing, hunters leaning against tree trunks, standing silent like they sprouted from the ground. Each had a waterskin like mine slung around their bare shoulder. One of them had a beat-to-hell day bag strapped to his back. Another moment of dissonance, of wrong-ness, like when I noticed the speakers hanging from the trees.

The woman was no longer tied up beneath the pine tree; she stood in the middle of the pack, the rope still around her neck. The end of it was wrapped several times around the old man's fist. She stared at the ground, didn't so much as lift her gaze to meet mine. Whatever moment we'd shared had shriveled up in the cold light of day.

The Woodkin's conversation dwindled and died when they caught sight of me.

I shivered and took a drink of water. The thudding headache from last night faded, and I was grateful. I struggled not to look at the rust-red patch of dirt a dozen feet away. To not hear the screams echoing in my memory. A lot of those going around, it would seem.

Without a word, Father started walking, hunters in tow. I followed—I didn't have a choice.

I thought we were headed back there—back to the box canyon. Nervous sweat broke out above my hairline. My heart sledgehammered against my ribs.

The skin at the base of my neck crawled at the memory of what I'd seen: a wriggling, reaching bundle of pockmarked black tentacles buried deep beneath the huge black slab. The sensation of sinking beneath the dirt to see it for the first time lingered in the recesses of my brain, constant and insoluble. A mass of black malevolence, a many-armed bundle of fury.

I'd walked into the canyon and come out alive twice now. Something primal in my gut whispered I wouldn't a third time.

Much to my relief, though, we didn't head for the winding game trail to the narrows. Instead, the old man picked up a thin path cutting west toward the valley wall. Our trail meandered through the forest, through meadows of late-season raspberry plants pressing against the trail. Remnants of rainwater dripping from the canopy managed to find its way beneath my shirt, ice cold. I kept looking at the valley wall with growing uncertainty. Was this the last walk I would ever take? Would we stop in a small, out-of-the-way clearing, where they would bash my head in with a rock and be done with it? The faces surrounding me, still masks and cold eyes, gave no hints. My extremities grew cold and began to tremble.

We passed a handful of clearings but didn't stop. We entered a field of black granite boulders littered along a steep slope.

Father picked his way over and up the slope with ease, walking a trail visible only to him. He and the other men leaped from boulder to boulder. I was not so quick. My wrist screamed with every bump, making a scramble up boulders an almost laughable endeavor. I was holding up the rest of the group. The man behind me snapped at me in frustration, almost hurling me by the scruff of my neck up the scree. By the time we made it back to the trail high above the valley floor, sweat was dripping from my face. Shakes racked my frame from the pain and effort. The two Woodkin behind me shoved me forward.

Above the boulder field, the trail followed a ridge, curving upward. Steep limestone walls riddled with stubborn plants rose on our right. The only thing keeping us from the drop into empty air beside us was two feet of beaten dirt. Far, far below, a river frothed with white rapids. I looked ahead, but low-hanging clouds obscured the tops of the mountains. Rain spat in thick curtains onto pine trees carpeting the valley beneath us. The hunters picked their way with goat-like surety, like it was a Sunday stroll. The man with the backpack hiked it higher on his shoulders.

A drop to your death. The expanse of empty air and rain pulled my eyes until I couldn't look away. *Hey, hey,* it said. *Take two steps, and it's all over.*

A long fall and a sudden stop, and everything would end. The worrying stiffness working its way through my wrist, the fear and uncertainty, the tiny, glimmering pieces of hope I clutched to my chest. It could all be over. I could be done. I could sleep.

But I knew I wouldn't do it. I wasn't brave enough. Wasn't brave enough to take that step, take the gamble. Because what if I didn't die immediately? What if I bounced off the cliff face and found myself broken and bleeding among the limbs of a pine tree. Besides, I still had a chance to escape. Still alive, wasn't I? I wanted to keep it that way.

The trail turned rocky and steep, sometimes cut into the limestone cliff face with handholds for a still-dubious level of safety. I panted with effort, hot enough I imagined steam rolling off my skin. I pulled the waterskin from my shoulders and took a drink, trying with only moderate success to ignore the dull pounding in my head.

I looked back; the valley stretched away to the south. Unremarkable, as valleys go: dirt and rocks beneath the misty pine trees. An airplane pilot wouldn't even look twice.

No, no one would be coming to rescue me.

Ain't nobody gonna miss him.

The path pivoted right around a huge spur of rock. Ahead of us the ridge rose in a flat, angled plateau, stubbled with stunted shrubs and heavy with clouds. Here, the wind pulled and clawed, a thing alive, constantly brushing cold mist against my skin. We climbed into the clouds and left the world behind.

Visibility sucked—which would work in my favor, but they outnumbered me by fifteen to one. If I could get far enough away, I might be able to hide in the fog until they stopped searching for me. I could stand a chance. How far was that, though, a hundred yards? I couldn't hold on to a lead when the little demon chased me into this situation. What made me think I could do it now?

The thought no sooner popped into my head when the mist rang with a strangled cry of anger. The woman with the noose around her neck went scrambling down the rocks and sand, making for the ravine gaping below us. The men didn't hesitate, didn't flinch with surprise. They flung themselves after her, hurtling down the slope with reckless abandon. They rolled, skidded, leaped like devil dogs.

"Ah, son of a bitch!"

Someone behind me grasped a fistful of my hair, tight enough to jerk my head backward. One of them had stayed behind, just for me.

The heavy touch of a hatchet pressed against my leg to soothe any doubts I may have had; he'd break my leg in three places and never flinch. He didn't say it, but I got the message all the same. The old man stood in place, arms crossed over his bare chest. He didn't look concerned. He waited.

She was getting small in the distance, lost here and there to the dips and curves of the mountain slope. Her limbs grew pale and indistinct in the mist. The men's cries moved through the fog around us, bodiless and hollow, echoing.

She might make it. She'd chosen her moment well and had a head start. She might hold them off long enough to disappear in the mist or throw herself into the river flowing north. I cheered for her, heart slamming against my chest.

My breath came in short, shallow pants.

Come on, run, you can do it you can make it—

I clenched my teeth together. I imagined the rocks beneath her bare feet, scratching and treacherous. The rough pull of the rope fibers against her throat. The icy touch of the wind mixed with the feverish burn of effort. Terror gleamed in her face. I could see it from here, the way she threw glances back at her pursuers, but she had a lead, she could do it—

It was the rope that got her. The rope snapping in the air behind her, she dove behind two boulders, making for a dip in the terrain. The rope got stuck in the rocks. I watched in horror as the slack ran out.

"Watch out!" The cry burst from my mouth, unbidden.

The noose tightened and she was slammed flat on her back to the ground with a muffled *herk*. Her feet flew ahead of her and she grasped at her neck.

Her pursuers' cries turned to laughter. They fell on her like jackals, picked her up, dragged her back up.

Back to the old man.

She didn't fight—she knew she'd lost her one chance. She hung between them, limp, defeated. The wind pulled at her hair. Her cheeks were wet, and the air whistled in her throat as she fought for every breath. She didn't look up.

I wished I knew her name. The night before, when we were whispering, I was too wrapped up in my questions, too desperate for answers to care about the person giving them. Now, the woman trembled and cried, her face white as the fog wreathed us. And I didn't even know her name.

Father held out his hand. One of the hunters handed him the end of the rope.

He turned and resumed his pace, a cold smirk stretched on his ruined lips. We hiked.

I struggled for breath, trying to keep up. Each time I began to fall behind, the man behind me jabbed me in the butt with a stick. My wrist was in constant pain. My waterskin started to run out and I shivered in the sudden, bone-deep cold. Hadn't I been running hot moments ago?

A cave gaped in front of us. It wasn't huge; there was barely enough space for a man to fit. I eyed the too-small crevice with no small amount of despair and wasn't thrilled when the first man disappeared into the black depths.

One by one they filed past Father and the woman, sidling into the darkness. She wouldn't even look into the cave. Her face turned to the mountains, eyes running over the trees and hills. She trembled, either from cold or the stifled sobs shaking her thin frame. A tear welled in one eye and dripped down her face.

"Please—please, don't, please, I'm sorry, it won't happen again—" Her begging was low. Meant for the old man's ears alone. She might have had more luck pleading with the rocks beneath her feet. His face showed as much emotion as wood, long-since petrified.

The man with the pack pulled a handful of sticks free from the side of it before slipping into the cave. A moment later the dim recesses were lit by an orange glow. Even though it was illuminated, I didn't want to venture inside.

It was my turn. Sweat dripped down my face and I could smell the harsh rank of my armpits—

The Woodkin behind me jabbed an elbow in my butt, propelling me forward a step. I walked on baby-giraffe legs, trembling from head to toe.

For a brief second I smelled something. Beneath the rain, pine sap, wet limestone, beneath the smells of a wet morning in the mountains.

"What is that?" I sniffed.

Father's face tightened and he looked over my shoulder, jerked his chin toward the cave. The man pushed me forward.

The gravel beneath me gave way to empty air and I fell. I threw my hands out in an instinctive flail to catch myself, knocking my wrist against an unseen rock. My scream echoed in my own ears, too close. My feet were already on solid ground. I looked up; I fell less than three feet. Impressive, to fuck up my already fucked-up wrist in that small distance.

"God damn it!" I clutched my wrist to my chest, teeth clenched. Searing pain radiated from my elbow to my knuckles. They laughed, the sound pressing close beneath the crushing rocks overhead. Someone behind me snapped, impatient. I rolled to the side, allowing the rest of the entourage to enter the cave. The old man came last, hauling his prisoner behind him; she sprawled on the rocks, falling flat on her ass. No one laughed at her. She kept a tight hand on the rope around her neck, staring, unblinking, at the old man.

"Please, Father, please don't—I'll never break the code again, I'm sorry—" Her pleading was a blunted, constant razor blade against my frayed nerves.

One of the Woodkin handed Father a torch, and he led the way into absolute shadow. He didn't so much as turn around. The woman's words followed us in the ghosts of our footsteps.

I pressed a finger against my injured wrist.

Ah shit.

It was hot. Not warm, hot. Even to my own touch the skin felt flushed and fevered. My head crushed behind my eyes. I couldn't control my body temperature. I knew those symptoms—everyone knew those symptoms. I had a fever. A fever meant an infection, courtesy of my shattered wrist. Without real medicine, the Woodkin or my own traitorous white blood cells raced to see which would kill me first.

In several spots the ceiling dropped, forcing us to crouch, and the walls narrowed to press against us. The cold touch of rock was a blessing on my hot skin.

I inhaled and immediately gagged. The air reeked of the sweet, ammonic taste of rot, cloying and thick enough to coat my tongue. I clamped down on my nose with two fingers and breathed through my mouth. No way I was gonna throw up the precious water in my system. I wasn't the only one struggling; most of the others' twisted and broken faces pulled into masks of silent disgust. Even the woman's desperate begging stopped for a moment as she dry-heaved in step. The old man walked with placid calm.

We didn't go far. After five minutes of shuffling, we arrived at a shelf swallowed by inked darkness. I got the sense of depth beneath us; the air echoed with our hitched breaths. Water dropped from a height, somewhere close. The walls were slick with it. Water, and a curious shade of neon-blue mold, crawling up the sides of the well in thin strands. Where darkness reigned it thickened and bulged in thick ropes, plunging out of sight.

The old man nodded toward the darkness. "Go ahead."

The man with the pack nodded and set off down a path, followed by a majority of the group. They took a single torch with them. I didn't like the way the shadows followed, snarling beyond the nimbus of orange light. Like they were alive, real things with real fangs and claws, given life and limbs by the flame. Father, the woman, and I stood on the shelf, watching the glow of torches wind their way down the circular well, punching deep into the mountain. A single man stood sentinel behind us, his arms folded over his bare chest. His face was cold.

"Please." The woman sobbed in earnest now. She clutched the rope with a white-knuckled fist. Her shining, red-rimmed eyes were the size of half-dollars. "Father, please, I've done everything you asked of me. If—if they asked me to give my face to Him I would!"

The old man held out the torch. The man took it. He wasn't looking at the woman—his eyes were focused on the black rock weeping moss water in the torchlight. The corner of one eye twitched.

"Kneel," the old man said, soft as a prayer.

"Please don't do this," she whimpered. Her knees gave out, and she knelt on the rock. She shook like a leaf.

I didn't want to be here; I didn't want to see this.

"You came here to live by the laws. Embraced by His light, His love." His voice was almost too quiet. He looked down on her with an utter lack of empathy. "We embraced you. Embraced you as one of us, one who gave up her previous life of sin."

"He was going to rape me!" The word echoed around us. "Would you have me submit to that—that—bastard?"

"Many more before you have, and many more after you will. Through the Reaper, the pure-born of the Woodkin are brought into this world. It's our way."

"That's bullshit!" She seized the rope, hauling on it. He let it go with a careless flick. "Let me out of here! I didn't do anything wrong! Please—I didn't—I didn't do anything wrong." Her struggles faded into incomprehensible tears. She fell back on her knees, crying into the backs of her fists, still clutching the rawhide. "I want to go home. I don't want to do this anymore. Please. I just want to go home."

I thought I might be sick. I turned away, back toward the entrance of the cave.

"No." His voice was hard. "No. You watch."

He stared at me. His face was wreathed in garish shadow from the torch, his scar puckered, clawing deep into the skin. His eye glared at me, milky and surrounded with boils, swollen and ready to pop.

"Please. Please let me go home." The woman's voice was barely a whisper, circling around her. Tripped in the dark.

I turned back around. He held out his hand, and the other man reached behind his back, placed something in the old man's palm.

A hunting knife.

My fingers went cold.

"What are you doing?" My words sounded far away.

"No! No, you—you can't!" Her screams rose in pitch, straight into hysteria. Her face was a ruin of tears and raw panic. She turned to me.

"Don't let him, please don't let him, he's fucking crazy, he'll kill you next—"

"I'm sorry. I'm sorry." I muttered the words over and over, like they'd shield me from what I was about to be a part of. She shook, crying.

"We live by a code. You knew this, and still you violated it. The balance is due," Father said.

The hunting knife blade brushed the fine hairs on her neck with a sound that drew goose bumps along my arms. Father's eye gleamed bright in the darkness. His excited whisper:

"Are you afraid?"

The woman didn't answer—didn't want to give him the satisfaction. A muscle in her jaw clenched.

"Answer me!" A bead of spittle flew from his lips.

She flinched, then nodded.

"That's good. He wants you to be afraid."

The hunting knife severed her windpipe with a thick crack. The air tasted of salted iron. A red cloud consumed the still air, and the woman went limp. Her face shifted, meat fresh and hot off the bone.

"Fuck!" I screamed, pawing at my face. My skin was slick, wet, and warm. "Fuck, what the—"

I jerked backward, but there was no more rock behind me. My heel slipped into black nothingness and I tottered, lost my balance—

A fist caught the fabric of my shirt. Father's grip was as brittle as cast iron, every bit as strong. With no effort at all he pulled me back from the brink, dropped me to the ground. My outstretched hands touched the fresh corpse and I recoiled.

"Glory be to the Feast." The man's voice was husky, his gaze still locked on to the rocks across the gaping darkness, at the dripping water, the bright blue mold. Anywhere but the woman at his feet.

Father wiped his face with the back of a hand. Blood coated his lower lip and cheeks, beading and dripping. He flicked it from his fingertips, handed the blade back. He placed a hand on the hunter's shoulder, squeezed it. He seemed almost relaxed. At ease.

"Her sacrifice is the final step in His plan. Do not mourn her; she is with the Feast, and with the Feast, all will be born again."

The scarred man nodded. The old man approached the edge of the shelf.

He looked down, past me. "We'll all be born again."

His voice reverberated down the cave from a hundred different mouths.

The group was a full fifty feet below us, picking their way across rocks encircling the edges of the well. Something lingered in those black depths, touched by the torchlight. At first I thought it might be an underground body of water, the way it chopped and roiled. As the party approached, I saw the truth.

Hundreds of them, stacked in piles like firewood, empty faces staring at the black rocks sealing their tomb. Men, women . . . and children too, young faces unscarred by the markings of the Woodkin. Slow rot took hold where the dead touched the water-slick rock walls. Bright blue mold grew in skeletal fingers along slack arms and legs. Their cheeks and eyes and lips and hair were rough, textured in round-shaped . . .

Mushrooms.

Growing from their faces, sprouting from their lips and gums and eyes.

The man with the pack knelt, another reached inside. Removed a cloth-wrapped bundle of familiar shape and size. The wasted and weak bastard child of Ronnie Coors, laid to rest with its people. Beyond torchlight, gaps of black shadow flickered and danced into unseen corpse-choked depths. How many scarred corpses lurked there, in the darkness? How many "paid the balance"? The others bent too, reaching out and caressing the faces of their dead. Collecting their crop. Even from all the way up where I was, I could see the color: an electric, neon blue.

My stomach flipped and I turned away from the stacked corpses, trying not to breathe through my nose. I tasted it now, that reek and rot, tasted them coating my tongue like a disease. Father's face flushed red around the white scar. His eyes bored into the piles of bodies, alive with an inner light. He laid a foot on the dead woman's chest. I thought for a second he was going to genuflect, contemplate what he'd done. Expose himself as someone with emotion, with an actual beating heart.

Without so much as a change of expression he pushed the dead woman's body over the edge, into thin air. She fell like a rock, graceless and thick-limbed, leaving a wet smear of dark maroon on the rocks in her place. The cave swallowed her. She crashed with a nauseating wet thump, the last sound she'd ever make. A person, who at one point had lived in the real world, went to school, fell in love, smiled, cried. Who went on a midnight hike and lost her entire life and everything in it. Who now would molder and stink like the rest of the nameless corpses around her.

The torch popped on a piece of sap, sending a firefly of cinder floating through the wet air after the dead woman. It tumbled end over end, borne on a ghost of wind, floating down to join her. The fingers of mold followed the ash down, hungry.

"The Woodkin feast." Father grinned. I squinted, sure that my eyes were lying, sure the darkness of the cave was playing tricks on me. His mouth was suddenly packed with too many teeth, thin and long like needles. Like the mouth of a horrid fish from the crushing darkness at the bottom of the sea. His lips stretched clear to his ears, bending the flesh of his skin like putty.

I blinked, and the teeth vanished. His face was normal save for the digging cleft of scars in his cheek. He grabbed my shirt and hauled me to my feet like I weighed nothing.

I emerged from the cave to the pouring rain hammering on my frigid skin. If death was coming for me, it wasn't going to be today. I inhaled deeply, let the clean air of the mountains cleanse the stink of the dead.

13

DEBORAH

THE FRONT DOOR SQUEAKED OPEN, SPILLING A SILHOUETTE ONTO THE icy front step: a sagging Santa hat with a bell on it perched on its head.

Oh God, here we go.

"Hey, you made it!"

"Todd, hi! Oh, it's so good to see you!" Deb exclaimed, spinning on her heel and smiling wide. The switchover from fighting to delighted was natural, so smooth no one but me would notice. I looked at the back of her hair, coiled in neat ringlets, and swallowed my retort. Her hair looked nice. It should; it was the subject of hours of effort and swearing earlier in the afternoon. I swallowed that too. Only Deb could pivot in the middle of a knock-down, drag-out fight and slap a smile all across her teeth. Me, I was about ready to push her into the bushes. But we had to do what she wanted to do. We always had to do what she wanted to do. All because of a sweater. She couldn't let me have even that one, tiny victory.

"Come in, come in, it's freezing out there." The man flattened himself against the door frame, beckoning us inside with enthusiasm bordering on frantic. We squeezed into the hallway, stamping the slush from our shoes onto the overworked floor mat.

"You must be Josh! I'm Todd, Mary's husband." The man stuck out a hand, and I shook as best I could with one arm still trapped in my heavy jacket. On Todd's chest a three-dimensional reindeer burst through a knitted screen door. At the end of the hall a dozen people stood in subdued conversation beneath Michael Bublé belting out his latest wretched holiday album. Todd and Mary's "ugly sweater" Christmas party was one of the hot-ticket social events of the year. The fact that "we" merited an invitation had been the primary source of excitement from one-half of my household for weeks.

"Is that Deb?" A mousy woman with an expensive haircut rounded the corner, a huge smile splitting her red cheeks. She had decided to forego the theme of the party and wear a glitzy neon-blue cocktail dress. It was only five thirty, but judging by the flush working up her neckline, she'd been "celebrating" for a few hours. Upon seeing Deb, she burst into ear-rending squeals, blowing away any questions about her sobriety. I tried not to wince.

"Ah! Debbie, there you are, darling, Katie and I were just talking about the drama that went down in Home and Furniture today!"

Debbie? No one had called her Debbie since grade school. I thought she couldn't stand the nickname.

"Oh, with Damian?" my wife gushed, instant excitement lighting her eyes. Nothing got Deb going like juicy gossip, and she was already running hot from the car ride over. She stuck her jacket out behind her without looking. I took it automatically, nodding in thanks for the hangers Todd pulled out of the hall closet. "God, wasn't it a bloodbath?"

"Claire thinks they're gonna fire him." The woman lowered her voice to a whisper, looking around like she was revealing state secrets. Too late, she noticed me, the obligatory husband. She straightened, waving. "Josh, hi! So good to have you! How's everything over in marketing?"

"Hi, Mary." Deb's boss had everything Deb was too scared to admit she wanted. Vapid and wealthy after fifteen years of seventy-hour weeks for Amazon. Rumor was she spent more time on the pull-out cot at her tiny office than sleeping next to her husband. I wondered if Deb wanted that part too. Oh, I'm sorry—Debbie.

My own boss at Amazon was a slightly mellower sort. Still a dick, but in his defense, that could be mostly Amazon's fault.

"Do you want a drink, dear?" Mary turned back to my wife.

"Oh my God, so badly," Deb said with a not-so-subtle sideways glance at me. She slipped an arm inside Mary's elbow, and a split second later they were gone, eaten by the crowd.

"Boy, they get along well, don't they?" Todd offered me a good-natured smile I didn't feel like returning.

"Like a house on fire," I said. The irony of the words slipping off my tongue wasn't lost on me. "Beer?"

"Oh, right out by the sliding doors."

"Thanks." I turned and left him standing in the front hallway. I wasn't exactly in the mood to make conversation with strangers. Not after the events earlier today.

A chance I was being rude, but I didn't care.

The ugly sweater theme was out in full. More three-dimensional reindeer, and a few with swanky, built-in LED bulbs. In most cases the sweaters had more to say than the white milquetoasts poured into them. I squeezed past the cliques and snagged the first bottle I touched from the ice chest without looking.

Beyond a pair of glass doors, festive string lights lit the landscaped back lawn. There was a fire pit beneath a wood portico with a view of the Olympics over the Puget Sound. They even had a clay pizza oven. I guess throwing your life away for the sake of a mindless corporation came with its benefits.

Not that I could talk. *Amazon* was printed on my paychecks the same way they were on Deb's. I, however, just worked there. Deb lived there. She loved every minute of her sixty-hour weeks. She was fully drunk on the Kool-Aid.

The beer was malty and crisp, with a sharp sting of alcohol. I glanced at the bottle; a barrel-aged porter with 11.8 percent alcohol by volume. A hint of something sharp wafted from the top of the bottle, some smell I should recognize but didn't. Sweet but with a bitter undertone. Tell you what I did recognize, though: that sweet, sweet ABV percentage.

"Hello, you," I murmured. I looked down into the ice chest and swiped a backup, slipping it in my back pocket for a quick reload. I promised Deb I'd be sober enough to drive us home so she could cut loose. I shrugged; two beers wasn't gonna be that bad.

"Mallorca!"

I spun, daring to hope. Only one person who swam in these circles called me by that nickname. A thick black beard rushed me, arms outstretched. Behind it, an all-teeth grin gleamed. I took a breath of relief, the first in hours.

"Rakesh! Hey!" He smelled of expensive cologne layered over the faint tang of spice.

"I didn't know you were going to be here," Rakesh said, pulling away but keeping a grip on my shoulder. "I would have worn something a little more risqué."

The big man wore one of the LED-rigged sweaters, each over a scrawled letter of the alphabet. A knitted attempt at a Demogorgon lurked just under his armpit.

"*Stranger Things*. Nice. Does that technically count as Christmas, though? Isn't it set in, like, October?"

"It's Christmas lights," Rakesh said, gesturing at his gut like I was oblivious. "Besides, my only options were either this or a sweater of Santa taking a dump in someone's chimney."

"You mean like that one over there?" I took a sip of beer and nodded at a mid-thirties man wearing the exact garment. He also sported a peach-fuzz mustache. I'm sure he would chuckle and assure me it was ironic . . . but he refused to shave.

The smell of the beer sharpened. New plastic, a little bit, like a fresh shower curtain. Whatever. I wasn't here to break down the flavor notes. It was good, it was strong, and that was all I cared about.

"Oh, yeah." Rakesh craned his head for a quick peek and shrugged. "Well there were only so many options in Prime, what are you gonna do? I see you went with . . . that." He gave me a doubtful side-eye, his smile slipping.

"It's my dad's. My mom made it," I said somewhat curtly, washing the words with beer. My choice of sweater was the spark firing off a six-hour shouting match between me and Deb, and I didn't particularly feel like talking about it at length. Luckily, Rakesh knew the play when it came to my family. He murmured a generic compliment and dropped the conversation like a bad habit.

"So what are you doing here, anyway? I haven't seen you at T and D's before."

"Deb got an invite after she did . . . I dunno, something with a crisis a few weeks ago. I'm riding shotgun for designated driving purposes, not because I merited an invitation."

Rakesh raised an eyebrow at the mostly empty bottle in my hand, but didn't say anything about it.

"Well, what do you think of your first party at the glamorous home of the VP of Finance?" He turned and gestured at the milling expanse of people. The doorbell had rung three more times since we arrived. The islands of talk grew as people gravitated toward who they knew and worked with. The house itself was lovely, a mid-century craftsman

Todd and Mary had put either a lot of money or effort into. Or both. Charcoal cabinets and white marble counters lined the kitchen; the living-room ceiling was high and lent an airiness to the room. Even an indoor fireplace—I wonder if they got a two-for-one deal with the one outside. A painting hung over the mantel—some modernistic wash of grayscale with a hint of brilliant neon blue.

I caught a glimpse of my wife at the home bar along one wall, giggling into a flute of champagne.

I looked away, but not before the burn of irritation brought a heat to my collar.

"It's . . . nice. Not my vibe, but nice."

"Your vibe is playing *Destiny* in your pajamas, which doesn't make for a fun Christmas party."

"Uh, strongly disagree."

We laughed. My chest was lighter, a little looser. Like the events of the day were being shuttered away. Did I want to be here? No. But, there were worse ways of spending an evening than goofing around with Rakesh.

"Where's Deborah?"

"Over there." I nodded to the bar.

"How are the two of you doing?"

"Oh, you know. Same old." Another drink, this time to wash down the lie. Wash, wash, wash. Maybe one of my sentences would taste pleasant tonight. He was asking out of politeness, there was no reason to dump all our shit on him. Besides, we were work friends, not real friends.

The hours rolled by, and more people showed up. Someone turned up the music. The conversations grew more animated, people shouting and shrieking with glee. The ice chest was emptied, refilled, and emptied again. I pounded down my pocket beer and went back for another, then another. Ah well, I thought, so we have to take a Lyft home. At least I was finally enjoying the life my wife wanted so desperately.

A born-and-bred hippie who'd give her left foot at the ankle to have the life promised her by Corporate America. The irony turned my stomach, and I doused the rising bile with more beer.

I wasn't above a little self-improvement by corporate ass-kissing; that was the way the world worked. But I liked hiking and backpacking and paddling on Lake Union on the weekends. My free time was exactly that—mine. Deb, on the other hand, hadn't taken a full day off in three years. Not even when we flew to Decatur last Christmas. She worked from the guest bedroom. Dad and I had turkey and stuffing silently in the living room.

Rakesh introduced me to people whose names I forgot as soon as I heard them. I stood in on a conversation about the merit of PNW-centric IPA. Someone bemoaned how expensive the Seattle housing market was, to much-muttered agreement. It took everything in me not to laugh outright; everyone in the tight circle, including me, made low six figures, if not more. We were the reason studio apartments were closing in on eighteen hundred dollars a month. But sure, let's sit here and mourn the loss of the city's identity, ignoring the fact that we're the ones forcing the original residents of Seattle out of their homes and neighborhoods. Hey, we can drink our expensive beers in a multi-million-dollar home while we do it, isn't that a gas?

After a few minutes the irony became sickening, and I left, pounding down the dregs of my fourth—fifth?—beer. The chemical smell was all around me now. Lingering in the back of my throat like an oncoming sickness. I'd pick a different beer this time. Because that was for sure the issue.

"Did he just . . . leave?" A not-hushed-enough murmur behind me. "What's his problem?"

"Ooooh, let me tell you," I mumbled to nobody in particular. I bumped into someone and apologized to a sweater-clad shoulder, making my way back to the ice chest. The floor was being a tricksy hobbit, bobbing underfoot as I tried to navigate the packed living room.

Deb. Deb was my problem. Deb and her desperate need to climb a cold, corporate ladder. To please faceless goons who didn't give a shit about her or how hard she worked. And the way she chose to do it was to micromanage my wardrobe, apparently.

"You can't wear that," she'd told me as I emerged from the bathroom, hours earlier.

"What are you talking about? It's a Christmas sweater," I said, looking down.

"It's not funny enough. It's an ugly Christmas sweater party. That's not ugly. Well, it is, but it isn't funny-ugly."

"My mom knitted it for my dad. We're about the same size. Come on, it's not a big deal." It wasn't a great sweater. Loose in the armpits, sagging from the gut, it was knitted from wool long since gone to seed and it smelled a little like mold. But I wanted to wear it—I didn't want to blow sixty bucks on a sweater for a meaningless party. There was a Christmas tree on it, and it counted. Besides, we ordered from the Thai place down on the corner even though I hated Thai, so it was my turn. That's how a relationship worked, right? Based on score?

"I don't care if your mom made it, it's not on theme. Come on babe, this is Todd and Mary's ugly sweater party. It's important. Go change."

"I don't want to."

"I don't give a good goddamn what *you* want, Josh."

And we were off to the races.

RAKESH FOLLOWED AT my shoulder, mouthing apologies for me as I bumped into a handful of other people. I didn't care. He steered me toward the upper floor, but I fought against him, angling toward the cooler. People were staring; I was making a fool out of myself. I didn't care about that either.

The stink of chemicals, jagged in my throat, in my nose. Every time I breathed, it choked me. I knew that smell.

She was still standing at the bar, but her coworkers were gone. Instead, she was talking to a guy I didn't recognize—tall, dark hair, broad shoulders. His sweater wasn't an ugly sweater at all—some sleek charcoal number molded to his muscles. Like she felt my gaze across the room, my wife looked up at me, a smirk touching the corners of her eyes—private, just for me. Just for a second, then back to the conversation, enthralled, nodding along. He cracked a joke, and she sputtered into a fit of giggles. She laid a hand on his, caressing the skin of his wrist. She wasn't wearing her wedding ring. On the underside of her wrist, a delicate curl of neon-blue mold crawled across her skin.

Looking at it, I knew where I'd smelled the scent threatening to block my throat. It wasn't a beer smell. That was just my brain playing tricks on me. My perspective.

Chemical, yes.

Ammonia.

Rot.

I snapped awake. Air, sharp with frost, pressed against my face, slipped beneath the ragged edges of the blanket. A dream, it was a dream. It had to be: I'd never been to Todd and Mary's house. Mom had never knitted a day in her life. I blinked, trapped between the lingering clutches of bad sleep and uncertain reality. It was dark, cold. I pulled the blanket over my head, and a finger of unwelcome cold air brushed my ankles. I tugged it back down and my shoulder popped out.

I sat up, groaning. My stomach felt small, tight. My wrist burned, too hot. I didn't have a watch, but no moon lit in the sky, no stars lit the woods; it was as black as frostbite, twice as cold.

It didn't help that my shirt had absorbed the wood-rot water as I slept, and now clung to my back. A shiver rocked through my gut, making my teeth chatter. My headache woke up with me. Grown from its origin behind my eyes, it now wrapped around the front of my head. A gripping vise winched tighter every time I moved. Despite the unwelcome chill in the air, sweat slicked my armpits and forearms.

Something pinched my thigh, bundling in the fabric I adjusted for the fiftieth time, trying to get comfortable. I panicked and slapped at it, imagining a rat or bug, but nothing went skittering into the underbrush. In my pocket. A hard piece of metal. I fumbled for it.

That fucking fire starter. God, a fire would be so welcome right now, the warmth slipping over me like dropping into a hot bath. Muscles relaxing one by one until I could finally sleep. I remembered the sensation like the aftertaste of a meal too far in the past.

So why not try again? *Because it never worked, that's why.* But hope springs eternal, and I sat up with no small amount of effort.

I grasped around for the remains of my last attempt, tapping the sticks to dislodge left-over ash, stacking them one by one. I had plenty of leaves—the rain and wind from the last two days had blown a tumbling talus of gold and crimson into one corner.

I sorted through them with painful slowness. I tucked the dry ones inside my trusty Lincoln Log arrangement of sticks. I knelt, clicked the starter near the leaves, and blew. Nothing. I tried again; same results. The leaves were cold, stiff to the touch. Like corpses, piled on top of one another.

It's fine, I told the cold weight of disappointment dropping my stomach into my pelvis. *It'll happen.*

A lie, and I knew it. It was my own fault for getting hopeful. Now I lived and died with each raspy click. It's the hope that kills you.

A fairy-dust cinder leaped from the metal, landing on a leaf. I inched close, blowing on the spark, trying to feed it a constant stream of air while not blowing it out of existence.

It worked. The spark grew to a red glow, which curled into a tiny finger of flame. Just like I'd done my first night, I fed it a leaf at a time with trembling fingers, nudging it beneath one of the charred sticks until the flame caught.

The inside of the cell flickered into distinction with orange light. I scrounged around, building a pile of dryish leaves and the occasional twig. After fifteen minutes a palpable heat bloomed from my tiny flame, and I warmed my hands on it. I leaned my head back against the wall and finally relaxed, smiling, relishing the light. I'd spent a long time in the dark.

The wall sagged behind me. Like, properly sagged—I almost fell to one side, thrown off balance.

I turned, curious, careful not to threaten my baby fire. Dozens of pin-sized holes had been drilled into the waterlogged wood. Winding lines connected them, some rough and crisp around the edges. Others had been scoured smooth by time. Termites. Without the fire, I never would have seen them. Never even have noticed.

I swallowed the immediate excitement surging to my fingertips. It could be nothing. I probed, pushing against the wood. A two-foot section facing the backwoods, close to the floor where I huddled for warmth. Even with a small amount of pressure the wall bulged outward, creaking a soft, sad sigh.

Holy shit. I sat backward in a rush, pulled my knees up to my chest.

The wall stood on its last legs. I'd guess a few decades of nonstop termite nesting combined with water damage did that. A few sharp kicks, and the whole section would buckle and tear away. This was it; this was my chance. I knew it in my bone marrow.

Then what? Then I'd run, my wrist be damned. I'd take three months in a cast over an immediate and, if I had to guess, painful death.

I'd go south. Toward the end of the valley, away from that box canyon with its wretched, writhing secrets. A river ran at the other end, flowing toward Bedal. I remembered it from my first sob-riddled and heart-pounding run for my life. It was either run and risk it or wait to die. Not much of a choice, when you came down to it.

I leaned down, braced myself. Beyond the confines of my cell, the forest slept, silent save for the breath of wind through the pine boughs, rustling like fingers. I kicked out, wincing at the dull thump echoing along the tree hollows. I froze, my ears straining. No rustles or cries, no sound of movement beyond the trees. The seconds crawled by. Another kick. My heart slammed in my throat now, threatening to choke me. Any minute they'd come rushing through the darkness, teeth sharp and blood in their eyes. They'd drag me back to that canyon, where the thing lived.

A last kick, and the wall crumbled outward with a wet pop, giving me a two-foot section to the free world. I waited, gritting my teeth and clenching every muscle in my body. I heard no alarm raised, no crashing of knife-wielding men breaking through the trees. I peered out of the hut, half expecting to see a twisted and scarred face leering back at me. But there was only the forest, black and cold.

They waited for me out in those trees, I knew. With their teeth and fingers, with their scars and milky eyes. Watched me in my feeble attempts, watched my hope building.

Now or never. I looked around my cell.

The fire. It crackled in earnest now, snapping at the moisture left in the leaves' crumpled-up crevices. A cheerful sound audible from a hundred feet in any direction, not to mention the light blowing away the shadow in every corner.

Figures. The one time I got a blaze going out of nothing in the backcountry, and I needed to smother it.

"Sorry," I muttered. I grabbed a fistful of leaves and batted at the flame, sending it to smolder and smoke against the wet floorboards. Darkness surged back inside the cell, leaving after-images floating in my eyes. They huddled in the corner, buried beneath a tattered blanket.

They cried. A gentle susurration, ringing in the edges of my hearing like a mirage. I'd left him, abandoned him. His blood stained my fingers just the same as the Woodkin's.

No, not my fingers—Switchback's. Never me, never mine. None of this was happening to Josh. This was just a nightmare for Josh, and now was his chance to snap awake.

Time to go. I wriggled through the hole head first, gritting my teeth as the termite-riddled wood scraped against my shoulders. I tried not to imagine dozens of hourglass-shaped maggots falling from the wood to crawl over my skin. The wood pressed tighter, and tighter . . . and suddenly I couldn't move forward anymore. I pulled with my hands, uprooting fistfuls of grass and dirt, kicked with my feet.

Nothing. The splintered remains of the wall clamped down even tighter, like teeth, crushing me. I took a breath and tried wriggling back inside. A different angle, that's all I needed. The wood scraped against my skin, drawing hot blood.

Stuck. Half in, half out of the wall.

Jesus.

Around me the forest came alive with sound, wind rattling the tree branches, leaves skittering across the ground. A snap, just to my left. My breath burned my ragged lungs, and panic flooded my senses. A crunch of dead leaves, a footstep. Teeth, grinning at me in the shadows. Real or imagined, it made no difference to me. They'd eat me, still stuck here. Crack open my back and start with my soft organs, still steaming and pulled from my twitching and howling form. Just like when the boy chased me into this valley the first time, when I stopped at the winding rivulet—hiding in the trees, watching. Letting me get my hopes up until the last possible moment.

I clenched my jaw, took a double-fistful of grass, and *pulled*. My wrist popped, something molten poured into my veins and muscles and a scream pressed up against my teeth, but the wall gave with a dull, wet sound, and I fell forward. I almost kissed the dirt. I army-crawled through dead leaves, soggy and freezing to the touch, sharply smelling of rot. I stayed low, not risking standing up yet. Toward the trees, trying not to gasp as my wrist jolted against unseen twigs.

Oh my God, I did it. I made it outside. I couldn't tell if I shook with excitement, fear, or fever. I tried to focus, but my heart was pounding hard enough to shake my vision. The distance between me and the trees stretched, a hundred feet of bare, open ground. Stepping into that no-man's land upright would expose me. They'd see me. I ignored the soaking moisture chilling my skin, the soft give of mud and dirt beneath me. When I closed within ten feet of the trees I couldn't take it anymore. I jumped into a stagger, desperate for the safety of the shrouding darkness.

The sky was a rolling layer of charcoal-edged silhouettes, backlit by a silver moon. A ridge was outlined against the far side of the valley. I kept it on my left, ducking around trees and over exposed roots dredged from the dirt like heavy limbs. I didn't look behind me, didn't slow or pause for breath. I forgot about the agony in my wrist.

I burst through the same meadow, wreathed in thigh-high grass, from three nights ago. Clouds roiled in the fogged black reflection of the scummed-over pond, thick and heavy.

A stick snapped twenty feet behind me. A ghost of movement, the smallest suggestion. I whipped around, my throat closing to a desperate whine.

I saw him first this time. A silhouette against the dark clearing, a shadow against a shadow. Running straight at me.

Oh God.

I dove into the forest, weaving around a pine tree, going south, or what I hoped to God was south. The fever tripped another breaker in my head; suddenly it was hot and muggy beneath the black layer of leaves and limbs. My breath clawed into my lungs, and blood pounded in my ears.

His alarmed shout followed me through the many-fingered forest.

Fuck.

The valley shifted and dropped down, the walls closing in on either side. I had to be close—I heard the muted white static of rushing water. I had a huge lead, but they were fast, so fast, like wolves in the dark with sharp teeth, snapping—

A sudden burst of motion out of the darkness to my right, and a pale hand lunged for me, missing by inches. I screamed, fear and anger ripping my vocal chords. Twigs and leaves snapped and ruffled to my left, too close. In front of me the woods opened; water rushed below. The river. If I could make it to the river . . . I lunged for it, breath coming in ragged pants.

I almost made it. The woods fell away behind me, turning to rock, stubbled with pale forms of fallen and long-dead trees. I couldn't see the river, but I could hear it, drowning the sounds of chase and fear, of my own panting desperation. I saw them for the first time, six or more, emerging from the black shadows behind me, twisted and scarred faces contorted in rage. One reached out, grabbed my shirt. My momentum slowed to a grinding halt.

They caught me. Panic, black and raw, took what little breath I had. They were going to take me back. The man who held me smiled wide. Moonlight winked in the holes riddling his face.

The deer skull in the clearing. The roiling smoke.

"No!" My high-pitched shriek barely made it above the roar of water. I kicked out in desperation, my foot making contact with the side of his knee. He released me, grunting in pain. Twenty feet below me the river churned and roared in a mad rush.

I careened over the bank, limbs flailing at empty air. Only twenty feet, but it felt like two hundred.

The surface of the river came out of nowhere, forcing what little air I had in my lungs outward in a stream of desperate silver bubbles.

Crushing black water surrounded me on all sides. Blind motion rushed against my face, but I couldn't see. The water stung my eyes like salt, a thousand fingers trying to pry them open. I flailed against the current and a rock slammed against my toes, hard enough to make me yell and swallow water. I broke the surface long enough to try a choking inhale before I sank back under, fighting. It was cold. Everywhere there were rocks hammering against my feet when the riverbed shot up to meet me.

I tried to kick backward to slow myself, but the riverbanks on either side of me were already streaming past in a blur of shadows.

I didn't see the tree trunk hovering over the surface until it was too late. A blinding flash of light and a roaring noise, and the volume knob of my life turned all the way down. My escape, the canyon, the black writhing thing, even my struggle to breathe. Fuzzy, indistinct things I couldn't bother to draw into focus. A relief, to just . . . let go. Let death come for me if it wanted to. The river swallowed me, and I floated on.

⟫ ⟪

I WALLOWED IN and out of consciousness, grasping at incoherent details slipping out of reach. A looming riverbank carved into a curved cliff. Trees, arthritic and hanging over the water like outstretched claws. Twin lights of a car on a late-night (early morning?) drive. A car. People. I felt like there was something there, some important bit of information I needed, but I couldn't focus. The river flowed slower now, lazy. I looked up at the sky. At the stars glittering in a patchwork spiderweb behind the heavy silhouettes of clouds. It wasn't cold anymore. That was nice.

A hand grabbed my shirt and pulled me out of the current. Water splashed and rolled in my ears.

"Hello." A voice, distant. I wanted to look, but I was fading back into the darkness again, sinking back into myself. A glimpse of tan coveralls and a face wreathed in a thick beard. Black, beetling eyes stared at me in cold speculation.

"What have we here?"

14

BEDAL

IN MY FEVER DREAMS, THEY CAUGHT ME IN THE BLACK DEPTHS OF the forest. They pinned me to rocks, scraping and cutting into my skin. Their mouths were all lined with long, needle-thin teeth. They bit me, one after another, jaws extending like some horrid fish from the deep, and I screamed—

I woke up thrashing and kicking, the scream still reverberating in my throat. It was dark and sweltering; something thick and wiry covered my legs. I struggled out of it, pulling the vague indistinct edges, gritting my teeth at the sharp pain in my legs. My hands and legs dripped with sweat, God why was it so hot—

A door opened with a creak, blinding me with a beam of light. I squawked in rusty fear and threw myself backward, right against the wall behind me. "Son of a—"

"Whoa, whoa, what's going on?" A silhouette consumed the light, looking in. It moved closer and I recoiled, pulling my legs up to my chest. "Oh, it's okay. Sorry, I didn't mean to scare you. Here, let me just . . ."

A light flickered into life overhead, sending shooting pain through my sensitive eyes. I blinked and squinted.

Behind him the walls were god-awful plastic laminate painted to look like wood. I squatted on a mattress eight inches off a stained and ragged carpet. The heavy wooly thing around my feet turned out to be a thick blanket. An electric heater wheezed in the corner. Sweat beaded beneath my hairline and slid down my face and back. My clothes were mostly dry. How long had I been here?

Like he was answering the voice in my head, the man spoke again. "I found you in the river this morning, pretty messed up. I brought you here, I hope that's okay. I—I heard you screaming."

The stranger knelt to the floor a few feet away. A black beard covered most of his face, but no twisting, melted scar carved through it.

"Where—where am I?" I croaked. My throat was dry. It hurt to swallow.

"You're in the guest bedroom," the stranger said, a smile playing at the corners of his lips. Something silver glinted in his teeth. When I didn't burst into hysterical fits of laughter, the smile vanished. "Sorry, little joke. You're in my house, on the outside of town."

"Town?" He only added to the headache I felt gathering force at the tip of my spine.

"Oh, right, sorry. Bedal. I live in Bedal."

Bedal. Sarah's Diner, the General Store. Ronnie Coors, before he went tits up. The memories lurked in the too-close past, many-toothed, waiting for me to bring them into the light.

"Would you like some tea?" the stranger asked. I swallowed past the dry lump of concrete in my throat and nodded. Tea, dirty wastewater, a muddy puddle—I'd take pretty much any form of liquid I could.

"I got you. Be right back." He stood up and left.

I swung my legs over the side of the cot and raised my hands to grind the images out of my eyes.

"Oh, shit."

My wrist was . . . bad. Covered in a livid riot of purple and black, the swelling reached from my fingers to the middle of my forearm. Even rotating it a fraction forced lancing pain to shoot up all the way to my armpit. Broken. Shattered. Perhaps beyond repair. I wondered if it needed amputation. I heard footsteps on the stairs and he shouldered open the door, holding a chipped mug.

"Here you go."

I took it in my good hand, wincing. I ached in a dozen places, from my back to my shoulders to my shins . . . but I was alive. I took a careful sip of the tea; it was terrible. Watery, weak, and lukewarm. I sipped it anyway. The stranger sat down on the floor, didn't say anything. He just . . . looked at me.

"Do you have a phone?" I had a single number memorized. Nine-one-one would ask questions, too many questions. I'd call Deb, get her to drive me to a hospital in Everett, maybe Bothell. Could be the trauma talking, but I was excited at the prospect. She'd call me Puggs and pretend not to be terrified at my wrist. Fuss at me every second of the drive for being stupid.

"Naw," the man said. I waited for him to follow the statement up with qualifiers. Why he didn't have a phone, and wasn't it a funny story, see there he'd been down by the river et cetera et cetera, but he . . . sat there.

"Oh. Okay . . . do you know where I could find one? I need to arrange a ride."

"I can give you a ride."

I looked up. "Really? I mean, I don't need to go too far. Maybe just Verlot, or even as far as Granite Falls."

"Yeah. Yeah, no worries. Happy to do it."

Something in the way he smiled. So eager. Happy to do it, happy to help.

"How about that phone, though? I gotta, you know . . . make some plans," I said.

A flicker of something in his features, half hidden in the shadows from the overhead light. Disappointment.

"Sarah's got a phone, in the diner."

Again, I waited for a follow-up sentence and got nothing. Was he being unhelpful on purpose? No way, right? He took the trouble to drag me out of the river and get me inside. If he wanted to be unhelpful, he could've let me float on by. He wanted to give me a ride.

I just needed to think about it differently. My filter, skewing things in my vision. He's helping. Let him help.

"Is the diner open? Can I go right now?" I set the mostly full cup down, struggled to lean forward and get on my feet. Even the small amount of movement almost sent me careening to the side. My sense of equilibrium had apparently gone out for a drink and hadn't returned yet. Spots flashed in my vision.

"Whoa, whoa, partner, go easy." The stranger came alive long enough to lean forward, ushering me back down to the cot. "It's almost ten thirty at night; Sarah's been sleeping in her armchair for over an hour by now. I go over before I hit the bait shop every morning; I'll take you. You need to get some rest anyhow. You look like you been through it and back. Tomorrow morning you and I'll go down to the diner, then I'll give you that ride. No problem. Happy to do it."

I slumped back down—even that little effort left me hollow and drained. His words, like magic, echoed and stretched, growing farther away. My eyelids turned heavy and dragged over my eyes like ten-pound weights. He grinned down at me, and his teeth winked silver.

"I'm Mike, by the way." He shucked up his canvas coveralls and knelt back down, extending a calloused hand. I shook my head, trying to pull myself together. Mike. Mike with a beard and a glint of something silver in his smile. Gilded onto his grin. I shook his hand, my vision weaving and folding on itself.

"Switchback. They call me Switchback." For a second, my real-world name hung on my lips but I kept it back, bit it off at the last second. He didn't get my real-world name. If I said it, then all this was real—it was happening to Josh Mallory, and I'd have to deal with the fallout. But Switchback? I could forget Switchback, crumple him up like a newspaper and toss him away, trauma and all. Switchback lived in the nightmare, not me.

"I bet they do. Get you some sleep, Champ. I'm sure it will all be better in the morning. And hey." I looked over. He swam in the light from the hallway, nothing but an empty silhouette. "Don't forget about that ride."

The gritty blackness behind my eyes replaced reality before he could leave the room.

The nightmares waited for me. Fresh deer carcasses with smoke pouring out of their eyes, stacked deep in a cave like cordwood. Their cold bones clattering, they stood, row upon row, staring at me with hollow sockets. I turned to run, but they surrounded me, trapped me. Something writhed beneath me, disturbing the bodies. I tried to run, but I was too slow. The cave swallowed my screams.

"Hey, brother." A hand shook my shoulder and I tore through the veil of sleep with a shuddering gasp of relief. Mike's bearded face loomed over me, lit by a hall light filtering through the cracked door. "You good?"

"Yeah." My voice was rusty and my throat still hurt. I swallowed with some difficulty and sat up. "Bad dreams."

Goddamn, it was still hot in here. I should have had the foresight to turn off the space heater before I fell asleep.

"Want some tea? I just brewed some."

I shook my head. "Water, if you got it."

"Sure, sure. In the kitchen, come on. Up you get."

Standing took no small amount of effort. My thighs and calves screamed in exhaustion, and my ankles refused to hold any weight at all. I cradled my wrist against my chest and attempted a sort of half hobble to the door. To no one's surprise I wobbled and fell back onto the mattress.

"Ah, God damn it," I swore, hissing more in irritation than pain.

"Easy there, my dude." Mike helped me back up. "Here, let me." He threw my arm over his shoulders and helped me out of the room.

The second floor of the house consisted of the coffin-like room I woke up in and a bathroom, lit by a bare bulb swinging from the ceiling. I caught a glimpse of myself in the smudged mirror and grimaced; dirt and sweat trails caked my face. My skin was stretched too tight over my bones like a cheap Halloween mask.

We descended a flight of stairs that creaked and groaned beneath our weight into a dingy and dark living room. The street outside the window was still black. No surprise, because the clock over the oven said it was a quarter after five in the morning.

Mike deposited me in a chair, shoving various fishing rods, lures, and tackle boxes out of the way. Hard to tell which of us was more relieved when I settled down. A flush had crept up his neck, and his breathing came in unsteady snorts. I shook from effort, already starting to sweat again. My head felt like someone had stuffed it full of napkins, which I guess was a relief from the crushing headache. God, I was already tired.

"Sorry," I muttered. "I'll find something to use as a crutch."

"Don't worry about it, man. Tea, you said?" Mike asked over his shoulder, going into the kitchen. The kitchen had seen better days, as well—the sink was piled high with dirty dishes, spilling over onto the counter. A cheap tin pot stood on the stove, full of whatever dinner Mike made days ago and forgot.

"Ah, no. Water, please." Tea sounded great, but my voice still rasped whenever I spoke. I blamed that godforsaken electric heater.

"You sure? It's good. Freshly brewed."

I swallowed a snarky comment. He was just trying to help. "Water's great. Please."

"Here you go." He came back with a glass of water and I pounded it down before he made it back to the stove. It tasted like rusty pipes, but I drank it so fast it didn't matter. "'Bout ready for that ride?"

The world fell still. A ringing, buried in the back of my head, like a single alarm bell.

"I need to use that phone first, bud." My voice didn't shake, a miracle in itself.

"Oh, shit. That's right, you said." Easy, carefree. I was being crazy, that's all. I looked at it all wrong. I just needed to look at it differently. He pulled me out of the river. He could have let me float on. I'd been through it, as he said. I needed to breathe.

"Mike, you got any ibuprofen?"

"Any what?" He asked over the clattering of mugs and glassware in a cabinet.

"Ibuprofen. You know, for fevers?"

"Oh, yeah. Bathroom's just down the hall there."

A bathroom.

"Actually, Mike, mind if I take a quick shower?"

His head popped around the corner, peering at me from the kitchen.

"A shower? Whatcha need a shower for?"

I almost laughed, but he was being serious.

"Mike, I'm . . . I'm filthy, man. Like, covered in sweat and dirt." I pulled at my shirt, as if to show him.

His expression didn't change a fraction. He stared at me. "Huh. Guess you are, ain't ya?"

I waited for a follow-up. He puttered around the kitchen to the sound of water pouring and metal clinking.

"Mike?"

"Yessir?"

You have got to be kidding me. "About that shower?"

"Oh, right. Sure, go on and help yourself. Bathroom's just down the hall there. Need some help?"

I looked around quickly, hoping there might be something useful. I also had to pee, and my pride demanded I at least attempt it solo before asking for a copilot. A hiking pole leaned against the wall beside a shoe rack stuffed with mud-coated boots.

"Nope, no I can manage." I grabbed the pole and limped past the kitchen. Not an ideal tool for the job, but hopefully it was short term. "Mind if I use this?"

Mike looked up from the process of pouring a steaming liquid from a lethal-looking tin teapot.

"Nah, knock yourself out. Holler if you need me."

The bathroom was around the corner, past two doors. One was cracked open, leading into a disheveled bedroom. The other was shut. I walked past it, made it three steps then stopped.

Surely not. My eyes were playing tricks on me. Not here.

I turned and limped back toward the door, bending with much effort, to scour the baseboards. Something caught my eye, a flash of color. There, along the dirty and scuffed crease where the beat-up wooden runner met the linoleum. A spider-web of vibrant indigo strands crawling up the door frame. Mold. Electric-blue mold.

Reeking of ammonia and rot, the rippling forms of their dead packed and buried in the darkness.

No—it couldn't be. I shook my head. I cast a backward glance down the hall—no sign of Mike. Regular old house-grown mold—I bet if I pulled his kitchen sink open, I'd find a science-lab of the stuff down there. But the color . . . so vibrant, almost neon. Once it caught my eye I couldn't look away. It crept from inside the room, moving up the frame and along the baseboards. So what if it looked similar? Mold was mold, Josh, and jumping at shadows ain't gonna get you home faster. An easier argument to make in my head than in practice.

I reached for the doorknob, slowly, mechanically. I didn't want to look, but I didn't have another choice. I had to see, had to know. Sweat beaded on my brow, and the hallway grew stuffy and still, heat hovering and pressing against my skin.

The knob didn't turn. Locked. I breathed a little easier; I didn't have to look inside. Average, everyday mold.

I moved on, ignoring the screams from the shadows of my imagination.

I fumbled for the light switch in the bathroom with my free hand. Two out of four lights set over the mirror buzzed into life.

Cramped and out of style, but semi-clean, which I was grateful for. I closed the door behind me, debated for a moment, then flipped the lock as silently as I could. I didn't want to be rude, but there was something . . . off about my host. I couldn't put my finger on it yet, but if the last three days taught me anything, it was to be better safe than sorry.

The shower squeaked to life with a rattling of ancient pipes, but the water ran hot. I undressed with as much grace as I could under the circumstances and stepped beneath the spray.

My muscles relaxed one by one, unknitting in the steaming cascade. I almost sagged against the wall in outright bliss. Five minutes went by before I could bring myself to go through the actual motions of cleaning, I was so happy. An anemic bar of soap sat on the corner, smelling faintly of laundry detergent. Building a lather with one hand ain't easy, but I made it work. Scrubbing my face and torso, the water ran as brown as mud, forming an almost-cake batter at my feet. I had to waffle-stomp it through the drain, but it went down after a minute. I rinsed my injured wrist as fast as I could, gritting my teeth against the heat needling the swollen skin.

Stepping out of the shower, I felt a million percent better. A limp and gray hand towel was the only means of drying off, but I made it work. A change of clean clothes felt like a lot to ask for, so I knocked the worst of the dirt off my clothes and put them back on. My not-quite-drowning in the river had flushed most of the blood out anyway.

A mostly normal person looked back at me in the mirror. He'd caught the rough end of a business out in the woods, going off the bruises on his face, the split lip and overall gauntness. His wrist was pretty much garbage and needed an immediate looking at. But his face was clean. He tried for a smile, but it came out grotesque and he stopped almost immediately.

I wondered who I was looking at: Josh . . . or Switchback?

The steam and hot water weren't doing great things for my fever; I swayed in place, catching myself on the counter.

I slithered to an awkward sitting position in front of the under-sink cabinet. I opened the double doors. Half-used toilet paper rolls and several gunk-slathered combs spilled into my lap.

"Oof, Mike," I muttered, wrinkling my nose. A definite funk, rolling in a wave from the sink somewhere. If I had to guess, beneath the fuzzy-looking drainpipe punching a not-so sealed hole into the wall. See? Fuzzy looking. Mold happens, it's fine. I dumped the junk to one side and began sorting through it, looking, hoping. My fingers touched on a square box, too small to be anything but pills. Aspirin, three hundred milligrams. I pawed the flap open and shook out an aluminum-and-plastic tray. Three pills rattled, safe in their sanitary pockets. I clutched them to my chest and leaned my head back against the wall.

"Thank you, God."

Nine hundred milligrams of aspirin wasn't going to take down a high-grade fever all on its own, but it was better than nothing. I dry-swallowed two of the pills and pocketed the third. I leaned forward, searching through the debris for anything else useful. More aspirin, or something a little stronger. I wouldn't say no to a bottle of oxy or Vicodin right now, I'd earned that much. I found it lodged beneath a moldy towel and a box of men's hairspray.

"What the . . .?" I snatched at the object, a furrow digging between my eyes. It didn't make sense. He dragged me out of the river, put me in bed, made sure I stayed alive. Did he forget it was there? I had to excavate it from beneath a mound of forgotten toiletries; it wasn't front and center. Hardly used too, unlike everything else in the house. He could have bought it a long time ago, used it once and forgotten about it. A near brand-new wrist brace, still in its box. Perfect for a certain sudden house guest with a desperate need for first aid.

He also offered you tea instead of water. Old boy Mike was perhaps working a few tools short of a set.

A mistake. Had to be. I shrugged and slipped the wrist brace over my fingers. It took five minutes of hissed inhalations to get it over the swollen skin of my wrist, now growing stiff and unpliable. I tried not to think too hard about how bad a sign that was. I'd get professional medical attention, after I got to a phone and called . . . well, after I got to a phone.

Now the hard part. I took a handful of preparatory deep breaths and stuffed a handful of my shirt between my teeth. A-one, a-two, a-one-two-three. I jerked the Velcro strap of the brace tight. My vision blurred and went black. When I snapped back to the surface, the echo of my scream still reverberated in the corners of the shower.

"You all right in there, bud?" Mike called from behind the door. I blinked past the tears and spat the T-shirt out of my mouth.

"Fine." I was not fine. I must have kicked the toilet bowl in my thrashings, because my foot now hurt as well.

"All righty. Welp, I'm getting ready to head over to Sarah's, if you're about ready in there."

"Yeah. Be right out," I said through gritted teeth. The shadow of his feet beneath the door moved away and his footsteps faded down the hall. I slumped against the wall and took a minute. Sweat caked my face and neck, but my wrist was braced. I tested it against my thigh—it hurt, but nowhere near as bad as yesterday.

I got back to my feet with much effort and clumsy pawing at the laminate counter. I splashed some water on my face. I still looked okay.

Mike waited for me in the kitchen, sipping something out of a chipped mug. "Doing good?" He asked over the rim. A smiling face winked at me from the cracked ceramic.

"Yeah. I borrowed this. Hope you don't mind? I found it in your sink cabinet." I waved my wrist and the brand-new brace in front of his face.

"No sweat. Let's hit the trail!" He barely even looked at my wrist —his eyes passed over the brace with no trace of familiarity. He dumped his mug at the pile of dishes without looking. I followed, limping on my hiking pole turned crutch. "Sooner we get to the diner, sooner I can get you on that ride."

Outside, the street was steeped in the navy blue gray of early morning. Down the valley, a river slipped through meadow grass like a flat mirror, a filament of white noise. A beat-up Chevy Silverado with paint peeling on the side sat in the gravel driveway, windows down. The inside of the truck smelled faintly of fish guts and cigarettes; the ashtray was full of dead butts.

Curious. I hadn't seen Mike smoke yet. The silver edge of the diner winked at me from Mike's driveway, two hundred yards away at most. We walked, which I didn't love.

I didn't recognize the main drag of Bedal until we were passing the Shell station at the four-way stop. Only two buildings on the main strip were lit: the Shell station, with its MONSTER ENERGY DRINKS ad, and Sarah's Diner. There were already two cars and a motorcycle parked on the hardpan. The light from inside the diner cast warm yellow squares onto the street. The parking lot smelled like coffee and hashbrowns.

Everything is going to be all right. I'll find a phone, call Deb, and in three hours I'll be on my way to a hospital. I took a deep breath. For the first time in as long as I could remember, I believed things were going to work out. Optimism or medication, I'd take either one.

Three people sat on the plush bar stools, leaning over cups of coffee and newspapers. I recognized one of them, farthest away from the door, from my last visit. A thin-wire goatee surrounded his lips. He was the one Sarah shamed into eating with his mouth closed.

"Hey, Sarah," Mike called to the woman standing behind the counter.

"Hey there, Mike." Her smile turned on me. "And yourself, stranger."

Did I introduce myself last time? I wasn't sure. The diner saw a lot of people come and go, no reason to remember one guy who stopped in for a grand total of thirty minutes. Heads at the bar swiveled toward me, ears pricked up. I nodded to Andrew with the goatee, but he frowned and went back to his paper.

No nod, nothing—not even a flicker of recognition in his dull brown eyes. Weird. He and I had had what almost counted as a proper conversation last time I was here.

"Coffee?" Sarah reached for an orange-handled pot beneath an industrial-sized brewer. Almost on cue I smelled the sweet-smoky aroma of roasted coffee beans, thick enough to stand on. My mouth watered in Pavlovian response.

"That would be wonderful. Do you mind if I use your phone?" I asked. Priorities: the sooner I called Deb the sooner I got the hell out of there. Then—hashbrowns. Mike slipped onto one of the stools at the counter.

She stood, frozen in place.

Didn't bat an eyelash, didn't move a muscle. She was standing not three feet away, how could she not hear me?

"Sarah." Mike raised his voice. She turned. "My man here needs to use the phone."

"In the back, sugar." Sarah smiled, nodding to a hallway off to one side as she pulled a white mug from a rack. Like a switch had set her in smooth motion, free from her time offline. I set off as quick as my quivering leg muscles would allow, which was not very.

A plain black phone hung on the wall. I fumbled it in my excitement, whipping it off the cradle and nearly dropping it. Everything was lining up, things were finally going right—

I tucked the phone to my ear. I tried typing in the first few digits of Deb's number. No dice—just a long, drawn out dial tone. Must be a pay phone.

After a second I found it: in the back corner of the machine, a coin insert.

I hung up and grabbed my hiking pole.

"Psst. Mike. Do you have a couple quarters I can borrow?"

Mike slapped his pockets, frowning. "Ah, sorry friend-o, I don't have any cash on me. Sarah, you gotta couple quarters?"

"Here you go, sugar." The walls rang with a cheery ding as the register popped open. Sarah handed me two quarters with a dimpled smile. "On the house. You look like you could use it."

One of the patrons was missing from his stool. A plate sat in front of an empty space, still steaming.

"Thanks." I grabbed the change and hustled back down the hallway. All right, a minor setback, but we're back in business, ready to get the hell out of this nightmare—

I slipped one of the quarters into the slot and dialed the only number I knew, waiting for the tone to change. Nothing happened. Frowning, I slipped the other quarter in. No change. I pressed the receiver, punched zero, and tried punching in Deb's number again. Nothing worked. The dial tone droned on and on in my ear, uncaring—and then cut out entirely. No dropoff or click of an operator picking up: it just . . . went dead.

"Hello? Hello?" No answer. It took every ounce of willpower not to bury the phone in the wall, beneath a picture of JFK waving from a convertible. Fucking phone.

Could be I did something wrong. I'd never used a pay phone in my life, so it was possible I missed something big. Like I had to dial 9-9 or something stupid. For the third time I grabbed my hiking pole and limped back up the hallway. The man with the goatee was just settling back on his stool, tucking something into his back pocket. He gave me a disinterested glance and picked up his paper. Sarah stood at the register, chatting with one of the other patrons. At my place a mug of something hot steamed beside a breakfast menu. I ignored it.

"Excuse me, ma'am? I think I'm missing something with your phone back there. I put the change in, but it's still not dialing out." I tried to keep the lighthearted smile plastered on my face, but my heart boom-boomed in my chest and a staccato message pounded in my head. *You're trapped-you're trapped—*

"Oh, that old thing." Mike shook his head. A single movement, one side, other side, center. "It's always acting up. It was working last night—Sarah, looks like you'll have to call Don and get him in here to look at it again."

The waitress frowned at me. "Sorry, honey."

The phone. My last visit, a problem with the pole outside, now it was just . . . acting up?

No, no it's nothing, it's fine. Nothing's wrong, it's an inconvenience. My stomach flipped, and I swallowed the not-so-nice retort that sprang to my lips.

"Does anyone have a cell I can borrow? It's an emergency." It wasn't the 1950s. People had cell phones. I wasn't crazy.

The diner patrons shifted in their seats, looking everywhere but at me. The newspaper covering Andrew's face didn't so much as waver.

"Please? I'll stay right here, I won't walk off with it or anything." Even I heard the ring of desperation in my voice. It all came down around me—the last dregs of my optimism drained from my extremities.

Someone cleared their throat, and that was all the answer I got.

"Mike?"

The Carhartt-clad fisherman's coffee cup froze halfway to his lips. He didn't blink.

He turned to me slowly, almost robotic, and an easy smile stretched over his lips as his eyes held mine. A little unsettling, watching his lips spread like that. Like they were going to keep stretching, the folds at the corners building until his face ripped in half. Exposing bleeding muscle and cracked flesh.

Jumping at shadows. You're acting crazy, calm down—

"Sorry, brother. Don't have one. Never did trust those little machines." His voice was light, carefree, but something empty hid behind the faux friendliness. Why did he call me brother too? He knew my name—I told him last night. I remember, because I almost spilled my real name.

Had he referred to me by name? I tried to remember. Champ, sport, friend-o—Mike hadn't once called me Switchback, even once. It could be nothing. I was emotional, hovering on the edge; who cared if Mike called me by name? Maybe he was forgetful. None of this helped me. A phone, I needed a phone. Or a computer, or something. Some way to reach the outside world . . . and quick. Because I saw the flash of dull brown over the edge of Andrew's newspaper when he thought I wasn't looking. Sarah hummed and bustled around her side of the counter, chipper as the breaking dawn outside. But she never went into the back kitchen, never let me out of her sight.

I looked outside. The sun peeked over the valley ridge, slanting rays of burnt orange on the valley wall above us. A bird chirped, a gust of wind sent early-season leaves tumbling along the sidewalk. Across the street, at the General Store, a CLOSED sign hung in the window. Unsurprising, considering the owner would never see the light of day again.

Ronnie Coors. Ronnie the lecher, the drunk. The owner of the white Jeep with the bottle of whiskey and black duffels.

The sleek iPad.

What were the odds there was a phone in that store? Pretty fucking good, I would say. Only one way to find out.

"I—uh—I'm gonna go check with the Shell station. They might have a phone." I nodded across the street in the other direction. I needed to lie, keep my real destination unknown. If you asked me why, I wouldn't have been able to tell you.

"All right, well you hurry back, darling, I'll get some coffee brewing for you." Sarah smiled wide. I tried not to look at the full coffeepot sitting not two feet from where she stood. I bobbed my head in response and backed out of the diner. A needles-and-pins feeling started in my hands as I crossed the street.

15

THE BASEMENT

BOOKED IT TO THE SHELL STATION, GRIPPING MY MAKESHIFT CRUTCH
with white knuckles. I felt their eyes watching me—the skin on my
neck prickled like a hot weight had settled on it.

Don't look behind you, don't look behind you—they would turn
away just before I did, I knew.

The morning air was cold, and I took a deep breath, trying to calm
myself down. Maybe I was freaking out about nothing. It could be
nothing.

*Keep your shit together, Josh. One phone call, and you can get out
of here. Everything is going to be okay.*

My inner voice lacked conviction.

At the *ding-dong* of an electric bell, the teenager behind the counter of the gas station looked up from his magazine with a mixture of

confusion and surprise. Not a lot of early-morning visitors at the Bedal Shell, it would seem.

"Do you have a phone?" I asked, interrupting the bored "Can I help you?" coming out of his mouth.

"Uh . . . no." A brief flicker to my dirty clothes, to the hiking pole in my hand.

"Not even a cell? Come on—look, man, it's an emergency." I snapped.

"Sorry, bro. Corporate policy." He sniffed and turned back to idly leafing through his magazine, wishing I'd go away. Or at least, he made a decent play at it; had I been a little calmer I might have missed the way he kept peeking at my shoes, or the too-long way he lingered on a page with a deodorant ad.

He was watching—they were all watching. No nineteen-year-old ever went anywhere without a cell phone.

Not in this day and age.

"Well how 'bout a bathroom? Got one of those?"

"Outside, 'round the corner." The teen jerked his head at the parking lot without looking up.

I couldn't see inside the diner across the street, but a pale smudge turned away from one of the windows as I walked out of the gas station. Just in case, I waved and pointed around the corner. "Bathroom! Be right back!"

Totally normal, just shouting about taking a piss at the top of my lungs.

I limped around the corner of the gas station and hustled right past the steel door with a stenciled man and woman on it. I made a beeline for the road, safely out of view.

Ronnie Coors's General Store sat kitty-corner to the Shell. The front windows were dark, and the CLOSED sign hung lopsided in one window, but I wasn't interested in trying to get in through the front door. For one thing, it faced the diner across the street and the patrons inside. If they saw me force my way into Coors's shop, they would know the jig was up.

I crossed the street in a limping run, slipped behind a beat-up Chrysler and over a brick wall. A bird called from the trees across the way. A battered Prius trundled down the road, slowing to a courtesy rolling stop at the blinking light. Another totally normal morning. Nothing to see here.

Behind the store, a trash can-lined alley punched twenty feet into the block before ending at a chain link fence choked with a decades-neglected rosebush.

Still no cries of indignation or rage. Likely as not people were watching me sprint pell-mell across the street like an extra in a Jason Bourne movie for not a single goddamn reason.

A windowless steel door, set into the wall. I approached as quietly as I could manage, looking over my shoulder. I tested the doorknob . . . and it turned. It wasn't locked.

Ronnie was an unmitigated piece of shit, but he didn't strike me as stupid. He wouldn't just leave his back door unlocked. Unless he did lock it and someone else had been here. Someone, maybe, who knew I would go looking inside, desperate for a way out of this town and these godforsaken mountains.

One of the trash cans thumped and rattled against the fence, loud enough to make me whip around in a blind panic—just in time to see the dark blur of a rat scuttle its escape down the alleyway. I sagged against the door frame, waiting for the bitter taste of adrenaline to fade from my mouth. A rat. Just a rat.

Pull your shit together, Josh. I slapped my cheeks, blinking. I took a deep lungful of dumpster-scented air, then another, ignoring the taste of rust and rotten garbage on my tongue. The sooner I found what I was looking for, the better. Everything would work out.

Against pretty much every single instinct in my body, I pulled the door ajar. I peeked around it. Nothing to block the door open—no piece of rock or brick. Nothing indicating a hasty exit, like someone loading a car who might have forgotten.

I looked over the silhouetted rows of shelves. The lights were off, the shades at the front drawn . . . everything sat silent and still. Waiting for an owner who would never return.

And the door was open.

I slipped inside and closed the door behind me with a click that echoed too loud in the large space. There was a deadbolt installed over the brass handle and I flipped that too, for good measure.

The golden light of dawn barely penetrated the heavy shades. Fishing rods, tackle, jackets, backpacks, and endless supplies stood in neat rows cloaked in shadow, looking like so many wretched-formed monsters lurking in my peripherals. My heart pounded and sweat dripped down my temples, but I took a few steps anyway.

I needed to get to the counter, where he kept that shiny new iPad. I crept like a burglar, down as low as possible, moving from the cover of one rack to the next. The open door was a fluke. Nothing sinister about it, old boy. If I was a burglar, I wasn't a very good one—I slipped and fell in a crashing heap twice, trying to stay sneaky for no good reason, and once almost took a rack of Yaktrax down with me. The fourth time I ate it, I gave up and limped up the aisle.

The air smelled faintly of store-bought cleaners. But underneath the chemically clean smell something sharp and acrid lingered. Body spray used as a hygiene replacement, if I had to guess. It smelled like a locker room from high school, in all the wrong ways. It got stronger as I approached the counter: the ghost of Ronnie Coors, hanging in the air.

The countertop was bare, with not so much as a speck of dust in the single narrow strip of sunlight cutting it in half. I dropped to my knees with a grimace and started going through the honeycombed shelving underneath, pulling out invoices, catalogs, guides, and maps, shoveling it all to the floor with increasing frenzy. God damn it, where was that fucking iPad? I pulled every single thing off those shelves, and it still wasn't there. I sat in a pile of paper and plastic clenching my fists in frustration.

The shop crept in around me, hungry. I didn't have much time—my absence must have been noticed by now. They would be looking for me.

I wanted to scream. Of course it wasn't here; why would it be, in this *Truman Show* nightmare? I just needed a fucking phone or internet connection; it shouldn't be that goddamn—

There, in the ceiling. A banister. It was tucked into the far corner near where I walked in, subtle. A second story. Of course—Ronnie owned the building, and his apartment would be upstairs. Yes! I scrambled to my feet, grabbing my hiking pole and making a significantly less-than stealthy beeline for the back of the shop. Where the banister met the floor were two sets of stairs, well-worn wooden ones leading up and sharp concrete ones down to a black basement. I didn't even make a conscious choice—the last thing I wanted on this earth was to see what kind of monsters Ronnie Coors kept in his basement.

A length of chain requesting no one to cross ran the width of the first step leading upward, and I smacked it aside. I made it three stairs up when a thought stopped me in my tracks. I turned and straggled back down to the shop, hunting through the aisles.

Two minutes later, I found what I was looking for. I used the sharp end of a can opener to tear open the heavy-duty safety packaging and hefted the weight of my new camping knife in my hand. It was a big boy—six inches long, serrated on one section. It looked sharp; I didn't have a spare hand to test the edge. It would do. I slipped it into a handy reinforced leg-pocket in my hiking pants in easy reach of my good hand. I didn't care if it cut a hole in my pants; going upstairs armed with only my wits and a hiking pole didn't seem like a great idea.

The upstairs was smaller than I expected. Three rooms shared a single hallway. A bathroom reeking of the same body spray, a bedroom ankle-deep in dirty clothes and empty beer cans, and a part laundry room, part closet, set farthest from the stairs. Someone had made an attempt at decorating; the bed had an actual frame, and there were posters of early 2000s movies I didn't recognize on the walls, but the overall theme was one of neglect and poor hygiene.

I rifled through the one bedside table and closet, flinging clothes and boxes to the floor. In a box stinking of mildew I found an ancient laptop with no juice and (of course) no charging cord. I threw it on a pile of underwear and swore, tapping my makeshift cane against the floor. No time, I had no time for this shit.

This didn't make sense. The iPad, his phone . . . he had the tech, knew how to use it. There had to be something else here, something I could use. A small table sat next to the bed with a folding chair beneath. A cheap desk, just lacking the computer. It had to exist; I wasn't fucking crazy. Did he take it with him? Was it sitting in the back of the Jeep, way up in the valley with the Woodkin? If he did, I was fucked. Unless he had another computer around—something bigger than a laptop.

The answer, of course, was obvious. It was all in the basement.

I considered leaving. That's how strongly I didn't want to delve down those concrete steps into the darkness. I could walk back out into the alley, find a side street, and hobble my ass out of this nightmare town. I could hitchhike, or find a bus driver with enough sympathy to let me on board free of charge. Assuming, of course, I opened the door to the alley and Mike wasn't waiting for me. Or the bus driver didn't pull a U-turn and take me straight back to the diner.

Bedal closed in around me.

I had to go into the basement.

"God . . . damn it," I muttered aloud. My voice sounded weird to my own ears—shifting and echoing in the confined space. For the third time I limped back downstairs. God, it was hot in here. The fake cork handle on the hiking pole was slicked with sweat. The vise at my temples ratcheted tighter. At the landing I fumbled in my pocket for my last aspirin and dry-swallowed it.

The stairs were steep, ending in black shadow. No light switch up on the landing, of course, and I didn't have time to go back into the shop to find a flashlight. I made too much noise, going down. I didn't care—the bang and rattle of my pole on the stairs was better than the gaping silence of the shop, sitting in wait.

In the half-light at the bottom was a door. I tested the handle, and it creaked open. I fumbled at the walls beside the door with a clumsy hand, groping for a light switch. I flipped it, and a flimsy yellow IKEA lamp flickered to life, suspended from the raw concrete ceiling by a bare wire.

It was everything an unfinished basement aspired to be—damp, cold, and lit like a torture dungeon. An ancient boiler ticked an irregular heartbeat in the corner, framed by rotting two-by-fours. The walls around the boiler were streaked with mold clawing up to the ceiling like fingers from a grave. It smelled sour and somehow green, but not a fresh green found in a forest; a putrid green, the green of rot and dying things.

Tick tick tick.

The boiler counted the seconds for me, reminded me that time wasn't on my side. Against the wall sat a sleek black-and-silver desktop tower and monitor. And, even better, another laptop, discarded to one side. My heart beat faster. Fucking finally.

I pressed the power button on top of the desktop with trembling fingers. The monitor hummed to life and began loading. Behind me the boiler ticked in too-fast measures.

The walls around the computer were covered with black-and-white photographs taped hastily into place. The quality was grainy and zoomed. Curious, though, was the angle—each of the pictures was taken from overhead and to the side, almost like a security camera. Women, wearing blouses or low-cut sweaters.

"Fucking charming, Ronnie," I muttered.

A single login profile, and it wasn't password protected, praise God. I clicked through to the Chrome app, heart in my throat. I was so close—I'd log into my Facebook and shoot Deb an instant message; I knew she kept her phone on her.

On the screen, an error message popped up.

No internet.

Tick tick tick.

I checked the corner of the screen, where the little ethernet picture had an X over it. Motherfucker.

Over my head, a floorboard squeaked. I froze, the sweat at my hairline turning cold. I told myself it was nothing, just another rat or the house settling around me, but the butterflies in my stomach whispered something else. One more, if I heard one more squeak I'd pull my knife, run upstairs . . . but nothing. Silence, and the ticking boiler in the corner. The heartbeat of the basement.

Tick tick tick.

I clicked through the usual suspects for internet access with trembling fingers.

"Come on, come on." Network was active, ISP address connected . . . just no juice coming through the line. I pawed at the back of the desktop for the cable, maybe it came undone—no, it was where it should be. The neon-blue ethernet cable snaked down to the floor and followed the wall, leading behind me. Maybe it was unplugged at the other end?

The blue wire followed the length of the basement and ducked into an unfinished room off to one side. I practically ran, stumbling and haggard in my desperation.

"Jesus Christ!" I staggered backward, tripped over my feet, and fell flat on my ass. My crutch went flying, my foot struck something hard, and my head smacked against the floor. The massive buck skull looked like it was screaming, crucified on the wall. Its antlers stretched six feet across, drilled straight through with shining silver studs. It pulled at me, snagged my vision. *You know me*, it said. Its mouth open, gaping dark and hungry.

Appletree, lying in a scarlet pool of his own blood, spilled by his own hand, already half eaten by the greedy dirt.

The angry boils covering Ronnie's hand, outstretched in desperate hope. Black smoke, pooling from the base of the dark rock slab like thick, poisoned honey, moving along the ground, swallowing the earth. I closed my eyes, trying to not picture it all over again, but the black space between blinks was all too alive, happening in real time. Like I lived two lives. Stuck, trapped with no way out.

A link back to the valley.

—black smoke coiling, thick like molasses and moving upward to pool in the eye sockets—

"God damn it." I sat up, wincing and grateful the blade I stuck into the side of my pants had, by some miracle, not gone sideways into my knee.

There, plugged into the wall, an ethernet cord. For a moment I forgot about it entirely, lost in the clutches of my nightmares. But I was here, I'd come this close to getting out of here for good; I just needed to reset the switch, and . . .

The blue cord lay in a slack heap on the floor, coiled around itself, plugged into the single pale outlet punched into the wall. And three inches from the wall, it was cut in a neat horizontal line. Not torn. Not unplugged and taken. Cut.

The last piece of the puzzle sank into place. I was funneled, like a rat in a maze.

"Well, well." The voice came from behind me, and I spun to see Sarah standing on the stairs, the filmy yellow light illuminating a sly smile on her lips. Her eyes were lost in darkness.

"You got down here quick. Aren't you the crafty one?" She still wore her blue apron.

My mind raced, trying to think through the details. I'd only get one chance, and if I fucked it up . . .

"We thought it would take you longer to figure it out. They usually take longer to figure it out." Her grin spread wider. She didn't move—she waited.

Waited? For what?

The rest of them. Shit. As long as she stood on the stairs, I wasn't going anywhere. I swallowed. One of her, one of me. Soon, it would be several of them and still one of me. I had to take my chances, no matter how shitty.

"Get out of my way," I said, hand sliding to my knee. "First and only warning."

Her laugh was high and mocking.

"Okay—okay, I get it. Small-town murderers, is that right?" I said. "Maybe you get your jollies off, killing innocent hitchhikers. Well you won't—"

She took two steps, and the words sputtered and died on my lips. She was still smiling, but her eyes were blank; they stared through me, through the floor, straight to the wriggling worms in the dirt beneath us.

"What the fuck? Can you see me?" I waved.

"Oh, we can see you, Switchback," Sarah all but purred. There was something familiar in her voice, now. It resonated, echoed on two levels. Her voice, sweet and charming . . . and something high-pitched and angry. Like shattered glass. "We can see you just fine. You thought you could run from us."

She took another step, and the grin on her face stretched even more. She stood on the bottom step, still blocking my way.

It wasn't possible. God didn't hate me that much.

"Clever little man. Running into the river. You thought that was it, right? Thought you could run from us." She dropped off the step, her thousand-yard gaze pinning me to the ground. "Look at you—thinking you're the first one to escape the Woodkin. So very proud of yourself. Amusing, to watch you flail and struggle. So many times you allowed yourself to hope. I love hope—it makes the fear sharper."

The glass-voice grew louder now, overpowering. It was cold, it was angry, and it was very familiar.

"But here we are, at the end of the game. No one escapes. All must pay the balance. The Feast arrives."

Sarah continued to smile, but it wasn't Sarah, not anymore.

"Who—" My voice didn't seem to want to work properly. The wriggling black tendrils beneath the slab. Her laughter was too loud for the small cellar; it boomed and echoed off the hundreds of imperfections and nooks in the concrete walls, cold and sharp.

I lunged for the stair, sweeping outward with the knife in my good hand. It connected with something solid, and she sagged backward with a deep grunt. The knife stuck on something and I let go, already fumbling up the stairs. Crutch, step, step. Crutch, step, step. My head down, focused on my footing; if I fell, if I faltered . . . my breath came in desperate wheezes, almost sobs.

A change in lighting announced the top of the stairs. I looked up—someone stood at the back of the shop, blocking the door to the alleyway. We noticed each other at the same time, his eyes wide in alarm.

"Hey!"

I ducked into an aisle and pulled down a rack of hand tools behind me with a crash.

The front door. I made a beeline for it, pulling anything handy, throwing shirts, packets of food, backpacks behind me. The slapping footsteps of pursuit didn't slow—I was wasting my time.

I fell against the door, pulling on the handle, a high-pitched whine building in the back of my throat. He was right behind me, jumping over a large backpack, his face flushed and angry. The door was locked; I fumbled with the deadbolt with trembling fingers.

Ten feet away, then five—

The lock turned and I yanked the door open, throwing myself through it, missing his outstretched hands by inches.

The sun burned bright, too bright. I stumbled and almost fell off the porch, shading my eyes with one hand. The hardpan parking lot and street were lit with rays of slanted orange light over dark shadow, deep enough to consume me. I whirled in a panic, vague shapes and silhouettes dancing in front of me. Something hit my foot and I fell, scrabbling at the dirt as I tried to get back up.

Unseen hands grabbed me. They pinned my legs, hoisted me upright.

"Hey! Get off me, you—" I wriggled and tried to free myself. The guy from the diner—the man with the goatee—and Mike. I tried to kick him in the gut, but he batted my foot aside with no effort.

They held me, silent.

I heard the steps first, from the inside of the shop. Slow, steady. A scattering of leaves tumbled over the empty street. Bedal closed in, vacant and staring. Hungry.

It wasn't Sarah. A man stepped out of the open door. A shimmering banner of carmine ran down the front of the blue apron, centered around the hilt of my knife buried in his gut.

"No." The whimper escaped my lips like a prayer. It wasn't possible. Not possible. His eyes found mine, black and dead as a shark's.

"You can't run from us, Switch."

"You're dead. You're dead—I saw you die."

"Life ain't always what it seems to be, brother."

16

PERSPECTIVE

SHOOK MY HEAD. THE COTTON WAS BACK, SLOWING MY THOUGHTS. I felt slow, stupid. Confused.

My name is Joshua Mallory. I'm twenty-eight. I'm from Decatur, Alabama. My mom died on the third of August, 2003.

I'd seen him die. That night in the clearing, in the box canyon. I'd watched the pool of rust red spread beneath his body, dripping from the ragged ruin of his throat.

Appletree's brows furrowed in cartoonish sympathy.

"What'sa matter, bud? You look like you're having a tough go of it."

"I—I—" My mouth was so dry it could have cracked. I swallowed with difficulty. "This isn't real. It's not real, it can't be. I'm—I'm dreaming, I'm asleep, this is all a dream."

Appletree laughed. The sound echoed from Mike and Andrew's lips, hollow and dull. They stared at nothing. He stepped closer. His pupils were huge and black, frayed at the edges. "Oh, it's happening, brother. Believe it."

"I don't understand." My arms and legs twitched almost of their own accord, trying to pull me from the iron grasp of the men behind me. "You're dead, you're dead—"

"Of course I'm dead!" His sudden bellow made me jump. He threw his hands into the air, spun in a delicate pirouette. The hilt of my knife still stuck out from his stomach, drooling maroon stains down the front of his apron. He was all smiles, radiating joy.

"Or I'm not. Or I never existed in the first place. Or I'm inhuman, or a nightmare. You all ask the same pathetic meaningless questions instead of the big one, the one that matters. Even if you saw me die, Switch, you have to ask yourself—for you, for your circumstances, does it matter? Do I need a pulse for you to believe what's happening? Hmm? Would that help, bud? Here, here, touch me—touch my skin!" He seized my hand, heedless of my desperate thrashing. He pressed my fingers against the skin of his neck. Hot, fevered. My fingers pressed the skin inward like it was warm wax. I recoiled with a cry. The indents stayed for a second before disappearing.

"There you go, I'm real enough for our purpose here. Better?" He bared his yellow teeth. The humor faded beneath a hyped-up maliciousness. He dropped my hand.

A flash of bulging eyes, staring at me from the water. Green-Eyes. He'd broken his leg, running.

"The body—the body in the woods I told you about."

"A waste." He turned and spat, thick and rust colored. Matching the stains crawling down the apron still tied around his waist. "Spilling the gift of his blood on the rocks. He tripped, the clumsy idiot, fell and reached out for my hand. Saw the truth and fled. Before the kin could snatch him, he tumbled. Dead before we could taste his fear." His face puckered, and he closed one hand tight enough to make the veins stand out against his papery skin.

Appletree had walked out of the storm. When I met him in the high mountain pass, in the rain and thunder—he'd materialized like a wraith. I didn't see where he came from, he was just . . . there. He didn't help gather logs, didn't help build a fire, didn't shake my hand . . . didn't touch anything *real*, anything we shared. A trick of the light, a sleight of hand. Don't look too close, you'll see right through it.

"You told me to go to Bedal," I whispered. The dead buck on the trail, with the hunting knife buried deep in its throat. The eyes, watching me from the trees. Waiting for me, just off the trail.

His lips stretched wider. His eyes never left mine. "Ding ding. Amazing the difference one of the kin can make on your state of mind, ain't it? You know, I thought you got him that night, when you went up to piss. Thought we were done for."

That high-pitched giggle, floating from the trees.

Bedal, where I met Ronnie, Ronnie who'd paid for the access trail leading back to the PCT. The trail leading to the ridge, where the scarred boy found me again, corralled me in the valley.

The valley. Everything led back to the valley.

"You did this. You did all of it."

Appletree gave me a mock bow. "Thank you, thank you—no, please, hold your applause."

The men holding me were silent, still. I wanted to rip the grin right off his face. I wanted to skin him alive.

"So . . . so the story that night? About your . . . I mean—?"

He shrieked, laughter so raucous it must have splintered in his throat like rusty nails . . . unless the nerve endings were dead and long-gone cold.

Unless the body he used was nothing but a shell, covering up the malice inside.

"Wasn't that the funniest tale you've ever heard? The first time the old man told it to me it was all I could do not howl in laughter on the spot. So much there, so much to use. He's become my favorite, now. Everyone likes him, everyone trusts him without even thinking about it. You did, just like all the rest. Sheep, slow and stupid, waiting for the slaughter."

The parking lot. I couldn't link the facts together. I didn't have perspective. I wasn't thinking about it right.

He circled me, quickstepping. "Now ask the question. The big one, the one they all ask. Go on, do it. It's my favorite part."

His voice floated in the corners of my head, stabbing, mocking.

"Why? God damn it, why? Why didn't you kill me and get it over with? Why did you have to play all these fucking games?"

He closed the distance between us in a blink. He smelled like iron and salt . . . and rot. The same smell from the clearing, from the cave. The edges of his eyes grew jagged. It might have been my imagination, but the pupils seemed to be growing, taking over the red-rimmed whites.

Sitting in front of the fire, telling stories. Whose idea was it, to tell the story about my mom? I'd forgotten it, pushed it away, deep down. I never breathed life into those words. What brought it screaming back to the surface?

His voice floated back to me over the smoke and flame. He'd reached in and pulled it out of me. He'd asked me why I was on the trail.

Running from my problems, I'd said. He wasn't surprised. Because he knew.

Sitting on a petrified log, shedding a filthy flannel. A deep-oak tan, gaunt cheekbones.

"Boots?" I whispered.

"In the flesh, dah-lin." That same drawling, good-old-boy accent. A single wink, a stretching of a sick smile. I told him. I told him I was running from my problems.

I closed my eyes.

There had to be something I missed. Some piece of information that made this make sense. I needed perspective, that's all. I needed to see it differently.

My knife, still buried in his gut.

I remember the tactility of it, punching through flesh, muscle, and sinew. It wasn't a parlor trick, done with acting and makeup; it was as real as the moment I'd touched it in its packaging. His skin, hot to the touch and stiff like Play-Doh.

"What are you?" The words came out as soft as a prayer, and every bit as hollow.

His grin turned stone cold. I watched the inked black tendrils move and take over his entire eye.

"I am the Plaguebringer. The All-Seeing. I am the One Who Came Before, the Absolute." His voice changed, losing its dusted-off flower-power vibes. It grew high-pitched. Like glass, shattering in my eardrums. "I am He, the one the children call Feast."

The skin above his left eye bulged. Something beneath it swelled, pressing the skin outward before slipping back down into his skull. Something lurked inside the mask he wore. Always there, laughing at me. The mass of wriggling shadow, buried not deep enough beneath the granite slab in the clearing.

Movement in the corner of my eye. I turned to look.

The man called Father, crossing the bridge coming from the forest. His face hit me like a punch to the gut, pressed the wind out of my lungs like a vise—his twisted and gnarled face, the scar pulling the corner of his mouth in a perpetual frown. His eyes were chips of stone. Behind him came the priest, limping and hacking into a half-clenched fist speckled red. He looked like he'd lost weight. Behind him, the rest of the split-faced faithful. They were here, all for me, walking across the bridge between the diner and the Shell station. Crossing into the real world.

"Can you smell it?" Appletree inhaled, his thin and blood-drenched chest swelling with the morning air. The smell came back as soon as he said it; a bittersweet sting of ammonia and woodsmoke.

I needed time. My heart trip-hammered a million miles an hour. He killed himself, I watched him die . . . and what happened next?

The beast of the black shadow.

The grin on his mouth spread, the skin at the corners ripped like wet cardboard, stretching from ear to ear, splitting his face in two hanging flaps. His teeth were needles, jabbed into his lips, which welled and filled with blood.

"Fear," he whispered. More blood dribbled over his split lips, down the gray-and-white beard. "It smells sweet, doesn't it? So sweet."

He was close, too close; he leaned forward and laid a single, dainty finger on my forehead.

Mother, screaming in the kitchen, thrashing. The shattering china, lancing her skin as she writhed over it, trying to get to the door. Why, why did he do this? The stupid, idiot boy. He killed her. It was his fault. Fire spread everywhere—it licked her skin, spreading red-hot blisters over her flesh like melted wax. She screamed. She didn't want to die, not like this. Not in fire and pain.

I didn't realize I was screaming until he pulled his finger from my head—it echoed in my throat, pulling my vocal cords tight.

Don't tell my father, please don't tell my father . . .

"Fear," Appletree repeated, savoring the word. A different intonation now—intimate, hushed. I sagged against my captors, the ragged edges of my scream turning to a sob. He stuck a finger beneath my chin, raised my head to stare into my eyes with his black, dead ones. Measuring, weighing.

"He's ready. Bring it to me."

I knew what they were going to bring before they stepped into the sunlight. I heard their slow footsteps and felt cold in my gut. The massive buck skull looked somehow more macabre in the daylight. Its curled shadow followed the Woodkin from a distance as they walked it down the porch. Behind them came the priest. He chewed on something, the muscles in his jaw flexing, trying to keep whatever was inside down. I knew what he was forcing into his stomach. Each time he took the mushrooms, he unchained the beast from his cellar grave . . . and took another step closer to his own.

A touch of air moved through the street. It smelled like gardenias. Gardenias, and fresh, acrid smoke.

"Are you ready?" Appletree looked at me and whispered.

It started with the skull. The connection to the ravine, to a box canyon not enough miles away. A tendril of black, pooling from the bleached jawline still frozen in its last scream. It moved of its own accord, writhing along the chipped and worn asphalt like a snake.

Coming for me.

I writhed, but the breathing statues clutched me tight. They hadn't made a sound, hadn't blinked.

"No, no wait, just wait." The words poured from my lips like water, unbidden and frantic. "Please, wait a second, I don't—I'm not ready, I—"

I sounded like Ronnie.

The smoke crawled over the streets, consuming the bottoms of signposts, the roots of trees. It moved between cars, curbs, and the chalk markings of children at play.

Appletree held out his hands. The muscles in his forearms bulged as the skull's huge weight settled in his hands, but he hefted it without a problem, lifting it like I would lift a basketball, holding it above his head. The black tendrils dripped like fat raindrops from the beast's jaw.

"Look at me." Appletree's voice sounded far away and close, too close. I stared at the ground, at the fingers of black shadow on the street as it surrounded me, closed me off from the rest of the world. This was it. My last few minutes.

"Look at me!" The high-pitched voice sounded like china shattering on floorboards. It boomed in a huge echo. One of the men who held me gripped my jaw with a hand stinking of sweat and sour ammonia and lifted my jaw.

Appletree stared at me with those black, unblinking shark's eyes.

I didn't want to watch, but I couldn't tear my eyes away. He forced the narrow opening of the buck skull onto the crown of his head. Tighter and tighter he pressed. Bones broke with a deep snap and spray of blood. He finished with a huge, final push, and his head crumpled and fell away. The buck skull was buried deep into his ragged neck, splintering cruel shards into the paper-thin skin.

The air stank of bittersweet smoke.

In the early-morning sunshine, the thing that I used to think of as Appletree turned to me. The skull hollows bore into my eyes, empty nothingness calling my name. The shadows expanded, pooling, growing, until they were deep enough to fall into. I felt my knees shake, felt my balance shift. I couldn't move.

Run, run, you have to run, the lizard part of my brain screamed at me in cold, skin-wrinkling fear. But my muscles locked up. I felt a cold touch on my legs—the shadows coming for me. They wound their way up my arms and shoulders, heavy as chains.

"Please don't," I whispered. I didn't want to know what waited for me in black shadow.

A choking, hollow sound echoed from the buck skull. The monster beneath the rock, laughing at me. The last sound to reach my eardrums before the black smoke wound up my neck and forced my jaw open. I tried to fight it, but it wound tight around my chest, squeezing the air out of my lungs, painfully pinning my arms to my side. Something pressed against my eye, insistent, urgent. I breathed in, and smelled the first touch of ash—

The blackness behind my eyelids swallowed me whole.

I didn't go alone.

The details of the house I grew up in surged from their long-lost grave in my memory, buried beneath years of nightmares and blackout drinking. The flowers on the wallpaper. The too-short door beneath the stairs that opened to a coat closet. The framed pictures, marching up the wall. A sideboard with a clay bowl I made in kindergarten. It was a miserable thing, crooked and misshapen to the point of barely standing on its own power, but she loved it. Rose red and cracked because I did a predictably shitty job glazing it. I'd forgotten about the bowl. Mom kept her keys in it.

I was standing in the hallway. Just in front of the door. Exactly where I stood the day she died. I could see my reflection in a mirror hanging on the wall.

This day.

Don't worry about that. The voice sounded different—calming, soothing. It sounded like a neighbor I recognized but couldn't put a face to, but I didn't worry about it too much. A neighbor, always there to help me.

She's in the garden. You can see her, there. The voice was right— the door to the kitchen stood open, I could see through it to the back-yard. It moved my eyes, it showed me. She was trimming the flow-ers. Always trimming the flowers. I couldn't see her face, but I got a glimpse of what she referred to as her "gardening couture"—a big hat and denim jacket. I laughed when she said it because she laughed, but I didn't know what she meant until long after she'd left.

It's going to happen any moment now. The voice whispered, deep in my ear like a wriggling worm. *You can smell it, can't you? You knew right away and did nothing. You didn't tell the firefighters. You didn't tell your dad. You didn't tell anyone.*

I could smell it—ash at first, but then it changed, lightening, shift-ing. Smoke cut with something bitter. It smelled like burnt sugar and hot wires.

I wanted to scream. I wanted to cry.

The eyes of the boy in the mirror watched me, boring into mine. I knew what that smell was. The urge to act was instantaneous.

"Mom! Ma!" My voice scratched my vocal cords raw and echoed down the hallway, but she didn't look up. The door stood open, the window hung ajar, she should have heard me. I tried to step forward but didn't move. I stayed where I was, frozen in the hallway. I looked down. My legs, still in my tattered and bloodstained hiking pants, but immobile. Frozen in place.

Sorry, Joshie, the voice whispered. *It's not that kind of dream.*

I hadn't heard the name Joshie in twenty-two years. The only person who ever called me Joshie stood outside the window. Trimming her gardenias with deaf ears. I hated the nickname; it reminded me of . . . here. This house, reeking of flowers and ash. This house, where she lived. She called me Joshie, and she was nothing but a dirty urn sitting on Dad's mantel.

She smells it. Here she comes, watch.

The jean-clad shoulder froze in place, moved an inch, then froze again. A dull clatter heralded the heavy-duty shears, dropped against the deck. Dad had built the deck for us with his own two hands.

The screen door slammed against its frame, and the hinges of the back door squeaked in sharp protest. Her feet against the floorboards, and then a flash of white and blue in the kitchen. She went for the stove. I didn't see her face, but I could imagine it with painful clarity. I caught glimpses through the open kitchen door.

A three-note electronic chime floated down the stairs from the upper level. Twelve-year-old Josh, sitting on his bed staring at the TV screen on the wooden bookshelf against the wall. Playing *Final Fantasy* with the sound cranked all the way up, not a single thought in his head except how to stick it to a pixelated dragon. He wasn't thinking about the crash his mother made, sprinting into the kitchen.

Ten feet. The distance from his bed to the banister, where he could have leaned over and heard the footsteps. Smelled the already-sharp scent of burning electrical wire. Ten feet, and he could have done something.

"Josh! Josh, God damn you, get up!" My voice echoed against the walls and stairs, but no one moved. No one cared.

Go ahead. Try all you want.

Whatever hold gripped me released; I surged away, nearly doing a face-plant on the floor.

"Hey! Anyone!" I lurched to my feet and spun, going for the door handle. There were neighbors on their lawn, watching the blaze. But outside, the street was pixelated. Blurred, like a video game unrendering before my very eyes. The neighbors on their lawns, nothing more than suggestions of smudged color.

Where are you going, Joshie? the cold voice in my head whispered. *The show's just about to start.*

From the kitchen a sharp cry of surprise and pain, and a ringing sound of metal on stone.

She burned herself. The voice inside my head whispered. *You heard it. You heard it and did nothing. What did she burn herself on, Josh?*

A snack. Twelve-year old Josh just wanted a snack after school. A secret buried so deep he'd never let it see daylight, no matter how long he lived. The smell of burning electrical wires as the pot of Ramen cooked down to nothing on the stove. Started to burn as the last bit of water evaporated. "No. No, no no no." My groan sounded weak and far away. There were too many details for this to be another nightmare—the gardenias, the clay bowl. This was a memory, come back to exquisite, agonizing life.

A memory a boy did everything he could to bury deep. His fault, his fault. He heard the words like a chant, every time he closed his eyes to sleep. Just like he heard her screaming.

A whoosh from the kitchen, the sound of fire exploding into life. The smell of burnt sugar changed, morphed into charred paint. Peeling away from the burner in fractured curls as the gas pipes running through the decades-old range groaned and hissed apart.

I could see seams running the lengths of the pipes, spots where invisible gas seeped through in harmless increments. Clear as a documentary, a micro-camera zooming through the cracks in the enameled-steel stove.

Here, it said, that nameless neighbor I'd known what felt like my whole life. *See here? A ten-minute replacement of the valves, and your mother would have been fine.*

She backed up, clutching a hand to her chest. Her hair the way I remembered it, wavy in undefined ringlets, framing a face I still couldn't see. I craned my neck, but my view didn't change.

Please. Please just let me see her face. It had been sixteen years since I'd seen her face outside my ash-steeped nightmares. The fire reflected against the curtain of dyed-blonde hair, dull orange and red. It grew, alive, clawing at the ancient fan above the range, consuming the faded and stained wallpaper behind the backsplash.

The cabinets are next, the voice whispered. Breathless, eager. *There's a package of black tea in the corner that burns like uncut diesel.*

For a second, something grazed against the skin of my arm—a flash of heat, maybe from the fire already spreading in the kitchen.

Red boils surrounded by livid flesh. I remembered them, rising in dime- and quarter-sized pustules, bulging and full. They had started in his arms.

It's happening to me. The thought came, small and distant, a sentence spoken in a mumbling crowd. In the real world.

But the real world was out there, far away, turned down to a tiny dot of noise and anger and light. Only here and now mattered. Because the kitchen door slammed shut, slipped from its butcher-twine mooring my dad had improvised to keep it attached to the wall. An old door, heavy. The door would trap her in the kitchen. Little Josh would come down and stare at it and know. Know that something was wrong.

The smell was exactly as I remembered it. Sweet at first. Sweet from the white flowers outside the kitchen window, already wilting and curling into brittle carbon from the heat.

"Hello?" There I was, too late, poking my head out of my room, guilt written all over my face. I wasn't supposed to be playing my PlayStation on a school night. "Dad?"

The door slamming shut alerted you. Too late. You were too late.

I was too late.

"Call someone! You little shit!" Nails scraped against my throat, my screams shaking the walls of the house. "You bastard! *Help her!*"

But of course, the boy did nothing.

I did nothing.

I remembered this part. This is where the nightmares started. Coming down the stairs, wondering why someone closed the kitchen door—it wasn't supposed to close. I wondered if Buster caught the corner zooming around the house . . . but then the smell touched my nose.

The dot of the real world grew smaller, condensing. The touch of hot pain stayed with me the next time it brushed against my arms. It wasn't a bother. It would all end soon. I had a vague impression of hot excitement deep in my head, stinging me as I touched on it, like the whirling blades of a fan.

China shattered on the floor in the kitchen, muffled behind the big door. Orange fingers crept along the space beneath it.

"Mom?" Little Josh stood in the hallway, staring at the kitchen. He sounded confused, but I knew better. He knew. We both did. As soon as the first plate shattered, as soon as the first whiff of smoke reached us, we knew. We knew it was our pot, sitting on the stove, forgotten over a computer game. Mother was in there, trapped, in need of help . . . and we did nothing. We stood there. Cowards.

I inhaled, but the air was shallow. Hard to breathe. The burning sensation broke the skin, seeping agony into my muscles. I swallowed, trying to pull my focus back on Little Josh. The memory flickered, grew dim. I didn't want it to stop. This was the closest I'd been to her in two decades.

The door to the kitchen slammed open, its handle leaving a splintered dent in the drywall. Hot air burst out. The wallpaper crinkled and combusted.

A hand emerged from the angry, sullen light, slapping against the pale floorboards. The skin was split and bleeding, charred in places.

Little Josh started to scream.

"Help." Her voice was hoarse, shot-through with rust but still loud enough to hurt my ears, rattling the walls and shaking the frame of the house.

She crawled.

Her teeth were bone-white against the black-red of her lips. Most of her hair was already burned away, leaving a charcoal frizz puffed around her ears. Her voice echoed in my bones, hot as molten lead. I wanted to scream with her, wanted to cry. Where her eyes should have been were empty sockets of heavy black smoke. The face I wanted nothing more than to see was torn and charred, bleeding, unrecognizable.

"Joshie! Josh please! It hurts so bad—"

I wanted it to be over. My heart could only break so much.

Little Josh turned and ran. He ran, leaving his mother to die in smoke and agony, alone. He ran out, screaming and crying, but I stayed. I stayed with her, so she wouldn't be alone this time.

My lungs burned for air. Even this far removed from the real world, I felt the pain; it connected these two worlds. Pain, suffering . . . fear. I wiped my face with a nonexistent hand—tears in my eyes.

This wasn't how it went. A single thought, clean and clear.

I remembered. I'd had the nightmares, waking me up every night for fifteen years. I'd lived through it, a thousand times and then a thousand more. This wasn't how it went. It wasn't my fault. It was an accident. Dr. K showed me, taught me the right way to think about it. Switchback killed his mom—just like the monster said—but Josh didn't do anything wrong. Josh was just a kid, just a little boy. He couldn't do anything. Brick by brick, stacked on the grave. Sealing it away. Sealing the truth away; it was an accident. Just an accident.

In a breath, two halves became whole. This is where they met, because this was where they split in the first place. A shearing of self, to seal away a trauma—a single thought so toxic it poisoned the depths of that little boy's soul. Switchback, Josh. Josh, Switchback. The fire and fury burned my skin like molten drips of glass, but for a split second, I didn't feel pain. I simply felt . . . whole.

Because I didn't do anything wrong.

I inhaled, and beneath the smoke, the ash, beneath the ugly stink of gas and burning, I smelled the flowers, out in the garden. Waiting for me. There, in the still silence, waiting after the pain and hurt. That's where she was. With her gardenias, and her bad mom jokes. I'd remember what her face looked like.

"See you soon, Mom," I whispered.

The fire howling down the hallway stuttered and froze. The dark creature wreathed in ash and pain froze in place, immediatcly silenced. Streaks of wheat-gold light strafed across the staircase from windows that weren't there. Outside the open door the street shredded, bits of color snatched by encroaching darkness, billowing like smoke. In the deep recesses of my head, a fury of motion and anger clawed upward, swirling up my spine in a series of writhing fingers.

Why would you say that? The voice sounded nothing like a neighbor, now. High-pitched, angry.

You stupid, pathetic human, why would you—

In a rumble of smoke and light, the memory dissolved.

17

FINALE

I SNAPPED BACK TO BEDAL WITH A GASP. THE AIR WAS SOUR AND REEKED of rot—it balled and hung heavy on my tongue, like rancid perfume.

"Why would you say that?" The voice booming from the bleached buck skull made the skin on the back of my neck shrink. It wasn't Appletree anymore—it wasn't even a voice of this world.

I inhaled again, struggling against the vertigo threatening to spill the contents of my stomach on my shoes. A bird lay on the street, crumpled and still.

Another lay on the slanted porch of the diner, where it had fallen from the sky.

"No!" The thing-that-was-Appletree screamed. The skin of its upper arm bulged as something thrashed beneath. The scarred old man ran into the street, his face pulled tight in sudden, raw panic.

The inked darkness stuffed itself back into the skull, forcing its way into the eye sockets in thick ribbons.

My arms loosened a fragment as the men holding me took stiff steps toward the skull.

Their eyes stared unfocused, their fingers twitched.

"No!" The skull-beast howled again.

This time the scream echoed from their mouths as well, stiff and unnatural.

I took the opportunity and shoved them back, overbalancing and falling to the street. I flipped over and one-arm crawled backward. The Woodkin ran toward us, closing in from the peripherals of town. The old man screamed something, pointing. The priest limped three steps but stopped and bent double, vomiting blood. When the thing screamed, it made a dull, tone-deaf keen. The priest thrashed with it, pantomiming agony.

In the skull's black sockets filled with angry shadow, a pair of eyes glared at me. Tiny, red-rimmed, swollen with fury and fear in measure. They were eyes not of this world—the eyes of a beast. The fault lines in the bone were traced in black, bulging and looping like skull was overflowing with tar. It smelled of hot ozone, the electric stink of threadbare wire.

"Oh . . . fuck," I whispered.

In a surge of limbs the thing charged me on all fours, heedless of the two men standing in its way. I watched a fragment of white antler pierce Mike's knee with a wet crunch.

He said nothing—behind the black beard, his lips murmured with the howling beast, flat and dead. His eyes stared at the rising sun, dull and blank.

"You pathetic wretch! I'll kill you. I'll crack you open like the sky and rain agony down on your every nerve—"

I bucked backward, desperate to get away, but the thing closed on me, rushing—it would kill me, eat me, take me with it—

A hand closed on my ankle, and I screamed hard enough to see spots.

"I will spend eternity exploiting your mistakes. I will bathe you in fire and put your every humiliation on display for the whole of time—"

Mike's fingers pulled at my clothes, thick-fingered and clumsy, a child's doll brought half to life. My wet hands slipped across the asphalt; I was losing the fight, they pulled me too close.

Run as I might, I could never get far enough.

I closed my eyes but found no peace in the dawn-tinted darkness behind my eyelids. The morning stank of iron and fury, resounded with the beast's eardrum-splitting bellows. Echoed with Mike's deaf-mute screams, a mockery of imitation.

This was the moment. I opened my eyes. Dawn crept over the mountains, spilling a flood of frost-hinted light against a pine thicket. I didn't want it to be like this. I looked at the ridge, rough with conifer-tops silhouetted against the gold dawn. I thought of my mom. If I was to die, I wanted to die looking at beauty, not hatred. I thought of Deb.

I watched the sun rise and sought forgiveness.

The beast raised its fists to the robin's-egg blue sky to slam them down again, but froze. A soft, surprised *herk* came from deep inside the buck's mouth, so faint I almost didn't hear it—almost human-sounding.

The world stopped in its tracks. Mike and the other guy froze in twisted, unnatural positions. Mike clutched my flannel shirt in a brittle grip. No wind sighed; no tree limbs moved. Even the river fell silent.

The beast collapsed sideways through the thick air. At first touch of the black asphalt, the skull shattered in a spray of glass-like shards, soft as snowflakes and twice as brilliant. They floated in the still air, borne upward in a shimmering column. Every inch of skull compounded on itself, broke into another wave of sky-borne pieces, until there was nothing left but the body, lying limp on the asphalt.

Where its head had been was a red ruin of still-wet flesh, merci-fully hidden from me by the still forms of two men. I wasn't looking at the twisted, heaped remains, though. I was looking just beyond it, where something struggled through the soggy viscera.

A single, wiggling black . . . thing slipped from the remains. The size of a thumb or even smaller, writhing along the pavement.

Father shoved the others aside, already running—he must have seen it on my face, the sudden decision.

"No!" The street split with his screech. I didn't care what he would do to me after, what they would do to me—blood roared in my ears, drowning out rational thought. All I saw was the black silhouette of pain and suffering pretending to be my mother.

The thing they called Feast made a wet, squishy pop beneath my hiking boots.

Father fell like a marionette with cut strings, propelled forward by his own momentum to tumble and roll like a sack of bones against the road. Behind him the hunched-over priest groaned through a mouthful of bile and collapsed. He didn't get back up. The scarred Woodkin stopped and stumbled in their tracks, confused, their twisted faces pulled tight. The echo of their hollow anger evaporated in the cool morning breeze.

For a single crystal, shimmering heartbeat, the world fell still. Nothing screamed or howled, cried, or shrieked. There was the soft white babble of the river, and the cry of a single bird, pinwheeling overhead.

Everything froze.

Groaning, I pulled myself into a sitting sort of crouch. Every mus-cle screamed with exhaustion. If they decided to kill me, there wasn't shit I could do about it. I couldn't run anymore—not for lack of desire, I physically couldn't run another step.

I heard them before I saw them. Creeping down the streets, peer-ing from their porches. Their faces pinched into tight suspicion. The same suspicion, I assumed, that they'd been living with for God knew how long. Their whispers were like leaves, skittering over the street.

"What the—?"

"Are they all together?"

"Who the fuck are they?"

"Are—are they part of—"

The anxious whispers turned to angry muttering. Fingers pointed at the corpses cooling in the early dawn light, then back to the scarred strangers creeping into town from the woods.

One of the split-faced Woodkin—the one who stood by to witness the death of the girl in the cave—whirled around. The eyes on them multiplied as people came out of their houses, outnumbering them in twos and threes. Frozen in place, the scarred men threw one another wide-eyed looks of confusion.

One man toward the front made the first move. He took a slow step backward. The others didn't know what he was doing. Some stepped toward him like they were going to huddle and regroup; others moved to the side, making room for him to pass. Still others held their stance, staring in open shock at the fallen figures of their former leaders. Whispers I couldn't catch ran through them like mist through the trees.

"Rich!"

The scream made me jump. A woman, wrapped in a threadbare rose-colored robe broke through the stiff-shouldered crowd, her bare feet slapping against the asphalt. A small child was pressed to one shoulder, secured with a strong-armed elbow.

"Rich!" I followed her eyes to a scarred man. His eyes were downcast at the hardpan beneath his feet. The Woodkin melted away from her like fish swam from a shark, peeling off toward the bridge. The man called Rich stayed where he was. He used one hand to cover one side of his face—the side split and frayed into their shared scar. The woman stopped a few paces away from him. Her hair framed her pale face in frizzy puffs, moving in the wind. The town surrounded them, closed in on them. Watched them, unsure of its next move.

"Is it . . . is it you? Is it—" She stood close enough that I could hear her breath catch. She covered her mouth with one hand. "What . . . where did you go?"

"I'm . . . I'm sorry, Kay. I—" His words were stilted, unfamiliar to his own mouth. He whipped around to face the rest of the Woodkin, but they weren't looking at him.

"Where did you go? Where—it was just a fight, Rich." Tears were taking over her words, now, stealing them from her lips. "Just a fight, and you went out for a walk."

He simply stood there. He didn't take a step back or go with the rest of them. He stayed, as if rooted to something in town. An anchor. He shook his head like a fighter in the ring.

"I was angry. I was . . . I don't remember. But in the woods, I heard your voice. Whispering to me from between the trees. I wasn't right in the head, Kay. You know I wasn't right."

Something stood between them; something invisible separated them by two feet, but it might as well have been a football field. He sounded almost like he was pleading—desperate for her to understand, to forgive. He stared at her, eyes huge and shining. "I'm sorry, Kay."

"It's been months. Months. You've been alive all this time? Why didn't you come back?"

The child fussed, whining and struggling in the mother's arms to turn around. The woman juggled the toddler without looking.

"I wasn't . . . I wasn't me." He wanted to leave it there, hunted her face for understanding, but there wasn't any to find. The hand still pressed to his face shook. "It was like I was in the backseat of my own brain. Not in control. I was so angry. All the time, angry."

"But . . . did you try to make it back to us?"

He opened his mouth, but before he spoke the child managed to twist around for the first time. They stared at each other, father and child. One in mild bewilderment and the other in awe. The woman stopped talking. The man's words died on his lips. Two seconds passed. The toddler scanned the man's face, calmly weighing, sorting through a mental catalog of faces he might or might not remember. And then, with the silent trust only a baby has, he just leaned forward. Rich didn't have a choice; it was either catch the kid or let him fall out of his mother's hands.

She covered her lips, but not in time to catch the breathless shriek. In the harsh light of the early morning, the scar on his face stood out in stark relief.

"Oh my God, Rich, what did they do?"

She reached up to touch his face, but he shied away, slow enough so as not to disturb the baby happily gurgling in his arms. He was lost in the child's face—either from love and adoration, or to avoid meeting the mother's eyes. The baby didn't care. He was already slapping spit-covered fingers along the man's jawline, babbling a story no one could understand.

"It's fine. I'm fine. It doesn't hurt anymore. It's . . . it's how they seal the bargain."

"The bargain? I don't understand . . ."

"I'm sorry." I couldn't tell if he spoke to the child or the mother, but there were tears in his eyes, running down his face. "There's . . . there's going to be so much you don't understand, Kay. We can talk about it—I'll tell you everything, I swear to God—but it'll take time."

The scene repeated itself along the street. One of the women, in a tattered smock, held hands with a man, whispering what I imagined were similar words. A man clutched a dog to his chest, laughing as the pup did its best to lick his scarred, split face.

But only a few of the Woodkin had someone, had a tie to the real world. The ones without an anchor drifted together, compacted by confusion.

They were the ones the scant handful watched, faces tight.

How long had they been watching hikers drift through town, never to be seen again? How long had they been hanging up Missing Person posters? I'd be pretty fucking suspicious too.

"Is that okay? Can it take time?" Rich asked.

"Yes. That's okay," the woman said. A weak smile pushed through, and she wiped her face with the heels of her palms. "It's okay. You're back now."

"I am." With every word, he came closer to sounding like he believed the voice coming out of his own mouth. "I'm here. I'm back."

Rich's eyes darted to the old man, still lying in a twisted heap on the asphalt.

One of the Woodkin turned toward the bridge and the trees looming on the other side. Slanted beams of early-morning sunshine sifted through the canopy, turning the spaces between the trees a filmy gold. The Woodkin whispered to one another, shoulders hunched, curled inward. Some of the women were weeping. Two men held hands. No one looked another in the eye. No one waited for them at home, looking at the door, hoping. They were too far gone for forgiveness, perhaps. For them, there was nothing but the valley. I wondered about their perspective.

Lost, suddenly alone. Abandoned by their . . . whatever.

I should feel sorry for them. I didn't. We watched them cross the bridge, watched them sift into the fingers of the trees. No one followed.

The forest swallowed them.

The distance between the couple in the parking lot evaporated. I watched it happen—they weren't together, and then they were. A measure of words between them, saying the right things, and they closed the distance. She pulled him close, buried her face in his smeared and stained shirt.

"Excuse me," I said from my position on the street with as much politeness as I could muster. "I hate to interrupt, but . . . could I borrow your phone?"

⇛ ⇚

THE "WHAT THE fuck do we do now" debate was like pulling teeth. People seemed unwilling to talk, unwilling to step out of their circles of trust and open their mouths. Three or four brave souls broke the silence. I listened absently, sitting on my red vinyl stool. One wanted to go into the woods and find the rest of the Woodkin, but it seemed like everyone else wanted to bury the evidence. To forget. Move on. I watched their faces. Quick, darting glances at their neighbors, at the people speaking. The ones who spoke did so quickly, spitting their words. Their eyes shot this way and that as they talked, too nervous to hold still. Plastic, tight faces, fidgeting fingers. Did their mouths taste of ash? Did they smell sweet-rot and dead flesh with every inhale? We balanced on the edge of a knife; I saw the uncertainty in their faces. They carried it with them.

The denizens of Bedal had suspected for a while. Had seen hikers stop for supplies in town and never return. Had whispered about this or that person who, like Rich, ran out after a fight and was never seen again. In the crowd I saw a few familiar faces—the parents waiting for their kids at the bus stop after school, the pinched suspicion and narrowed eyes, for some. Still clutching their bats and golf clubs. Their gaze still sneaking to the Woodkin who'd stayed behind.

"Ain't no one gonna believe what happened here," an older woman grunted, hammering a cane against the diner floor for emphasis. "I don't trust none of yous, and yous don't hafta trust me. But this'n something we gotta deal with."

So they agreed. Hesitantly, reluctantly. A group volunteered to take the three one-time residents to their last rest, loading Sarah, Mike, and what's-his-face in the back of a truck as quickly as they could. After all, a broad-shouldered man with the voice of a mouse pointed out, at some point they were part of the town. They'd had lives, families. They'd paid bills. No one knew when they stopped being themselves and became members of the Woodkin, but they belonged to the town, and deserved a decent burial.

"Wait." Rich, one of the handful who stayed, pointed out the obvious. He hadn't let go of the baby and didn't look like he would anytime soon. "What about . . . what about them?"

He didn't point to the twisted and malformed corpses, but everyone knew what he was talking about.

"What about them?" The old woman's upper lip wrinkled.

"We can't leave them there, Salma Hodgekiss. And you all know that damn well." His partner stepped in front of her husband, taking the brunt of the woman's disdain with no effort. She jerked her chin at the truck of corpses. "Take 'em with you. Bury them deep, and their secrets with them."

"Who says you get to make the call?" A balding, thin man called from the back of the crowd. He shrank from the gazes turned his way, fingers fidgeting at his sides. "You, Kay. How do we know you're not . . . you're not one of . . . one of *them*?" More whispers, sideways glances. Kay looked at her split-faced loved one, who shrugged uneasily.

"I don't know." Rich muttered, just for the two of them. He shrank beneath the combined suspicion they leveled at him. Like any moment his skin would distort like putty, revealing the deception. Like smoke would pour from his eyes, from their eyes. From anyone's. "It feels different now, but . . ."

"You can't," Kay said finally, looking back at the balding man. The whispers, the tension built in dissonance, splitting like the hydra's heads. One person, then two. They'd eat each other, given half the chance. Because any one of them could be just like *them*.

No one seemed to be able to look in the bed of the truck. It was like . . . like looking in a mirror and seeing a plastic version of your almost-self. So close, it could almost be you, if you looked at it just right . . . or it looked at you. The facsimile hit closer to home than any of us wanted to admit. Like wax dolls, frozen for now. But when the sun went away and the shadows crept back, would their skin melt and twist into something new?

The group agreed eventually. They dumped the three in the bed of a truck like sacks of flour and drove across the bridge. By some miracle, no cars came through the town, no early-bird hikers or logging truckers. No witnesses. Their secrets buried deep.

A few people, including myself, stayed in the diner. Some seemed at a loss about where else to go. Some melted back into their houses, clutching loved ones or kids. Others still stood in their tight pods around the streets and sidewalks, staring at the drying blood stains on the asphalt.

Muttering. Watching, waiting. Their uncertainty and suspicion carried like a knife pointed outward.

A woman—Maria? Mary?—got behind the counter at the diner and started handing out coffee, murmuring quietly to people. The coffee was bitter and weak . . . I'd never tasted anything better. People talked quietly. The same questions.

What now?

Who do you think?

It's like a dream.

The bell over the door tinkled and a bear of a man walked in at the head of a group. The chatter died down for a second. More than one person craned their head to get a good eyeful.

"How'd it go?" Maria/Mary asked from the counter.

He ran a hand across his scalp. A muscle in his jaw twitched. "It went. Brian Mayhew said some words over the graves."

"Where are they . . . you know?"

"Down the PCT trail along the river, before it splits and starts goin' uphill. There's a spot along the banks, in the sun. They loved that river, all three of 'em."

"What about the . . . the others?" Her disgust was palpable.

"Buried deep, in one of the ravines. Covered the graves in rocks. The wolves might get 'em, but ain't nobody gonna stumble over 'em by accident."

The quiet whispers offered approval, if only for a heartbeat. I said nothing.

Did they drive up to the valley, where that granite slab reigned? Bury them too shallow, where the others could dig them up, find them? Pull them apart with their bare hands, consume them? In the darkness behind my eyelids I could see their teeth, wet and red with blood and stringy muscle. Grinning.

Switchback would never leave that valley. He died there, between those teeth, pulled apart and left to rot. I was no longer Switchback but somehow not yet Josh. I stood in the limbo between my names, nothing and no one. I was alive—and for now, that was all that mattered.

"Someone's coming up the road," a girl in her teens by the window said, sitting up straight.

"Police?" someone asked, hustling to the window to peer outside.

"No, it's just a person."

Everyone moved to the window, staring.

I turned to see a beat-up red Subaru pull onto the hardpan of the diner's parking lot, a familiar pair of hands white-knuckling the steering wheel. I drained the cool dregs of my coffee and stood up. Time to step out of the valley.

I was nervous. A chill hovered in the pit of my gut, and my fingers weren't as steady as I wanted them to be.

Showtime.

I walked out of the diner unmolested. They'd already forgotten me, another blank face in the crowd. No one even asked my name.

No one looked up.

She waited for me outside, leaning against the car door. She wore sweatpants and a bleach-stained black hoodie, sleeves pushed up around the elbows, hair thrown up in a messy bun. My heart sledged against my ribs. A familiar high-pitched voice whispered in my ear. I could feel their gazes against my neck like iron bars.

"Hey."

"Hey."

I waited. I had the right to wait, even after everything. Because we were standing next to each other, but the distance between us was still measured in miles. It wasn't like I thought it would be, in the woods, in the fire and fear. Forgiveness wasn't immediate. Seeing her . . . all our problems were still very much there, still very real. Everything wasn't magically solved because we were together. I think down deep I'd hoped that would be the case, because it meant I wouldn't have to do the work. But that's not how life works, is it?

"Where's your stuff?"

"It's a long story."

"Are you . . . what happened to your wrist? Blech, and your ear? Are you okay?" She was a crap liar, her faux calm thin enough to be transparent.

"It's fine. I mean, it's not, but it's fine for now." It was too easy to fall into the patter, into the easy rhythm we'd had for years. I braced against it; we had to do the hard stuff first. If we stood in the parking lot of the Bedal diner and fought it out until the sun went down, fine. But we had to do the work. The lingering lessons from Dr. K, reaching over the years. You had to do the work. It doesn't just go away on its own. I had to leave everything here. The only question was, who would start? Except it wasn't a real question. She would—I'd already decided. Because I still wanted to punish her. She'd made my life seem foolish, and me in the process.

"So." She fiddled with her keys, running a finger over the jagged teeth.

"So." I waited.

"I'm sorry, Puggs," she whispered. She looked up from her car keys; her eyes were pale blue, shining. "I'm—I'm sorry. It was a stupid,

stupid mistake, and I . . . it was nothing, no one, just some guy—a vendor for some vacuum company, he came to meet with me to get onto the site and—"

I held up a hand. The images crashed into my brain, unbeckoned and unwelcome. "I don't want to know."

"Are—are you sure? Because I'll tell you. I'll tell you everything."

"Nope. Don't want details. Never want details."

"What do you want? What can I do? Because I'm sorry, Puggs, I'm so sorry, I never should have done it, but I was angry at you for something and he'd been charming and nice, and—"

"Deb, God damn it, I don't want details!"

She shut her mouth with a pop, her upper lip trembling. I hadn't meant to shout, but the voice was louder now, taking up all the space in my head. I pressed my good hand against my temple.

"Okay. I'm sorry," she said. She inched closer, her fingers running over and over the teeth to her keys.

"Puggs? Are you all right?"

"No, I'm not all right!"

She recoiled like I'd hit her, pressing up against the car door. Like a splinter pulled from an infected wound, the ichor rose to the top of my throat, bubbling over. "I'm not all right, Deb! How could you do this to me? I—what did I do? What did I do to deserve this?"

"You didn't—it was . . . it was complicated. No one did anything wrong. Or . . . I guess, I did. I'm sorry." One hand reached out, reached across the distance. I felt like a stoked fire, burning too high. My skin flushed, too hot; sweat poured down my face. I was yelling; why was I yelling? She wanted to apologize. All those hours on the trail, spent fantasizing about this, about this exact moment. And I still wanted to punish her. She'd made my life seem foolish. She'd made me seem foolish.

After everything I'd been through, was that really the only thing I wanted to keep with me?

The quarterback yells hike, and you have to do something. Fix it, or walk away. I had to do the work.

A matter of perspective. I wasn't mad at her—not even a little—anymore. Maybe it was Switchback who had been mad at her. Switchback, who had wanted to punish her, to see her beg for forgiveness over and over again until the words turned into mush. Switchback, who had craved the mean little details curling through the hurt in her expression.

I wasn't Switchback. Not anymore. I could leave him behind, crumpled and useless. Buried too shallow beneath the rocks in the valley.

My name was Josh Mallory. And I was alive.

I took a breath, grabbed her hand. I reached across the emptiness between us.

"Oh my God, Puggs, you're burning up. Do you have a fever?" She stepped in, brow wrinkling in instant concern. She put a hand on my forehead.

"Almost certainly." I huffed a weak laugh. Her hand on my forehead felt good, felt cool. A bridge across the divide. I took a breath . . . and crossed it. I left that cold, angry voice on the other side. It wasn't over, big things like this were never over right away, but we each took a step, which is all that mattered. A step toward the middle, to close the distance.

"Thanks for coming," I whispered.

She wrapped her arms around me, hugged me tight. When she pulled away, she gave me an up and down, a sly smile fighting against the last tears rolling down her cheeks.

"You look like shit."

I laughed, stronger this time. "You should see the other guy."

She smiled. I smiled.

"I really am sorry, Josh."

In one brilliant, effervescent moment, everything faded away. The Woodkin, the valley, everything. One sentence, and it became a bad dream, a wound that would eventually heal. I was alive; the rest would sort itself out. I became Josh Mallory once again, and left Switchback behind me. The cold, high voice in my head, all those miles away, stopped screaming.

I kissed her on the forehead and wrapped her in my arms. She smelled like coffee and bedhead.

"Let's go home."

THE END

ACKNOWLEDGMENTS

⟶⟫⟶ ⟵⟪⟵

T HERE ARE A BUNCH OF PEOPLE I WANT TO THANK FOR THIS. You can write in an empty room all you want, but to turn those words into something people want to read takes a community.

To my agent Becky, who took a chance on a sassy writer with a decent pitch. To my editor Helga, who turned a halfway decent manuscript into a polished and real-world book. To the entire staff at CamCat, who helped a first-time author with objectively way more questions than necessary.

And finally, to my critique partner Taylor, who's been with me from the very beginning, and who will probably be there long after I should have called it quits. Bomber Bros for life.

ABOUT THE AUTHOR

⟶⟫ ⟨⟵

A LEXANDER JAMES IS A WRITER FROM THE PNW WHO HAS WRITTEN four novels (worth of tweets). When he's not writing, he's attempting to keep his line cooks from slapping each other with fish. He's a big-time nerd who loves *Dungeons and Dragons*, video games, hiking, and backpacking in the mountains. After eight months of editing this book, he still doesn't understand how semicolons work.

If you've enjoyed Alexander James's *The Woodkin*,
please consider leaving a review
to help our authors.
And check out another horror read from CamCat:
Brendon K. Vayo's *Girl Among Crows*.

CHAPTER ONE

⸺∘⸺ ⸺∘⸺ ⸺∘⸺

April 22, 2021

M<small>Y HUSBAND KARL SHAKES HANDS</small> with other doctors, a carousel of orthopedic surgeons in cummerbunds. I read his lips over the brass band: *How's the champagne, Ed?* Since he's grayed, Karl wears a light beard that, for the convention, he trimmed to nothing.

The ballroom they rented has long windows that run along Boston's waterfront. Sapphire table settings burn in their reflections.

The food looks delicious. Rainbows of heirloom carrots. Vermont white cheddar in the macaroni. Some compliment the main course, baked cod drizzled with olive oil. My eyes are on the chocolate cherries. Unless Karl is right, and they're soaked in brandy.

At some dramatic point in the evening, balloons will drop from nets. A banner sags, prematurely revealing its last line.

<small>CELEBRATING THIRTY YEARS</small>!

Thirty years. How nice, though I try not to think that far back.

I miss something, another joke. Everyone's covering merlot-soaked teeth, and I wonder if they're laughing at me. Is it my dress? I didn't know if I should wear white like the other wives.

I redirect the conversation from my choice of a navy-blue one-shoulder, which I now see leaves me exposed, and ask so many questions about the latest in joint repair that I get lightheaded.

The chandelier spins. Double zeroes hit the roulette table. A break watching the ocean, then I'm back, resuming my duties as a spouse, suppressing a yawn for an older man my husband desperately wants to impress. A board member who could recommend Karl as the next director of Clinical Apps.

I'm thinking about moving up—our careers. I'm not thinking dark thoughts like people are laughing or staring at me. Not even when someone taps me on the shoulder.

"Are you Daphne?" asks a young man. A member of the waitstaff.

No one should know me here. I'm an ornament, yet something's familiar about the young man's blue eyes. Heat trickles down my neck as I try to name the sensation in my stomach.

"And you are?" I say.

"Gerard," he says. The glasses on his platter sway with caffeinated amber. "Gerard Gedney. You remember?"

I gag on my ginger ale.

"My gosh, I *do*," I say. "*Gerard*. Wow."

Thirty years ago, when this convention was still in its planning stages, Gerard Gedney was the little boy who had to stay in his room for almost his entire childhood. Beginning of every school year, each class made Get Well Soon cards and mailed them to his house.

We moved before I knew what happened to Gerard, but with everything else, I never thought of him until now. All the growing up he must've done, despite the odds, and now at least he got out, got away.

"I beat the leukemia," he says.

"I'm so glad for you, Gerard."

If that's the appropriate response. The awkwardness that defined my childhood creeps over me. Of all the people to bump into, it has to be David Gedney's brother. David, the Boy Never Found.

My eyes jump from Gerard to the other waitstaff. They wear pleated dress pants. Gerard's in a T-shirt, bowtie, and black jeans.

"I don't really work here, Daphne," says Gerard, sliding the platter onto a table. "I've been looking for you for a while."

The centerpiece topples. Glass shatters. An old woman holds her throat.

"Gerard," I say, my knees weak, "I understand you're upset about David. Can we please not do this here?"

Gerard wouldn't be the first to unload on what awful people we were. But to hear family gossip aired tonight, in front of my husband and his colleagues? I can't even imagine what Karl would think.

"I'm not here about my brother," says Gerard. "I'm here about yours." His words twist.

"Paul," I say. "What about him?"

"I'm so sorry," says a waiter, bumping me. Another kneels to pick up green chunks of the vase. When I find Gerard again, he's at the service exit, waiting for me to follow.

Before I do, I take one last look at the distinguished men and a few women. The shoulder claps. The dancing. Karl wants to be in that clique—I mean, I want that too. For him, I want it.

But I realize something else. They're having a good time in a way I never could, even when I could let go of the memory of my brother, Paul.

The catering service has two vans in the alleyway. It's a tunnel that feeds into the Boston skyline, the Prudential Center its shining peak.

Gerard beckons me to duck behind a stinky dumpster. Rain drizzles on cardboard boxes.

I never knew Gerard as a man. Maybe he has a knife or wants to strangle me, and all this news about my brother was bait to lure me out here. I'm vulnerable in high heels. But Gerard doesn't pull a weapon.

He pulls out a postcard. The image is of three black crows inscribed in a glowing full moon.

"I found it in Dad's things," says Gerard. "Please take it. Look, David is gone. We've got to live with the messes our parents make. Mine sacrificed a lot for my treatment, but had they moved to Boston, I probably would've beat the cancer in months instead of years."

"And this is about Paul?" I say.

"When the chemo was at its worst," says Gerard, "I dreamt about a boy, my older self telling me I would survive."

I take my eyes off Gerard long enough to read the back of the postcard:

$ from Crusher. Keep yourself pure, Brother. For the sake of our children, the Door must remain open.

Crusher. Brother. Door. No salutation or signature, no return address. Other than Crusher, no names of any kind. The words run together with Gerard's take on how treatment changed his perspective.

Something presses my stomach again. Dread. Soon as I saw this young man, I knew he was an omen of something. And when is an omen good?

"Your dad had this," I say. "Did he say why? Or who sent it?"

An angry look crosses Gerard's face. "My dad's dead," he says. "So's brother Dominic. Liver cancer stage 4B on Christmas Day. What'd they do to deserve that, huh?"

"They both died on Christmas? Gerard, I'm so sorry." First David, now his dad and Dominic? He stiffens when I reach for him, and of course, I'm the last person he wants to comfort him. "I know how hard it is. I lost my mom, as you know, and my dad ten years ago."

The day Dad died, I thought I'd never get off the floor. I cried so hard I threw up, right in the kitchen. Karl was there, my future husband, visiting on the weekend from his residency. I didn't even think we were serious, but there he was, talking me through it, the words lost now, but not the comfort of his voice. I looked in his eyes, daring to hope that with this man I wouldn't pass on to my children what Mom passed down to me.

"Mom's half there most days," says Gerard. "But one thing."

The rear entrance bangs open, spewing orange light. Two men dump oily garbage, chatting in Spanish.

"Check the postmark, Daphne," says Gerard at the end of the alleyway. He was right beside me. Now it's a black bird sidestepping the dumpster, its talons clacking, wanting me to feed it. I flinch and catch Gerard shrugging under the icy rain before he disappears.

The postmark is from Los Angeles, sent October last year. Six months ago, George Gedney received this postcard. Two months later, he's dead, and so is another son.

What does that mean? How does it fit in with Paul?

Though he's gone, I keep calling for Gerard, my voice strangled. Someone has me by the elbow, my husband. Even in lifts, Karl's three inches shorter than me.

"Daphne, what is it? What's wrong?"

"Colquitt. I need Sheriff Colquitt or . . ." Voices argue in my head, and I nod at the hail swirling past yellow streetlamps. "Thirty years ago, Bixbee was a young man. He might still be alive."

"Daphne, did that man hurt you? *Hey*."

Karl demands that someone call the police, but I shake him.

"It's fine, Karl," I say, dialing the Berkshire County Sheriff's Office. "Gerard's a boy I knew from my hometown."

Karl's calling someone too. "Some coincidence," he says.

Though it wasn't. Here I am trying not to think about the past, and it comes back to slap me in the face as though I summoned it.

Paul. The little brother I vowed to protect.

The phone finally picks up. "Berkshire Sheriff's Office."

"Hello," I say, "could I leave a message for Harold Bixbee to call me back as soon as possible? He is or was a deputy in your department."

"Uh, ma'am. I don't have anyone in our personnel records who matches that name. But if it's an emergency, I'd be glad—"

I hang up. Damn. I should've known at 9:00 p.m., all I'd get is a desk sergeant. I'd spend a good part of the night catching him up to speed.

"Daphne." My husband lowers his phone, looking at me as though I've lost my mind. "I asked Ed to pull the hotel's security feed. You're the only one on tape."

"What? No."

"It shows that you walk out that door alone," says Karl, gesturing, "and I come out a few minutes later."

The Door must remain open.

Dread hardens, then the postcard's corner jabs my thumb. I'm about to show Karl my proof when I realize that now there are only two crows in the moon.

"How'd he do that?" I keep flipping it, expecting the third one to return, before I sense my husband waiting. Distantly, I hear wings flap, but it could be the rain. "Gerard wanted me to have his dad's postcard."

"So this boy Gerard comes all the way from Springfield to hand you a postcard," Karl says. "And he can magically avoid cameras?"

"I'm not from Springfield," I say, shaking off a chill. *Magically avoid cameras.* And Gerard can turn pictures of crows into real ones too. How?

"You seem very agitated," says Karl. "Want me to call Dr. Russell? Unless . . ." Karl's listening, just not to me. "Ed says the camera angles aren't the best here. There's a few blind spots."

"I said I'm not from Springfield, Karl. Any more than you're from Boston."

My husband nods, still wary. "Boston is more recognizable than Quincy. But how does your hometown account for why Gerard isn't on the security footage?"

I lick my lips, my hand hovering over Karl's phone. When we first met, I wanted to keep things upbeat. Me? I'm a daddy's girl, though (chuckling) certainly not to a fault. In the interest of a second date, I might've understated some things.

"Here," I say, "it's more like I'm from the Hilltowns. It's a remote area." My lips tremble, trying to force out the name of my hometown. "I was born and raised in New Minton, Karl."

Somewhere between Cabbage Patch Kids and stickers hidden in a cereal box, the ones Paul demanded every time we opened a new Croonchy Stars, is recognition. I can tell by the strange flicker on Karl's face.

"The New Minton Boys," he says. "All those missing kids, the ones never found." Karl is stunned. "Daphne, you're from there? Did you know those boys? God, you would've been a kid yourself."

"I was eleven," I say. And I was a kid, a selfish kid. I came from a large family. Brandy was seventeen, Courtney fifteen, Ellie nine, and Paul seven.

The day before my brother disappeared, I wasn't thinking that that night was the last time we'd all be together. I wasn't thinking about the pain Mom and Dad would go through, especially after the town gossip began.

No. I thought my biggest problems in the world were mean schoolboys. So I ruined dinner.

"Daphne?" Now Karl looks mad. "That's a big secret not to tell your husband."

If only he knew.

CHAPTER TWO

----- ----- -----

March 30, 1988

M UDDY GREEN HILLS PITCHED AND ROLLED as far as I could see from my window. This time of year, the bare trees looked like thousands of needles stuck together.

We lived halfway up Hangman's Hill, about a mile from church. Our house had masonry and stone on the first floor, wood shingle panels on the second, a stone-end chimney on the gambrel roof. Six bedrooms, two baths, and a kitchen with teak countertops. Oh, would Mom talk your ear off about those teak countertops. They were the reason she moved back in.

While we waited for Dad to come home, I read Florence Parry Heide's Brillstone Break-In over and over in the room I shared with my younger sister, Ellie. Liza and Logan were siblings who investigated crimes committed against their neighbors. No matter if evil relatives tried to swindle a lonely old man out of his inheritance, they'd solve it no problem. I planned to do the same thing, except I'd solve mysteries all over the world for free.

Each time the hills reddened, I paced with Liza and Logan tucked under my arm. If the sun was a birthday candle, I'd blow it back up into the sky, keep us frozen in time forever. The end of today meant that tomorrow was Thursday. Thursday meant Rusty Rahall and David Gedney were back in school after a two-week suspension, and I was dead. Like totally, pond scum dead.

"He needs to . . ."

"Move out of the way, Court."

I followed voices to the bathroom. With all the drama I could muster, I placed my hand against my forehead and groaned. "I don't feel good," I said.

No reaction. No Get Daphne some lemon water. Here's a warm cloth, dear. Now stay in bed for the rest of the week.

Dang. I wasted my award-winning wooziness on Brandy and Courtney, my older sisters, who tucked Paul's shirt under his chin to reveal his bulbous belly. I could've backflipped into the bathroom and expected the same response.

Brandy unsnapped a button on Paul's pants. "There you go, Paul," she said. "It was just stuck." When she talked or laughed, Brandy sounded ditzy.

My brother's name was actually Brady, though only Mom called him that. Despite being the youngest and the only boy, Paul was perfectly capable of dressing himself and brushing his teeth. Not that you could explain that to Brandy and Courtney, who did everything for him.

"Where's Mom?" I said.

"You got legs, don't you?" said Brandy.

I whined against the doorframe. "I'd sell my soul not to have school tomorrow," I said.

"Don't say that, Daph," said Courtney, tugging at her hair.

When she hit puberty, it sprang into a copper-red bush unlike anyone else's in the family.

"What?" I said. "It's a joke."

Though Courtney's words dug in. How come when the other kids said it, everyone laughed? They did when Rusty was clowning.

Brandy frowned as though she could do a better job of urinating for Paul. When he finished, Paul snapped his underwear.

"Wait, honey," said Brandy. "You don't want to touch your face or anything until after you wash your hands, okay?"

"Germs are bad, right?" asked Paul, his voice raspy and thin. He watched Brandy turn on the faucet while Courtney lathered his hands with soap, mouth agape.

"Actually," said Courtney, "urine is sterile."

"No, it isn't," said Brandy to Paul. "Don't listen to her."

"I read it in a book, Bran. Urine doesn't have germs. That's why you can drink it."

Mom's voice bellowed from the kitchen. "What are you telling my only son to drink his pee-pee for?"

Brandy denied involvement. I took advantage of the mêlée to find Mom slamming the fridge, muttering that she had enough problems.

Mom had black hair and a low stomach bulging from her Levi's. With oval-rimmed glasses, she resembled a librarian, which she was part time, except her face was dotted with black scabs. They looked like bug bites but she said they were from chicken pox.

"Mom," I said, "my stomach hurts."

An armload of trash bags plopped on the kitchen tiles. My heart quickened as Dad patted my head, his hands cold. He was finally home, though he didn't pause for long.

"Girls?" he said, headed for the master bedroom. "After you finish your homework, think we could stitch a few pants and shirts for the penitent and less fortunate?"

Mom eyed me. "Was that your father?"

I turned into Brandy, who brushed me aside, Paul in tow.

"Hop up, big boy," she said, helping Paul into his seat. Then Brandy opened cabinets with no apparent purpose. "So, practice was totally awesome." She meant basketball practice. Brandy was the team's power forward. "Friday, Elkshire is toast."

That got Mom's attention, when I couldn't. "Friday," she said, "not Saturday?"

"Yeah," said Brandy, "I kinda . . . forgot?"

She snapped a carrot and Mom held her breath, as she did every time some tragic flaw manifested in her daughters. A cooking pan clinked onto the back burner. "Ahhh," said Paul after each glug of juice. Outside, branches sliced the wind into a whistle.

The front door slammed. Loud footsteps transformed into Ellie hopping over Dad's garbage bags. "Ta-da," she said, speckled in neon paint and nearly euphoric since her headlong plunge into drama this year. She chased us until Mom issued a decree.

"Only children recognizable as my daughters and son are allowed at the dinner table."

"She hasn't showered in four days at least," said Brandy.

"Maybe I'm going for the record," said Ellie, reaching for Mom.

"Maybe my soiled children could be civilized for one night," said Mom. Momentarily ignored, Paul rocked in his chair as if hoping to gallop toward us.

My sisters set the table. A prism danced on their backs. I traced the glow to a crack in the patio door, a thin line bone cold to the touch.

I never noticed before, but the crack pointed right to the church. Above it and the tree line, the moon floated, an unpolished stone with its large crater the hole where the setting used to be.

Now back, Dad flurried Mom's sweaty neck with kisses. "I missed you," he said.

Though his arms and legs were thin, Dad was naturally potbellied, which his simple white robe, untucked and unbuttoned, revealed as a smooth mound. He had deep dimples that, in the morning light, would make him look gentle and even boyish.

"Supper was ready twenty minutes ago, Brandon," said Mom. "It's just me and the kids." When a flushed Courtney walked by, her Walkman rumbling with classical opera, Mom snatched the headphones. "Unless you brought home some more transients."

"Hey," said Courtney. Halfway through his apology, we smelled the reason for Dad's haste to the bathroom. Courtney gagged. "Pee-you, Dad! Gosh!"

Dad shrugged. "Stink over substance," he said. "Happens when you get older."

Collective disgust kept us silent as Mom resisted Dad's affection. Seeing them together again was still a little disorienting. Kids called it a trial separation, the months Mom lived with a friend in Hyannis. The week after Thanksgiving, Mom came back with a suitcase, crying only when she held Paul.

We asked what was wrong. Were they fighting too much? Was one parent unhappy, or both? All Mom and Dad said was that they loved us very much. Of course, some more than others. Some dots I could connect. Mom made her distaste for New Minton well-known. Ten years later, she still didn't appreciate the way Dad moved us here.

Dad was the Minister of Second Unitarian Universalist. Before his calling in 1977, he owned a wildly successful marina in Hyannis. He sold fast boats to playboys, living like how you might imagine the Kennedys in the 1960s.

Dad was forthcoming about the drinking, the partying. The arguments he had with Mom. One day, he told Mom that he had a vision about becoming a minister in New Minton, a town in desperate need of a functioning church.

Mom, though, was dismissive.

Dad often had spontaneous impulses that he termed visions, sudden gusts of energy to change the world. Once, he proposed the family single-handedly clean the Blackstone River. Mom probably assumed Dad would forget about New Minton, and a few days later he'd chase another of his "visions" the way a dog chased the next car in the neighborhood.

Instead, Dad came home to announce that he'd sold the marina. He planned to build a Unitarian church in New Minton, the only Christian branch that accepted him and his ideas. And he would be known as Reverend Gauge. So long as we stayed, I wondered if Mom and Dad would be forever pitted against each other.

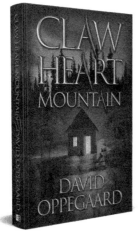
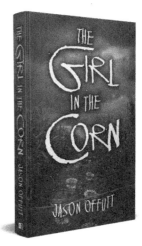
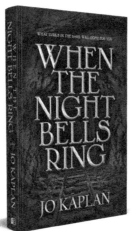

CamCat
Books

VISIT US ONLINE FOR MORE BOOKS TO LIVE IN:
CAMCATBOOKS.COM

SIGN UP FOR CAMCAT'S FICTION NEWSLETTER FOR
COVER REVEALS, EBOOK DEALS, AND MORE EXCLUSIVE CONTENT.

CamCatBooks   @CamCatBooks   @CamCat_Books   @CamCatBooks